# A Story of the West

## Susan Spence

For Tom

Also by this author:
**Liberating Sky**

# Book One: Matt

# Chapter 1

In the small frontier town of Kincaid, there didn't appear to be anyone appreciating the spring air. The few people out on the single street went about their business with little notice of their surroundings. In the early afternoon, a stage coach arrived, stopping long enough to swap horses at the livery stable before continuing north.

Matt sat in a chair. His hat and pistol lay on the bed, which was the only other piece of furniture in the room. The chair was positioned just to the side of the single window that faced east. Matt could see out without being seen.

Dusk fell, and then darkness. Still he sat. There was a half bottle of cheap whiskey he had brought from the bar up front. In between sips from the bottle, he rolled and lit a cigarette, scratching the match with his thumbnail. The three activities of drinking, smoking and watching seemed to keep him fully occupied. But it was his thoughts that held most of his attention. The noise from the bar up front swelled then receded as one day ended and another began. Finally there was silence as the night stretched on. Inside the cabin Matt still sat. There was a slight creaking when he shifted in the chair, followed by a soft thud as he set the bottle down, then, a while later, a flash of light and the cracking hiss of another match being struck.

He never even considered lying on the bed and sleeping. He didn't want to sleep. He only wanted to be alone with his thoughts. From looking at his face, sleep was one of the things he lacked. His face was haggard and worn. It made him look older than twenty-nine. The lines in it deepened as he frowned, recalling a day years earlier.

In 1883, Miles City was the center of the ranching industry in Montana Territory. Rich speculators bought cattle and fattened them on free grass. After selling the longhorns for a large profit, they deposited their money in the Stockman's Bank. When they were in town, they stayed at the Cattleman's Hotel. That was where Matt had rented a room the night before.

That morning in late August he was dressed in a white cotton shirt over which he wore a black wool vest. Instead of wool pants, he wore the new style of pants called Levi's. They were made of a heavy, durable, cotton fabric called denim that originated in France. Originally made as a rugged pant for miners, they were becoming popular with cowboys also.

On his feet Matt wore high heeled boots that were the trademark of men who made cowboying their way of life. The narrow toes slid easily in and out of stirrups, and the heels made it hard for a foot to go all the way through. The boots were scuffed and his clothes also had some wear. No one would mistake Matt for a newcomer to the cattle business. His hat also told his occupation. It was a Stetson and had a high crown that sloped towards the front, with a crease down the middle. The wide brim originated down in southern Texas for keeping sun as well as rain off the face and neck. Brims on hats worn up north were modified somewhat. They were wide enough to protect, but their smaller diameter didn't catch the wind as easily. The felt hat was light colored, called silver belly. The brim set off Matt's strong chin. It shaded his eyes, but didn't hide his friendly smile.

The final article of clothing that defined his line of work was a yellow silk scarf tied around his neck. The colorful scarves the cowboys wore had many purposes. Besides keeping them from choking on dust while trailing cattle, the cowpunchers also wore them for warmth in the winter. Other uses included a quick repair for tack when nothing else was handy and as an emergency bandage.

The purpose of Matt's trip to Miles City was to meet with cattle buyers. It was the first time he had taken on the responsibility. His father usually took care of the business end of the ranch, but an injury kept him home that year.

As the westbound train approached, Matt walked over to the station from the hotel. Because of his six foot height, and muscular build, he stood out amongst the few people waiting there. Curly brown hair was barely visible beneath his hat and his blue eyes were never still as he took in all within his field of vision. He waited, watching as passengers exited once the train stopped.

A family made their way down the wooden steps the conductor had placed below the door. First the mother cautiously descended, taking the conductor's arm, followed by two boys who jumped from the car, missing the steps entirely. Next a young woman appeared in the doorway, the older sister Matt supposed. She caught his eye as she managed the steps onto the platform gracefully and easily, despite her long skirt, ignoring the offered arm. An older man followed her. He must be the father. As they walked towards him, she glanced up. He smiled and touched the brim of his hat with one finger. She gave him a quick smile and continued on. Matt turned to meet the two men he was waiting for.

He couldn't remember the names or faces of the buyers he met at the station that day. He remembered the agreed on price for the steers he was selling, because that was his business. Mostly he remembered the young woman. She had big brown eyes and her hair was a rich chestnut brown. The reddish highlights shone in the sunlight. She was wearing a dark blue traveling suit. The skirt didn't quite reach the ground, and the short, tailored jacket showed off her figure. Her cheeks had a healthy pink glow. As she walked by, he had seen how small she was, not even coming to his chin. Her look had been curious and friendly. Even in that quick glance, he had felt pulled towards her.

That afternoon Matt rode the train as it continued west. He wasn't sure he liked having the second transcontinental railroad close by. It used to take two days on horseback from where he lived with his father to reach Miles City. Now he sat on the train for half a day. He supposed that was a plus. But the territory seemed to be filling with people who had no business being here. He thought of the young woman and her family, and wondered who they were and where they were going.

Matt's destination now as he rode the train was the town of Compton. It was one of many towns that were springing up along the tracks that paralleled the Yellowstone River. Situated just upstream from where Compton Creek joined the river, it was named when a trapper passing through years before had decided to immortalize himself. He had never been back, but his name stayed with both the creek and the town.

\*\*\*

Before the Union Pacific put the tracks through, steamboats brought supplies, as well as people, up the Missouri River to Fort Benton. From there long trains of wagons pulled by oxen transported goods along overland routes. Compton was one of the way stations to the south. It was here the route divided, with some of the wagon trains following the river west, while others went east.

The town was originally just a canvas tent with a couple of corrals that the freight line used. Spare oxen were fed and rested to replace the footsore and exhausted ones. There was a ferry across the river, which was the thing that most insured the town's survival.

Compton had grown to a cluster of wooden buildings

housing a couple of hotels and restaurants, and even a church. The freight company had built a barn, and the way station was expanded into a livery stable. A general store served the basic needs of the townspeople and nearby ranches, and a clothing store had opened as well. And of course, there were a number of drinking establishments along the main street, making it easy to wash the dust out of a man's throat.

Matt walked from the train station over to the livery. There were a few oxen dozing in the late afternoon sun, waiting for the next load of food, tools, and other necessities being sent west. Their route had become much shorter. With the train, Compton was the beginning of the freight route instead of the end.

The manager of the stable, a man by the name of Gust, straightened up from his task of nailing a loose board on the side of the barn as Matt approached. "How was your trip to the city?" His grin greeted Matt as he laughed at his own joke. Miles City was not much larger than the other towns along the train tracks. Its importance was in its meeting place for cattlemen.

"It was fine." Matt smiled back. He didn't know if Gust was the man's real name or one given to him to remind him of an event in his life from years before. The tall, wiry man never volunteered the information. He took good care of the animals in his care, and that's what mattered. The two men talked for a few minutes, but Matt didn't linger. He still had close to a twenty mile ride that day, and the afternoon was wearing on.

"I'll get your horse." Gust walked into the dimness of the barn. Matt's horse was waiting saddled in the nearest stall. The gelding was wearing a halter. Gust led the horse, a sorrel named Dusty, out into the sunlight. Matt automatically watched him walk, looking for any sign of soreness. He looked at the shoe Gust had reset on the off hind hoof, and noted the horse's overall condition. Matt had only been gone overnight, but it was habit, learned from long days of riding, knowing that his horse was his insurance on getting home safely.

The inspection completed, Matt settled up with Gust.

Taking the bridle from the saddle horn, he slipped the bit into the gelding's mouth and pulled the headstall over his ears. After handing Gust the halter, he turned and tightened the cinch before slipping his foot into the stirrup. He swung his leg over Dusty's rump and settled easily into the saddle. The horse and rider walked past the few buildings lining the dirt street and clambered aboard the wooden ferry waiting at the edge of the river. Gust watched them go, admiring the ease with which they moved together. He liked and respected both Matt and his father, as did everyone in the area.

Once across the river and off the ferry, Matt took the road that loosely followed Compton Creek north. He traveled along the edge of the plains. Along the horizon to the west rose steep, snow covered mountain peaks. Further east the land began flattening out. In between the ground rolled, with juniper and sage covered hillsides surrounding the bottoms. Intermittently, sheer, rimrock cliffs rose straight up, adding to the ruggedness of the terrain. Numerous creeks and springs surrounded by cottonwoods and willows provided water in the arid climate. There was grass too, lots of it, in the openings and up on the flats. That was why the Daly father and son were there, the abundance of bunch grass for fattening cattle.

The horse and rider trotted along, following the rutted tracks, slowing to a walk only once on a steep hill. After twelve miles, they came to another small town.

Turkey Creek was the next way station along the freight route. Its closeness to Compton seemed strange, seeing as it was almost forty miles to the next stop. But the country didn't care what was convenient. That was the last suitable spot with potable water.

The town had done all of its growing before the train tracks were laid. There was one hotel with a restaurant, a couple of saloons, the livery, and a general store. A few houses had been built around the edges. It sat next to the creek where the road forked. The main road continued north. A much less traveled road crossed the creek and headed west.

It had been dark for an hour when Matt rode down the

single street. He didn't stop, except to allow Dusty to drop his head and drink when they reached the creek. He gave the horse a loose rein, knowing he was capable of finding his way home in the dark. The gelding splashed through the water, taking the west fork, and continued at a walk as there was no moon. He never faltered as he strode over the rough ground. At such a slow pace, it took another two and a half hours to reach the home ranch.

The D Rocking D headquarters consisted of three hundred and twenty acres, which technically the Daly's were squatting on. The Homestead Act of 1862 allowed each head of household to claim one hundred and sixty acres. Matt and John Daly had each filed on that amount, but they wouldn't receive official ownership until the land was surveyed by the government. They, along with other settlers, had to trust that the land would remain theirs after that was done.

The Daly herd had grown to six thousand, small compared to many outfits in the area. The cattle grazed on land that was public domain, meaning anyone could use it. The prairie of Montana Territory, in fact all the short grass prairie of the arid west, was still labeled as desert on maps. The region was so large that no one could foresee any problems with livestock overcrowding. Before the grazing potential was recognized, the whole region, from Canada to Mexico had simply been a hardship for settlers crossing over in covered wagons forty years before, headed for Oregon and California.

Then it was realized how much grass was growing on the fertile prairie soils. This was how the speculators, many of them foreigners from Europe, were making so much money. The cattle, mainly young steers, were trailed up from Texas and turned loose on the plentiful and lush grass of the northern prairie. The cattle grew fat, and then were sent east to feed the growing population of the eastern United States. The railroad made it that much easier, and train loads of fattened steers were sent back each fall.

The investors were interested in making quick money. They turned the cattle loose on public land, some with only a crew of cowboys, calling a chuckwagon home, to tend them for the summer. They owned no land, and no buildings, which cut expenses even further. The condition of the range didn't concern them. As long as the cattle were gaining weight, which meant profit, they were happy.

The Dalys cared though. This was their home. They knew that the condition of the prairie was their livelihood and they wanted to prevent overgrazing on what they considered their land.

\*\*\*

When Matt rode in that night there was a dim light in the window of the one room cabin he shared with his father. He stopped by the small barn and dismounted. A coal oil lantern was hanging on a peg outside the barn door. He lifted it down and walked off a few paces before striking a match to light it. Inside the barn Matt hung the lantern next to the door, and then turned to unsaddle and feed his horse. Dusty had drank again at the creek before reaching the barn, so he could stand in the barn overnight with a full manger of hay. The hinges let out a creak as Matt swung the heavy barn door shut before walking to the cabin with the lantern.

Inside, Matt hung his hat on a peg near the door as he greeted his father. "How'd it go?" Big John asked his son as he stood and stretched. A well-read book sat on the table in front of him.

"Prices are still up. We did well this year. How's the knee?"

There was a plate of food sitting on the barely warm stove. Matt took it to the table and sat on a bench. He hadn't eaten since breakfast early that morning in Miles City. The fried steak and potatoes went down quickly.

The two men didn't say much more, except to finalize plans for the fall roundup. They were soon fast asleep in bunks on opposite sides of the cabin.

# Chapter 2

Two days later Matt led a team of horses from the corral over to the barn to harness them. The two were a fairly matched set of gray geldings aptly named Steel and Gray, Steel being the darker of the two. Matt pulled the heavy collars over their heads and slid them down the horse's necks. Then he heaved the harness onto their backs and buckled it into place. After bridling the horses, he attached the long driving lines.

Holding the lines and walking behind them, he guided them in a circle from the barn door, around and back underneath the leanto attached to the side of the barn. He steered them so the near horse stepped over the wagon tongue, and stopped the pair directly in front of one of the two wagons sitting there.

Once the horses were hitched Matt climbed up onto the seat. The horses pulled the heavy buckboard out into the open and they headed to town. Fall roundup was beginning in a couple of days. It was time to supply the chuckwagon, which would be the ranch crew's home for the next month or so. Matt made a list in his head as they ambled along. As usual he was also continually looking around, noticing everything from the vegetation, especially the grass, to the hawks flying overhead. He also read the brand on any cattle he passed.

He arrived in Turkey Creek two hours later, and stopped in front of the general store. It was made of boards hauled from the nearest sawmill sixty miles away. The building was already graying from the wind, water, and sun, one of which always seemed to be beating down on the flaking paint. The sign above the door read:

*Turkey Creek Mercantile*
*All Goods Big and Small*

The only building boom the town of Turkey Creek had experienced was when a stage line was added to the freight line. It was expected to be a major dropping point, but a mine in the nearby mountains had quickly played out. The town stopped growing, having become all it would ever be.

The owner of the Turkey Creek Mercantile was a man named Silas Riggs. He was in his fifties and had decided he wanted to sell out and move somewhere with a more hospitable climate. In his old age he wanted an easier life than running a store on the frontier.

Next door to the general store was the hotel, the only building in town with two stories. It also housed the only restaurant. It had the optimistic name of The Palace. In reality it had only a few small rooms for travelers to spend the night.

The only other businesses were the saloons, one of which had a barber chair in back, and a small doctor's office. Anyone wanting a haircut knew to catch the barber early in the morning, before he got hold of a bottle. There hadn't been a doctor in town since the last one, being drunk, had fallen off his horse and broken his neck the year before. The piano player once employed by the fancier of the saloons had long since packed up his piano and moved on. It was easier to make a living in the mining towns further west. A few small houses rounded out the town of Turkey Creek. The rail line was attracting most of the people moving in, but the few businesses hung on.

As Matt halted his team in front of the store, the stage was pulling out from in front of the hotel. He wondered how they made any money on this route. Few people passed through Turkey Creek, much less got on or off the stage.

He jumped down off the wagon and, after wrapping a lead rope around the hitch rail, climbed up the steps onto the porch and opened the door. Inside, to his surprise, was the family he had seen stepping off the train in Miles City.

"Mathew, hello!" Silas boomed out as he entered. "Come meet Theodore Lavold. He's come to look at the store." Matt walked over to shake hands with a large blond man. Lavold's mustache drooped around his mouth and mutton chop sideburns framed his cheeks. Matt looked into pale, blue eyes as he shook the man's hand. He judged him to be in his mid forties, about the same age as his father. "This is Mathew Daly. He and his father run cattle a few miles west of town."

"Call me Matt. Nice to meet you, Mr. Lavold." Matt's smile came easily, his friendliness genuine. He turned his attention to the man's family.

"This is my wife and daughter, and my sons Teddy and James. " Matt said hello to each of them. Mrs. Lavold was a small, brown haired woman. As she said hello, Matt noticed how her daughter resembled her.

"It's nice to meet you Mr. Daly. My name is Lavina" Her eyes met Matt's, but only for an instant before she looked away. The boys had been staring at Matt. When he looked at them and said hello, they mumbled a greeting and then looked around, bored at being inside. Matt guessed them to be around eleven and twelve.

Still smiling, he turned back to Lavold and asked, "How long you in town for?"

"We'll be on the next stage back to Compton. I have business to attend to elsewhere so we can't stay longer." Lavina was watching Matt. He nodded at her father's words and then

11

looked back at her. Once again she met his glance for only an instant before looking back at her father.

"The Lavolds came out here all the way from Illinois," Silas told Matt.

"Yes, I've always wanted to come west. I'm investigating business opportunities in the area."

"It's a nice place to live." Matt suddenly felt tongue tied, feeling Lavina's eyes on him.

After a pause, Silas asked how he could help Matt.

"Roundup starts next week." Silas knew what that meant.

"Excuse me," he told the Lavolds, before walking behind the counter and picking up a pencil.

"Okay."

"Two bags of flour, couple cans of sugar, sack of beans. Got any rice?"

"Nah."

"Well give me six cases of tomatoes, the same of milk, a couple boxes of dried apples. How about potatoes and onions?"

"I got some in last week, but they were rotten by the time they got here."

Matt nodded and continued. "Hundred pounds of salt pork, coffee." He arched his eyebrows. "Any raisins?"

"Those we've got."

"Throw some in. Salt, oh, and a hundred pounds of whole oats." Those were for the horses, mainly the team standing outside. He wanted them in good condition before they left, as they would be working hard for the next month.

Silas wrote everything down and started collecting the smaller items from the shelves. Matt walked over to where bags of flour were stacked. He easily lifted two bags, one onto his shoulder and the other under his opposite arm, and headed for the door. Lavina moved to open the door for him. Matt smiled down at her as he walked through.

Theodore Lavold had been listening and watching intently. His mind was still calculating. Being only twelve miles from the railroad, he expected they could get potatoes and onions before they spoiled. And no rice. Running a store out here would be different than back east. There would be a lot of outfitting for the twice-yearly roundups, plus people traveling long distances for staples. He looked around the store and saw a lot of room for improvement.

Meanwhile Matt continued carrying supplies out the door, filling the back of the wagon. "You better throw in a box of horse shoe nails." The horses would all be shod, but frequently shoes were lost and they would need to be replaced in camp. Silas helped Matt carry bags, boxes and tins to the wagon. When they were finished, the bed of the wagon was almost full.

"Why don't you go outside." Lavold saw that his two sons were bored. "You too Lavina, while I talk to Mr. Riggs." The store owner said goodbye to Matt on the porch as the three Lavold children came out into the sunlight. The two boys walked down the steps and paused, looking around.

"Come back up here. Stay by the door." Elizabeth Lavold's voice called out from inside the store. The two boys trudged reluctantly back up the steps.

Lavina walked over to where Matt was arranging the load in the back of the wagon and asked him, "What's a roundup?"

Matt turned towards her, his face again lighting up into a smile. Lavina looked quickly into his eyes and away again. Matt began explaining roundups.

"All the different outfits in the area round up their older steers in the fall and take them to the railroads. Then they're shipped back east."

"How long does it take?"

"It depends." Matt answered Lavina's questions while he continued working. It was warm out, on the verge of being hot, which is why he didn't stop He wanted to be home by the time the early September heat intensified in the afternoon. But he was as fascinated as she was. In his experience, most women weren't interested when he tried to explain aspects of ranching to them. Lavina's parents walked through the door. "We have to be going," Lavold explained.

Matt couldn't imagine where they needed to be going in

tiny Turkey Creek. But he kept the thought to himself. Instead he said goodbye, wishing he could stay and visit longer. Pretty, young women were a rarity out here. He climbed aboard the wagon and picked up the lines. "Steel, Gray," he spoke softly to them. Once he had their attention he maneuvered them around in a half circle and headed back towards the D Rocking D. He wondered if Lavina watched him go, but didn't turn to look. She watched his back until he took the west fork, crossed the creek, and disappeared in the cottonwoods at the edge of town.

***

It was mid afternoon when Matt arrived back at the D Rocking D headquarters. Besides the house and barn, there was also a bunkhouse. The buildings were all made of logs brought from the mountains, except for the leanto attached to the barn. It was enclosed only on the long side, with lumber that had been left over from a house that had been built in town a few years ago. An outhouse had been erected with the last of the milled boards. It sat in back of the two cabins.

The name D Rocking D signified the partnership between father and son. It was a bit of a joke as only the second D on their brand had a rocker underneath it, as if Matt were still a baby. All the Daly's cattle and horses were marked on the left hip with:

**DD̲**

The barn was the largest structure and it sat closest to the creek. There was a corral along the more protected east side that ran down to the creek. Coming off the west side was the leanto. This was where Matt drove the team, making the circle around back and then through one open end, stopping underneath. To his surprise, there was a man in the back of the other wagon that sat there.

14

"Hey there, Matt!" The other man had heard him coming.

"Curly! It's about time you showed your face." The two men jumped down and shook hands.

Big John and Curly had met years before when the cook had hired on for a cattle drive starting out in Texas. His real name was Henry Jacobs, but had gotten the nickname when, as a young man he had first grown a mustache. The whiskers had curled up at the corners instead of growing downward. The mustache eventually straightened out, but the name stuck.

Curly remained friends with the Dalys after they moved to Montana, and still cooked for them during roundups. For the rest of the year, he disappeared. Nobody seemed to know where he went, or what he did. He was one of the best cooks around, as well as being their friend. He always showed up a few days before the D Rocking D cowboys rode out, and had the uncanny ability to know just when that was, even though the date was never fixed. He had ridden in on a borrowed horse and immediately began getting the chuckwagon in order.

Matt unhitched the team, first unhooking the four tugs running along either side of each horse to the evener at the front of the wagon. Then he unhooked the neck yoke from the front of the horses' collars. He carefully set the wagon tongue on the ground. Walking back around the horses, he picked up the lines where they lay across the front of the wagon. The horses hadn't moved, but when Matt spoke to them, they walked forward a few steps, closer to the barn door. Knowing the routine, they stopped where they had been taught to, where Matt would have the least distance to carry the harness into the barn.

Matt unbuckled the lines from each side of the horse's bits and coiled them up before hanging them on the wooden hames pointing upward above the horse's withers. After unbuckling the belly band, Matt gathered up the heavy harness and carried it just inside the barn, hanging it neatly on pegs. He did this with both horses, removing the collars last. Once the horses were free, they went in the barn and into separate stalls to wait for grain. After removing their bridles, Matt fed them and left them to eat.

The two men lifted the supplies out of the buckboard and into the chuckwagon. Curly nodded and mumbled a few words to himself at each item, already planning meals. Everything had its particular place, and Curly made sure it was exact, knowing not only what was efficient, but also where everything would ride well.

Chuckwagons were developed for use on cattle drives, and were designed for sturdiness and efficiency. The reinforced box had to travel over rough country. Filling the back of the bed was the mess box. It was filled with compartments for storing cooking and eating utensils and dishes, plus containers of flour, sugar, coffee, and other food staples. The back of it swung down and formed a table when the attached leg was unfolded. Filling the remainder of the bed were bedrolls, and the bags containing the few personal possessions each cowboy brought for use on the roundup.

"No taters?"

"Nope," Matt answered the cook.

Curly nodded again. The ingredients he had here were more than adequate. Anything fresh would have to be used up quickly anyway.

Once the supplies were transferred, the two men took a break, enjoying the late afternoon. It had cooled off as the shadows lengthened, and there was just the hint of fall in the air. Matt reached for his vest, which still lay on the wagon seat. He took a pouch out of one pocket and rolled a smoke from the tobacco and papers he pulled out. He handed the pouch to Curly, who also rolled a cigarette.

"It'd be nice if the weather held for a while." Matt stated the obvious, after pulling a match from the other vest pocket, striking it on the metal rim of the wagon wheel, and lighting both cigarettes. Curly agreed, combing his dark mustache with the fingers of one hand. They leaned against the end of the wagon, catching up on the latest news.

"How you getting along with your neighbor?"

"Fine, as long as he keeps his cattle where they belong."

Matt knew which neighbor was being referred to.

The Spade was the closest ranch to the north of the D Rocking D. Their range was just over a high ridge that ran in between the drainage the Dalys ran cattle in and the next creek over. By way of the road it was close to twenty miles to the Spade ranch headquarters. It was a large spread, thirty thousand head, mainly steers, run by a man interested only in maximizing profit. The fact that he owned no cows for breeding proved that short term gain was his only concern in the ranching business.

"What's the guy's name?"

"Buehler. They call him Bully." That seemed enough of an explanation for Curly as to the man's character.

Just then John Daly rode up on horseback. He'd been out checking water holes to see which springs were still running this late in the summer. They would be slowly easing the cattle closer to headquarters as fall progressed. He had also been looking to see if cattle had strayed in from other outfits.

John was an older version of his son. At just over six feet, he was barely taller, and had the same square jaw and friendly smile. His eyes twinkled out from between thin lines at the corners, made by years of squinting into bright sunlight. But the creases were the only thing that looked aged about him.

"Howdy, Curly! Where you been hiding?" He smiled down from atop his horse.

"Big John! I've been here and there." He knew the question was merely a greeting.

"How's it look?" Matt asked.

"Pretty good." John swung his leg over the horse's rump and stepped down. He was still limping on his sore knee. Matt noticed that his father was well armed. There was a rifle in the scabbard on his saddle and a pistol hanging off his hip. Rifles were for hunting, pistols were for trouble. Matt knew his father was a little uneasy about their neighbor to the north to be packing so much iron.

Curly asked about the limp. "What're you slowing down in your old age?"

17

John smiled. "Nah. I had a difference of opinion with a knothead." He motioned with his head to a handsome buckskin standing in the corral.

Curly said, "He's a good looking son of a bitch anyway."

John nodded. "He'll be okay, and so will I," meaning he thought the horse would make a good mount. He was still looking at the animal.

"You expecting trouble?" Matt asked his father.

"No, and I didn't find any." Big John didn't want to worry his son, but he knew what could happen when one man coveted what others had.

"I've got to feed my dough." Curly went around to the back of the wagon to tend to his sourdough starter. Any cook worth paying had a jar of the white, pasty-looking, leavening that he carried with him. The starter Curly used originated down in Texas years ago. He had boiled potatoes and then let them sit until they fermented, the native airborne yeast spores colonizing the new food source. Once the potatoes had a strong smell, he continued to feed them by adding flour and water. After a week, the live yeasts were strong and plentiful enough to use for rising and flavoring bread, biscuits, pancakes, anything made with flour.

Curly took the jar out of the straw-lined, wooden box and set it on the back of the chuckwagon. He pulled back the wire holding the lid in place and sniffed the gooey mess. The sour smell was one he never tired of. He added flour and water in small amounts. If he filled the jar too full, the starter would bubble over as the warm weather kept it active. It needed to be used soon, before it outgrew the jar. The other option was giving some away, which he did frequently. The sourdough starter used at the D Rocking D had originated in Curly's jar. He snapped the wire back over the lid and returned the jar to the box.

Matt went back into the barn and led the two horses out, turning them loose in the corral. After closing the wooden gate, he went through a gate into a smaller pen next to the corral and pitched hay to the hungry horses. Meanwhile, Big John led his horse into the barn to unsaddle and grain him. Besides the team, only a couple other horses were up close. The rest of the remuda would be brought in off the range just before they left on the roundup. There was a milk cow with a calf out in the fenced pasture. They looked up as Matt pitched the hay, and then resumed grazing on the fresh grass.

At dusk Matt walked over to the cabin. He could hear laughter coming from inside and wondered what story Curly was telling. He opened the door, and sure enough, sitting on a bench was the cook with his arms outspread. "I'm telling you, it was this big, darn near knocked me off my horse!" Big John sat in the only chair, as usual. Another younger man sat opposite the cook. A young woman sat next to him. All were laughing. Matt didn't know what was so funny, but knew he'd hear the story another time.

The young couple sharing a bench was Kirsten and Jesse Branson. They had filed on homestead acres across the creek from the Dalys, and were working for the father and son until they could get their own place stocked with cattle and generating income. So far they had built a small cabin they lived in. A footbridge across Turkey Creek connected their home to the Daly's.

John Daly met the Bransons one day when he was riding through Compton. The young couple had stood out on the main street because of the milk cow tied to the back of the wagon they were riding in. Obviously new to the area, Big John struck up a conversation with them.

"Where you headin'?" It was a frequently asked first question.

"We're not exactly sure." It was the woman who answered. "We're looking to take up some land, run a few head of cattle."

"Well you better hurry up and get there. Winter's not too far off."

The man sitting next to her shifted on the seat. He knew they weren't in the best position. Their traveling had taken longer than they thought it would, but the milk cow had been bred before they left Nebraska, and they wanted her to remain that way.

"My name is John Daly." He came closer to the wagon and stuck his hand up for the other man to shake.

"I'm Jesse Branson. This is my wife Kirsten." The two of them jumped down off the wagon. Kirsten stood at the horses' heads while Jesse walked behind the wagon and looked underneath it. John followed him and watched as he bent over and checked the springs and running gear. There was a lot of wear and the axles needed grease.

"How much further you expect to go?" The wagon would need repairs before too long. The three of them ended up standing on the street close to an hour discussing the couple's options. John liked them so much he invited them out to the D Rocking D. Matt liked them too. They stayed the winter. And two years later they were still there.

Jesse stayed at the headquarters mainly. Although he was a good hand on horseback, he preferred working at home. He was a carpenter by trade, and the Dalys were fortunate to have him working for them. Actually the two homesteads were run more as a partnership, with everyone pitching in to help on both places.

Kirsten did most of the cooking and other household chores, besides riding. She was nearly as strong as the men and worked just as hard. Her long blond hair hung in a braid down her back. It got in the way of her hat when she pinned it up.

When her milk cow calved the next spring, there was the added bonus of fresh milk and cream. Mainly the Dalys enjoyed having the Bransons around for their happy, positive outlook on life.

The five of them sat down to supper, Matt and Curly sat on one bench and Kirsten and Jesse shared the other. Big John sat in the chair at the head of the small table. "I didn't see any pepper." Curly looked at Matt.

"You all out?" Matt looked up at the cook a little too eagerly. Curly supplied his own seasonings when he cooked. He used only a few, but usually had an ample supply. "I'll ride to town tomorrow and pick you up some." They all looked at Matt. Was he volunteering to go to town again tomorrow just for pepper?

"All right," Curly answered. Matt continued eating, but inside he was smiling at the thought of seeing Lavina Lavold again.

They finished supper. The dishes were washed and dried. Buckets of water had already been brought up from the creek and the wood box near the stove was full. Kirsten skimmed the cream off the top of the milk that she had poured in pans after the morning's milking.

"Is there room in the bunkhouse?" Curly asked as they were finishing up.

Matt nodded. John had given their three cowhands a couple days off in town before the roundup. Equipment, saddles and such, needed repairs before the crew spent the next month out on the prairie. Mainly it was an excuse to hit the saloons, but as long as they were sober and ready to ride when the time came, they could drink as much as they wanted to in town.

Curly preferred solitude when he slept. If the bunkhouse had been crowded he would have slept in the barn. He walked over to the smaller cabin, carrying a lantern and his bedroll. Inside he hung the lantern on a peg and looked around at the bunks. There were four of them, one in each corner, taking up most of the space in the small building. A wood stove sitting in the center of the dirt floor completed the furnishings. Three beds were claimed as there were blankets on top of them and personal possessions underneath.

The fourth, closest to the door, was empty. It was simply a frame covered by boards that was attached to the log wall on two sides. The outer corner had a stump for a leg. On top of the boards was a mattress made of strips of coarse muslin sewn together and stuffed with prairie grass. Curly bent over and sniffed it. The hay still smelled sweet and fresh. He'd sleep well tonight. He smiled to himself as he fluffed the mattress before putting his blankets down. The bare boards with a blanket would have suited him. A woman's touch around a place could sure feel good sometimes.

The following morning Matt left for town just after breakfast. "Your kid have a girl?" Curly asked as he and John watched Matt ride off.

"Not that I know of."

"He needs to find himself a wife." Normally Curly wouldn't have an opinion on a matter that was none of his business. But the Dalys were his friends. It was more a concern for Matt's well-being than telling him what to do. Big John nodded his agreement as they turned their attention to the chuckwagon. It was time to grease the moving parts on the underside. Then they would roll it out to attach the bentwood bows that held the canvas top in place.

It was a cool, crisp morning. Matt wore a wool coat over his vest. It was his favorite time to be riding. Everything was fresh as the sun rose, first turning the mountains pink, and then working its way down the hills before warming Matt and his horse. It felt good on his face. Matt thought about how quickly the sun went from unbearable heat to welcome warmth within a week once the season started to change.

\*\*\*

In the town of Turkey Creek, the Lavold family was at breakfast in the restaurant at the Palace Hotel. Theodore ate hurriedly and left his family before they finished. He walked next door to the general store to further investigate Silas Riggs' business. He preferred to go alone so there would be no distractions as he studied the books and talked to the store owner.

Lavina sat with her mother and two brothers, lingering over breakfast. "Well, now what?" She asked. Elizabeth sighed as she put down her tea cup and looked around. She didn't know if she could live in such a small, out of the way place. But she had agreed to come here with her husband.

Her younger son banged the table leg with his foot.

"James, stop that. Come along." She rose from the table and led her family out. The restaurant was so small that it was only a few steps to the doorway and out into the hall that served as a lobby. There was a bench against the opposite wall.

She couldn't very well expect her children to sit there all morning, so she continued out the front door. The porch, shaded by an overhang, was still cool so early in the morning. Elizabeth stood on the edge and looked down the single street. There was little going on. To the south the road disappeared as it followed a bend in the creek. Looking the opposite direction, she saw a fork where the road divided. Behind the buildings, to the east, the hills began flattening out. Below was the creek, lined on either side by towering cottonwoods.

"Let's go write a letter to Grandma Lavold. We'll ask at the front desk for stationary." The two boys slowly followed their mother back inside. Lavina reached the door last. As she was about to step inside, movement caught her eye. She turned to look. It was a man on horseback coming towards her from the forked road above town. The first thing she thought was how handsome he looked sitting tall on a fast-walking, long legged, bay horse.

It was Matt Daly. He had already seen her and was smiling. She couldn't see his eyes. As usual, they were shaded by the wide brim of his hat. He stopped his horse in front of the hotel, swung his leg over the back of the saddle, and stepped down in one easy motion.

Tying the bay to the hitch rail, he called out. "Good morning, Miss Lavold."

"Good morning, Mr. Daly." Lavina smiled back. "What brings you to town so early?"

"Pepper, and call me Matt."

"Well then, call me Lavina. Pepper?"

"Yup. The cook has to have it." Matt took off his coat and tied it behind his saddle before walking up the steps. Lavina heard the jingle of his spurs. That and the leather leggings he wore were the only differences in his appearance from the two times she had seen him before. All the cowboys dressed similarly. Not all of them were this handsome though, she thought. Matt was still smiling, so Lavina decided there must be a joke behind the pepper.

"You have a cook?"

"He also drives the chuckwagon. On roundups." He wasn't sure if she understood.

But Lavina remembered Matt's explanation of the bi-yearly gathers from yesterday. In fact she had thought about it a lot. It seemed so exciting. She wanted to ask him more about his life.

As if reading her mind, Matt asked her, "Would you like to walk with me down by the creek?"

"Let me tell my mother." She ducked her head in the door and called out, "Mr. Daly and I are going walking down by the creek." She backed out quickly as her mother called out.

"Take your brothers with you."

That was what she was afraid of hearing. For an instant she considered pretending she hadn't heard, but Matt went inside to where Elizabeth stood at the desk with her sons. "Good morning, Mrs. Lavold. How are you this morning?"

"I'm well, thank you Mr. Daly."After hearing her reply Matt turned. to the two boys. "Would you like to go down by the creek.? If it's all right with you." He looked back at their mother.

"Yes, sir," they each replied politely. They looked at their mother expectantly. She looked at her daughter who obviously liked the young man standing in front of her. Should she be worried? Lavina was no longer a child, and Matt Daly was polite and seemed respectable. With the two boys along, at least there was the semblance of a chaperone.

"Behave." She gave the two of them a stern look. "Be back by noon."

After Lavina and her sons walked out the door with Matt, Elizabeth turned and headed up the stairs to their rented room, smiling. It wasn't often she had time to herself. Once the door was closed, she sat on the bed, untying and pulling off her boots, feeling relief in her cramped feet. The boots were the latest style, narrow with pointed toes, but they weren't comfortable. Sitting back on the bed, she pulled out her knitting so she wouldn't feel too guilty about being idle during the daytime. Within ten minutes she was fast asleep without a care in the world.

As Lavina passed through the doorway ahead of him, Matt put his hand on the small of her back to guide her to the right. At the steps he dropped his arm, but they both felt the warmth of that touch linger, he on his hand and she on her back, as they started down the street.

They followed Teddy and James along a path that ran alongside the stream. The sun had burned the dew off in all but the shadiest spots. The creek made only the faintest gurgle as the water flowed slowly towards the Yellowstone.

"Papa went to talk with Mr. Riggs. I don't know if he'll buy the store. Mother thinks this is too out of the way, especially since there's no doctor. I think she misses home." Lavina felt like she was babbling, but it was a relief to be talking to someone. Her father hadn't said much, and her mother was reluctant to voice her concerns. And yet their future hung on his decision.

"Did you want to come out here?" Matt asked.

"Oh, yes. Papa and I both wanted to. It's as beautiful as I imagined. I want to stay."

"I hope you stay." He wanted to kiss Lavina right then and there. Instead he sighed and looked around. "I wish you could come see the D Rocking D." He then began talking about the ranch, and about his father's and his plans for the future. Lavina heard the pride in his voice as he spoke of his home.

They strolled along the creek as they talked, almost oblivious to the yells of Lavina's brothers. Finally Matt glanced up at the sun. "We better head back."

"James, Teddy, we need to go back," Lavina called.

Too soon they were in front of the hotel. Matt left them there. He untied his horse from the hitch rail.

"Don't forget the pepper," Lavina called out from the doorway. The pepper. Matt had almost forgotten. He waved as he headed for Silas' store.

The entire ride home Matt thought about Lavina. He and his father would be heading out within the week, which meant he wouldn't be back to town for five or six weeks. There was nothing he could do except hope that Theodore Lavold bought the Turkey Creek Mercantile. He didn't want to think that he might never see Lavina again.

She walked back into the hotel with her brothers, thinking only of Matt. Her mother's shrill voice brought her back to reality. "Look at your clothes!" It was directed at Teddy and James. Lavina looked at her brothers. They were wet and muddy. Next Elizabeth directed her ire at her daughter. "You know you have to watch them. What were you doing?"

"I'm sorry. I should have watched them more closely." Elizabeth looked at her daughter. Was she falling for Matt Daly? Normally she was much more responsible. The distracted look on Lavina's face told her all she needed to know.

"Well what's done is done. Get upstairs and change," she told the boys. "I don't know how we'll get your clothes washed. And it looks like you'll be wearing wet shoes for a while."

As they filed upstairs, Elizabeth was actually pleased. Lavina was twenty-four, the same age as Matt. She had never seemed serious about finding a husband. Maybe her daughter was beginning to realize it was past time to be married. Of course this young man couldn't be the one. They wouldn't be staying here. At least that was what she hoped.

\*\*\*

The Lavolds had lived a comfortable life back in Illinois. They resided in a medium-sized town where Theodore owned a store. It was similar to the general stores found in western towns, but as the town expanded out onto the farm land, it was changing. Factories were turning the town into an industrialized city. The air was becoming hard to breathe as coal smoke spewed out of giant smokestacks and chimneys. It was making Theodore's job harder as well. Instead of only providing food and necessary household items, he was finding himself having to keep up with current trends. Not long ago, people were content with well-built and functional household goods and tools. Now they wanted specialty items. It was becoming harder to stock his store.

He had always wanted to go west. He tried to persuade his wife to at least think about it many times, but she enjoyed her safe, routine life. Instead, he found himself discussing his adventuresome longings with his daughter. Lavina also wanted a more exciting life. He wondered if this talk wasn't the reason she hadn't found a husband. His sons, on the other hand, also seemed content where they were.

One day he made up his mind. A wealthy businessman came into the store and began talking about what he believed was the future of the town. He thought the way to make money was to start selling the newly manufactured luxuries people seemed more able to afford. Theodore offered to sell him the store on the spot. They agreed on a price and shook hands. He locked the door at noon and hurried home to tell his wife.

Elizabeth was as shocked as Lavina was thrilled. She looked around her comfortable home, wondering why on earth her husband and daughter would want to leave it. In the end she agreed to take her family west mainly because her husband once again had the fire in his eyes she had seen when she met him twenty-five years earlier.

Rinsing the mud out of her sons' clothing using a basin on the washstand in a hotel room in a frontier town, Elizabeth Lavold realized why her daughter had never been interested in her suitors back east. None of them had that fire in their eyes, no real passion for living. That was what Matt Daly had. Suddenly she was proud of her daughter.

# Chapter 3

Roundups were busy and exciting times. Each ranch had two yearly roundups, one in the spring and another one in the late summer or early fall. Even though the entire territory was public domain, the range had been divided into grazing districts. Boundaries were defined by the geography; mountain ranges and rivers were the main dividers.

Since the land was all unfenced, the cattle could and did wander long distances, and had to be brought back to their home ranges. Each ranch also sent a representative or rep to the neighboring roundups as well. Their job was to claim and bring back any cattle that had strayed.

The spring roundup was to brand the new calves and to see how the animals had overwintered. In the fall the purpose of rounding up the cattle was to sort out the older steers and send them to market. The Dalys set out with their crew. This included the three cowboys who had been occupying the bunkhouse, plus three more who hired on for the gather. Kirsten and Jesse waved goodbyefrom the yard. They stayed home during roundups. Although Kirsten was a more than capable hand, it was no place for a woman. She had wanted to protest the first time she wasn't allowed to go, but camping out with a bunch of crude men didn't appeal to her anyway. Instead she and Jesse kept watch over ranch headquarters while the others were away.

Each rider had a string of five horses assigned to him by Big John. Although the horses all carried the D Rocking D brand, each cowboy's string was considered his as long as he worked for the Dalys. No one, including the boss, rode a horse from another man's string without permission from that cowboy. As few cowboys owned their own horses, it was easy to tell who any individual worked for by the brand on the horse he rode.

It was barely light enough to see when they rode out that first morning. There was no frost on the ground yet, but they could feel it coming. The horses were frisky in the coolness and trotted out with no encouragement. The remuda followed John across the prairie, loosely encircled by the other riders. Curly drove the chuckwagon, pulled by four horses, in the rear. He would reach the first night's camping spot hours after the cowboys had started their first sweep.

John turned in his saddle to look back as he topped a ridge. The herd of fifty horses was loosely bunched and still trotting. Riders flanked them on either side. He watched as his son took off after the buckskin that had gotten the best of him the week before. Matt got in front of the gelding and turned him back before other horses followed him away from the herd. They would make good time since most of the horses had been out on previous roundups and knew the routine.

\*\*\*

Big John smiled, thinking back to his days trailing cattle. It had been a good life, almost as good as ranching with his son. With only twelve men they drove two thousand head of cattle over a thousand miles.

Each rider had a specific place to ride on the edge of the

herd. The two point men stayed on either side at the front, guiding the leaders. Behind them were the two swing men. Further back were two flank riders. The worst job was riding drag. These three men followed the herd, encouraging any stragglers, and they ate a lot of dust. The other two men in the outfit were the horse wrangler, and the cook, up on the chuckwagon.

The first couple days out were difficult, as the cattle weren't used to traveling. That's why John always had two older steers within the herd. They took the lead and the others followed. Once the herd got used to the routine of life on the trail it became easier.

As trail boss, Big John rode ahead to find places to water and feed the cattle, and where they could bed down for the night. Once he found a satisfactory camp site, he would ride to a high spot where the two point men could see him signaling the direction to take the herd. The cowboy on the side they wanted to turn towards dropped back, while the rider on the opposite side came in closer to the lead cattle. The herd would veer away from him and towards the opening that had been provided. Like a giant wave, the rest followed.

Sometimes all went smoothly and sometimes it didn't. There were always strange sights and sounds to spook the herd since they were wild cattle. Once they were lying down for the night, it was the cowboy's job to keep them that way. The men took turns, two at a time on two hour shifts, circling the sleeping cattle in opposite directions. Many of the cowboys sang as they rode at night, putting words to quiet, soothing melodies. In fact many western ballads came from cowboys riding night herd.

All it took was the flash of a match being struck to light a cigarette, or the flap of a slicker in the wind and the herd could spook. A cough might set them off. Of course the worst was lightening. Once the cattle were running, the only way to stop the runaways was to gallop to the head of the herd and turn the leaders by running into them until the entire bunch spiraled inward to a stop. It was dangerous, especially in the dark when the ground was slick from rain and lightning flashed nearby. A cowboy wanted a sure footed horse for night duty.

Big John remembered the worst stampede he'd ever experienced. A horse being ridden on the night shift snorted at a rabbit that jumped out from underneath him. The sound brought the herd to their feet and they were running in an instant. The cattle ran for miles, scattering into small bunches as they fled. It had taken days of tracking to locate them all. And it was luck that the handful of men was able to round the steers up into one herd again on the vast, rolling prairie.

One time something set the herd off and almost a hundred head never were found. John realized afterwards that the strange men who had been lurking nearby were rustlers and had caused the stampede in order to cut off a bunch of the steers. They were miles away by daylight and there were so many tracks that it was impossible to figure out which direction they had gone.

All in all, life on the trail was enjoyable. It was hard work for little pay, but there was a freedom out on the prairie that John had never experienced before. There was also a comraderie, of knowing that the men he was with would do anything to help him, and he felt the same about them. Of course once the drive was over he never saw most of them again. Moving on was the way of life for many cowboys. They were continually looking for new adventures over the next horizon. Big John was no exception, except he had a family to support.

*** 

By the time the first gather had been completed that evening there were a half dozen other wagons in the center, and the cooks were busy preparing supper for their crews. Curly had gotten there first and claimed the best spot near the creek where there was shade. He scanned the sky. It was clear so he decided there was no need to put a tarp up over his outdoor kitchen. The biscuit dough was rising as he put fresh coffee water on the coals. Tonight there was fresh meat and a pudding made with canned milk and raisins for desert. An hour later Matt rode in.

"How'd it go?" Curly greeted him.

"Real good. The cattle are fat and the grass is holding out. "Matt paused. "Coffee on?"

"Not yet. Matt looked around and spied his father off in the distance, visiting with the owner of a neighboring ranch at his camp. He loped his horse over and greeted the two other men.

"Young Daly. I hear you got yourself a girl." The man grinned at him.

Big John tried to act casual as he listened to his son's reply. "I can't imagine where you heard that. 'Course you fellows over on the Two Butte don't seem to have anything better to do than make up gossip." The three men laughed, teasing one another as they caught up on the latest news. Roundups were the only socializing many cowboys had, outside their own outfits, all summer.

Curly was the first one up each morning. He rolled out from his spot underneath the wagon long before daybreak and gave the ashes a stir to see if there were any live embers left from the night before. Once the fire was going, he put the coffee water on.

Meals varied at different camps, depending on the generosity of the owners. Unlucky cowboys ate a lot of beans and salt pork. More sympathetic owners made sure their chuckwagon was well-stocked with canned and dried fruit, sugar, flour, and rice, things that would keep well in all kinds of weather.

The cook was in charge of the camp. No one crossed him, not if they wanted good, hot food, well prepared and on time. John and Matt Daly backed him up. Not that they ever had much trouble. The D Rocking D was a good place to work and most cowboys were content to stay working there.

While the water in the huge pot was heating, Curly pulled out a coffee grinder. Once the water was boiling, he dumped in the ground coffee and let it roll for a few minutes. Then he pulled the pot off the fire and let it brew before pouring in cold water to settle the grounds. The pot sat near the edge of the fire to stay warm.

The horse wrangler came in. He had the horses rounded up into a rope corral, one end of which was tied to the chuckwagon, to wait until after breakfast. "Mornin'."

"Mornin'," Curly answered. "Have some coffee." The young man hadn't made a move until invited. Now he picked up tin cups and poured both himself and the cook a cup of the aromatic brew.

Curly turned back to the pancake batter he was mixing. He placed two large cast iron skillets on the coals to heat while he mixed flour and water into the batter. As he stirred, he hummed quietly to himself while the other man stared at the fire.

When he had the batter to his liking, Curly scooped chunks of lard out of a can and dropped them onto the skillets, spreading the grease to cover the entire surface. He dipped his fingers into a bucket and flicked the water drops onto the skillets. They hit the hot lard and sizzled. Satisfied the temperature of the skillets was just right, he poured ladles full of batter onto them, making eight pancakes at a time.

Half an hour later Curly yelled out into the darkness. "Come and get it 'fore I feed the coyotes."

Immediately bedrolls began moving as men squirmed out into the chilly morning. The men quickly set hats on their heads and pulled on their boots. Then they rolled up the blankets and tarps that were their beds. Heading towards the fire, they dumped the bedrolls in the front of the wagon before grabbing a plate and cup. Curly served a stack of pancakes to each man, topping it with a ladle of stewed apples. The men helped themselves to coffee and found a place to sit and eat.

John Daly was the first man to the fire. He was in his element and jumped up from his warm bed into the cold air ready to go each morning. Sitting on the damp ground to eat didn't bother him. He would dry out as the day warmed up.

Matt joined his father as the second man to the fire with

his breakfast. He looked over and grinned. The older man was so completely at home, sitting there in the dark, his face lit up by the fire. It was how Matt would always remember him.

They all ate quickly, washing the food down with hot coffee, while waiting for Big John to line them out. The boss thought about the terrain to be covered that day while sizing up his hands. Besides himself and Matt, there were six of them. The horse wrangler was just a kid and he would stay near camp to look after the remuda and help Curly. Three of the men had been living in the bunkhouse all summer. Two others had been staying in a line shack on the edge of their range. They all knew their way around the D Rocking D country. The last man had been hired recently and didn't yet know the area.

Big John turned to the new man. His name was Samuel, but John pronounced it with the emphasis on the second syllable. "Sam Yule, you head out with Joe here."

Samuel Sheldon had come out to the ranch a couple weeks before looking for work. After he had introduced himself as Samuel, Big John had automatically shortened his name. "Nice to meet you Sam."

"It's Samuel," the slight, serious looking man corrected the D Rocking D boss.

"Okay, Sam Yule." And that was how his name was pronounced from then on.

"Joe, take Sam Yule up the coulee." John motioned to the east with his head as he continued his directions. "On top, point out Eagle Butte." He turned to Samuel. "Ride to the base of the butte. There's a cliff on the far side with a sheltered spot below it. Take anything you find to the bottom and bring them back."

He turned back to the man named Joe. "Head on over to Lantern's and come back through the meadows." John instructed each man, the directions making little sense to anyone not knowing the country, the landmarks, or the names of the people who lived there.

There was just enough light to see by when John walked into the horse herd, hemp rope in hand. The horses snorted and began running in a circle around him as he stood in the center of the make-shift pen, shaking out a loop. The other cowboys waited on the outside. One by one, they called out the name of the horse they wanted caught for the morning's gather. John's rope flew out and the loop encircled the neck of a horse whose name had been called. It all went quickly, as Big John rarely missed. Once the targeted horse felt the rope settle around his neck, he stopped and followed it to the center of the circle. John waited for the appropriate cowboy to come with a bridle and claim his horse. As the man led his mount away, he carefully coiled his rope and shook out another loop. The procedure was repeated until each man had a horse. Finally he snared the buckskin who had been giving him problems as his morning's mount, confident that the horse was ready to go to work.

The horses were quickly saddled, and the mounted riders headed in the direction assigned to them at breakfast. The same thing was happening in the half a dozen other camps. As the first cowboys loped off, another man, a stranger, trotted towards the Daly camp, leading two spare horses. He was repping for another outfit further east.

"Mornin'," he called out.

"Go see if there's any grub left," John called out to him. The man was grateful, since he hadn't eaten since starting out from the distant ranch the day before. He turned his horses in with the Daly's remuda before heading for the chuckwagon and a hot breakfast.

Matt headed north, towards country filled with coulees and pine covered hills. Since he and his father knew the area best, they had the toughest ride that day. Once atop a ridge, miles from camp, he began scanning the hills below him, looking for brown and white patches in the landscape. The longhorns out in the open were easy to see against the yellowing vegetation. The ones in the trees were harder to spot, so he would have to ride down each canyon, pushing any cattle he found towards the creek flowing through the bottom. At the end of the day he would push them across, towards camp, and complete the circle.

He had also decided on a green horse for that day's ride, one who didn't yet know his job. The horse wasn't used to being out alone, and spooked when they came upon the first bunch hidden in the trees part way down a steep hillside. The cattle scattered downhill as the horse jumped sideways and galloped in the opposite direction, back up the hill. Matt urged him on and didn't allow him to stop until they were all the way to the top. By then the gelding was out of breath from his hard run. With the edge off, he settled down and began paying attention to the task at hand.

Depending on the size of the area to be covered and the terrain, each gather took from one to three days. Once all the cattle were in, the sorting began. Big John sat his horse on a hill above the growing herd. Small bands of between fifty and two hundred head came out of the hills onto the prairie from all directions, each group followed by a lone cowboy. Once the cattle were crowded into one bunch, it was time to change horses.

Each horse had a specific job depending on what he was best at doing. The tall, long legged ones were better at covering long distances. They went out on the longest gathers. The younger, inexperienced horses that needed the miles to gain experience with a rider on their backs, also were ridden out where they were less likely to cause trouble than if they acted up near camp.

The horse a cowboy chose from his string to use when they sorted was one who could cut a wild steer from the safety of the herd. These horses were quick and able to read a steer's movements. The best ones turned cutting into a game they were as determined as the cowboy to win.

Cutting and sorting was hard work. Each man could easily go through three horses in an afternoon. It was also exciting, sitting on the back of a well trained horse as he anticipated the moves of the steer, needing little guidance from the rider. In fact it sometimes became more about staying in the saddle as the horse worked. Many a cowboy had to listen to laughter from the other hands as he picked himself up out of the dirt after his horse turned out from under him. They all took turns at cutting, helping hold the herd while their horse rested, and watching the next guy show off his horse's agility and skill.

As the steers were cut from the main herd the reps from far away ranches claimed the ones with their brands. Each calf was also checked, and any that had been missed the spring before, as well as any mavericks, were roped, drug to the fire, and burned with the appropriate brand. Once the sorting was completed, the cows, calves and bulls were turned back out for the winter. The herd of D Rocking D steers grew as the roundup progressed.

The weather remained beautiful for a full month, with crisp, clear days. Bright, blue skies framed the brilliant, gold cottonwoods along the creek bottoms. The shrubs on the hillsides added reds and oranges as the heat of summer faded. Nights turned colder and they woke to a covering of frost in the mornings that turned the landscape an eerie gray in the predawn light.

The fall roundup went smoothly with one exception. One morning, Samuel was back in the hills chasing an uncooperative cow and calf. The pair threw their tails in the air and ran the opposite direction from camp. He would have let them go except they wore the brand of a distant ranch. They had to be brought in so they could be returned to their home range.

Samuel's galloping horse stepped in a badger hole and went down. Both horse and rider scrambled to their feet with minor injuries, but the horse headed back to the safety of the remuda at a full run and Samuel was left on foot. Great, he thought. He was miles from camp, so he started walking.

The riderless horse was spotted as he topped the ridge above camp. Most of the men had just sat down for a quick meal when the cry of, "Rider down!" rang out. Without hesitation, they set down their plates, and mounted horses already saddled for the afternoon. Leaving only two men to stay with the herd, the rest fanned out to search for the missing cowboy.

There were too many tracks to isolate one set, but they all knew the general direction to look. Samuel was found a couple hours later by Matt, who was relieved to see him on his feet and walking. The bruised cowboy mounted behind Matt, and the two of them rode the single horse back to camp, driving the cattle Samuel had collected in front of them. The afternoon was lost looking for the downed man, since it was evening before the last cowboy returned, happy to find Samuel safe.

When the last steer had been trailed to the pens near Miles City, where box cars were waiting, John met with the men who had bought the cattle, to receive payment. It was the Daly's one paycheck of the year and the first thing John did was hand out wages to his cowboys. Some of the men who had worked for the Dalys, as well as other ranches over the past summer intended to remain in town for the winter, at least as long as their money held out. Others planned on heading south for the winter, to seek work in a warmer climate. Only two kept their jobs on the D Rocking D.

Once the steers were at the loading point, it was time to celebrate. Many of the hard working, young men hadn't seen a town since spring, and they were feeling thirsty. Leaving two unlucky cowboys to stay with the horse herd, the rest galloped off to the nearby town.

Cow towns all over the west were festive this time of year. The saloons filled with rowdy young men, eagerly participating in the good times, drinking, gambling, and generally tearing it up. Some of them would spend their entire summer's wages in a few weeks. Others were more conservative, but the saloons and women of the night took a lot of money from the rowdy cowpunchers.

Once the crew was paid off and the remaining money deposited in the bank, Matt and Big John headed for the hotel. John had his mind on a hot bath. Matt was restless and distracted however. His job wasn't over yet as the plan was for him to go repping the next district over, as John repped at the Spade roundup further north.

"You think Joe can handle repping at Gillan's?" Matt

knew the man was capable.

"You got business somewhere?" John asked back.

Matt shrugged. "I just feel like getting home."

"Well go ahead. Joe knows the brands." John knew his son was thinking of the girl he had met in Turkey Creek last month. Otherwise he'd be joining the rest of the men in the saloons for some drinking and fun. And repping was an enjoyable job.

"Let's get something to eat." The two men left their horses at the livery stable where they were grained and fed hay. Matt wanted to let his horse eat and rest for a while before riding out.

Two hours later, and without much daylight, Matt was on his way home. He was riding his favorite horse, a handsome long-legged bay he called Easy. The horse got the name because, as Matt said, he was easy to ride and easy to look at. Matt had used the horse sparingly the past month because he wanted him fresh going into winter.

Most of the horses were turned out to fend for themselves until needed again in the spring, but a few were kept in the corral and fed hay for winter use. The ones that had been ridden hard all summer needed a vacation. Besides the weight that had been ridden off them, they had saddle sores and other bumps and scrapes that needed time to heal.

It was the horse wrangler's job to get the horses home. They would go at a leisurely pace with Curly and the chuckwagon, giving the tired horses ample time to graze each day.

# Chapter 4

**M**att could feel the weather turning as he rode west from Miles City. He scanned the sky. It was clear, but the temperature was dropping. If the wind picked up, he'd be riding into it. But he didn't worry, as he was dressed for cold weather. It was an easy, two day ride to the D Rocking D. There was even a road ranch part way, where he could stop for the night and he and his horse would get fed.

At the top of the next ridge, a cold wind hit horse and rider. Matt halted. Without dismounting, he reached around and untied his saddle strings. His coat was on top of the gear tied to the back of his saddle. He pulled it out, and retied the strings, pulling them tight. Putting the coat on, he could feel Easy's restlessness, but the gelding stood until Matt nudged him forward. The horse traveled at a hard trot. The wind picked up even more. Matt pushed his hat further down onto his head, turned up his coat collar, and bowed his head so his hat wouldn't blow away and the brim protected his face. The evening of the second day was colder with a wind that penetrated Matt's coat and slicker, and it was snowing when he came into view of the ranch buildings. There were a few inches of snow on the ground, cold powder that swirled around Easy's hooves with each step. But it seemed the clouds were lifting. There was a faint orange glow to the west after sunset.

Two horses, Kirsten's and Jesse's had been left behind, but now the corral was empty. The couple's saddles were gone from the barn. Matt glanced over to the cabin across the creek. It looked dark and deserted. He wondered where the couple had gone.

His own home was also dark and cold. After four and a half weeks, it had taken on an unlived-in feeling. Matt knew a warm fire and the smell of coffee would change that. He felt lonely and smiled to himself. Was he being womanized? He had thought about Lavina the whole time he was away, seeing her face as he lay looking up at the stars at night. What chance did he have of finding her? Matt woke the next morning before there was even the hint of light in the sky. After starting a fire in the cook stove and putting coffee water on, he pulled on his coat and stepped outside. Not too bad he decided, since the wind had died down. He went down to the corral and pitched hay to his horse, noticing Eva, the milk cow, had come up with her calf. They had been turned out into the pasture, but there was little grass left. He tossed out another pile of hay for the two of them.

Matt walked down to the creek at the bottom of the corral and made sure the water was free of ice so the animals could drink. He crossed it to close the gate into the pasture.

An hour later, after washing down biscuits he had stashed in his saddle bags the day before, with hot coffee, Matt saddled his horse and rode for town. It was no longer snowing, but as the clouds lifted, the temperature dropped further.

It was still early when Matt rode into Turkey Creek. He rode straight to the general store. Inside, Silas greeted him.

"Howdy, Mathew!" He was always happy to see anyone from the Daly ranch.

"Mornin' Silas."

"Coffee's fresh," the store owner called out from behind the counter.

Matt walked over to the wood stove in the center of the store to pour himself a cup. He stood with his back to the blazing fire, warming his fingers on the tin cup while they talked. Not that he had to ask any questions.

"Those Lavold folks never came back. He sent me a note sayin' he had 'found better business opportunities elsewhere,' I think he put it. That's okay. He's a smart guy. Turkey Creek isn't ever going to amount to anything. He'll do much better for his family in a bigger town."

Matt's heart sank. Silas continued on, but he wasn't listening. Lavina was gone and he didn't know where. He questioned Silas more about the note, but apparently Lavold had been vague.

Matt walked over to the counter and ordered a few food items, a can of milk, coffee, tobacco, small things he could stuff in his saddlebags. Silas asked how the roundup went. The two men chatted for a while after Matt poured himself a second cup of coffee.

"Here's your mail." Silas handed Matt a couple of envelopes as he was gathering up his purchases. As usual, no money changed hands. The total was added to the D Rocking D's account without anything being said.

Matt stuffed the mail into his coat pocket without looking at it. He said goodbye and walked out into the cold air, automatically looking up at the sky before stuffing his saddlebags. He patted Easy before crossing the street.

It wasn't yet dinner time so he headed for one of the two saloons. The Blue Bear had never been considered a nice place in any sense. The building was constructed of logs, and there was only a single window cut into one wall. Inside it was dark, dirty and cramped. The smoke was thicker during cold weather when the leaky wood stove added to the tobacco smoke. Matt ducked his head as he passed through the doorway, and squinted through the brown haze as he made his way to the bar.

There were already a couple men sitting at one of the

tables, despite the cold weather and early hour. Matt nodded at them as he walked by, not recognizing either of them.

"Howdy there, Daly," the bartender greeted him.

"How's it goin', Bobby?" The man poured a small glass of whiskey without being asked, since it was the only thing he served. He was a big man with thick black hair. His beard matched, except on his left cheek where no hair grew because of a thick scar that ran from just below his eye down to his chin. It gave him a sinister look that helped keep order when trouble was stirring in his bar. Actually he was easy going, as long as everyone behaved.

"You know, there were some men in here the other night, said some interesting things." Bobby's deep voice lowered as he spoke to Matt. Like a lot of men seemed to do when they lived on the frontier for a while, he shortened his sentences.

Matt didn't like gossip, but he had never heard Bobby run off his mouth. He was usually quiet, listening to the conversations around him. "A couple of Buehler's men were in. They're starting to act like they own the town. Seems the boss wants to expand his range and he don't care how it happens."

Matt shrugged. "They can talk all they want." He put the empty glass down and thanked the other man. Heading for the door, he paused a moment as a stream of tobacco juice shot out from the mouth of the man sitting closest to him, splattering on the dirt floor. Once outside he walked over to The Palace for a meal before starting for home.

That evening he was still thinking of Lavina. He hadn't given up on finding her, but he might have to get lucky. He carried his saddlebags and rifle into the cabin after pitching hay to Easy, and Eva and the calf. There was still no smoke coming from the stove pipe across the creek.

He pulled out the can of milk and shook it. It hadn't frozen. In fact the temperature was comfortable once the sun came out. The snow had melted, and there hadn't been enough moisture in it to leave mud.

Matt pulled the other items out of his bags, and then reached into his coat pocket for the fresh bag of tobacco. The mail fell to the floor as he pulled his hand out. Matt picked it up, noticing the handwriting on the top envelope for the first time. It was definitely a woman's, and not his mother's. He moved to the lantern, turning up the wick so the light became brighter. The letter was addressed to him. He opened it and read:

*Dear Matt,*

*I am writing to let you know we are safely settled in Cedar Junction. My father has already shook hands on a store here. The town is busy, as there is much building, so we shall thrive. So far, ours is the only general store. It is called the Cedar Junction Mercantile. I don't know if Papa is going to keep the name.*

*I hope all is well with you. Thank you for your hospitality when we were in Turkey Creek.*

*Sincerely,*
*Lavina Lavold*

By the time Matt finished the note he was grinning. He had found Lavina! Cedar Junction wasn't too far away. Like many towns along the rail line, it was shorter to ride there cross country from Turkey Creek, but the train could get him there quicker. And Matt considered the train schedule. He could leave right now if he rode. Not that he was going to. The horse herd was due back and it was time to prepare for winter.

The next afternoon they arrived, and Curly made it back, driving the chuckwagon, just before dark. Matt had put on a pot of beans that morning in anticipation. It wasn't fancy, but the biscuits were fresh.

No one said anything to Matt about his early departure from Miles City, and he stayed silent on the subject. Instead they wondered where the Bransons might be. But since nothing seemed amiss over at their cabin, no one was worried.

Curly prepared to leave. He emptied his few personal belongings out of the chuckwagon before taking the canvas top down and storing the wagon underneath the shed. Matt helped haul the remaining food into the house.

"Back already?" Kirsten called out as she and Jesse rode into the yard. "Things must have gone well."

Matt nodded as he greeted the couple. "Where you been?"

"We took the train over to Bozeman to look at cattle."

"Oh?" They had talked before about introducing other breeds of cattle into their herd to improve the quality of their beef. "What did you find out?"

"There's a fellow over there selling Hereford bulls. They're nice looking animals." For once, Jesse did the talking.

"Well, I'm off," Curly announced a few minutes later. He mounted the horse he borrowed from the D Rocking D as they all said goodbye. He would leave the horse at the livery in Compton before boarding the train. They all knew better than to ask where he was going.

***

The weather remained warm and dry for the next month and Big John returned home from the Spade roundup. He had experienced no trouble from Bully Buehler's outfit. Because of the high ridge separating the larger outfit's range, there was little mixing of cattle. This gave Buehler nothing to complain about.

Although Big John hadn't questioned his son about the woman he met, he had thought about it. He had also been planning. That night at supper he looked down the table at Jesse. "What are the chances of the weather holding for a while?"

"It's been pretty nice so far." Jesse didn't want to commit to predicting the weather. "What are you thinking?"

"I think it's a little crowded in here." He nodded towards the wall on his left. The logs for an additional room were already piled up outside, the trees having been felled and hauled home for that purpose. John hoped his son would

45

eventually marry and he couldn't expect his bride to sleep in the same room as her father-in-law. Besides, there wasn't the space. The addition would almost double the size of their home.

Matt knew what his father was thinking. Word of his walk with Lavina had spread fast. During the roundup he had been the butt of many jokes. Everyone knew he was sweet on a girl he had met in Turkey Creek. "Hey, Daly, you better take a bath before you get home," one man had called out to him after a particularly dusty day of cutting steers. "Can your girl cook as well as Curly here? I hope she smells better," was heard one night at supper. It was true. He was thinking a wife might do him good. He thought about how lonely he felt the night he arrived home. That had never happened before.

So the three men began making plans for building the new room. Jesse retrieved a scrap of paper from the wood box by the stove, found a pencil stub, and began calculating.

As he worked out the details, John announced he would take the wagon to town the next day. Besides the hardware needed for the addition, it was time to settle his account at the store, plus they had let their food stores dwindle before the roundup. It was time to restock for winter. "You won't need me, will you?" Matt decided to make other plans.

"Where are you going?"

"To Cedar Junction. To see a man about a horse." Although it was a plausible explanation, no one believed him. But there was a horse trader near there, who despite his occupation, was an honest man. He handled only quality horses, mainly ones that had been driven to Montana, where there was always a demand for them.

Once again, no one questioned Matt. They were curious why he was acting so mysterious, but it was his business. He'd explain himself when he was ready. Actually there was no reason he was reluctant to tell anyone about Lavina. He didn't think there was anything to tell. He just knew that he wanted to see her again.

It was still pitch dark when Big John rolled out of bed. He struck a match to light the lantern, and then glanced over at

Matt's bunk. His son was gone. John chuckled. She must be some girl. He thought about Matt's mother as he dressed.

Easy was fed a skimpy breakfast that morning. The horse ate a scoop of oats while he was being saddled, but received no hay. Matt hurried in the darkness. They had a long ride ahead of them, as Matt planned on returning home that night. The shorter days meant more riding in the dark, but it was something they were both used to.

Pausing at the first creek crossing to let the horse drink, Matt began to have doubts. Maybe he should have written. What if Lavina didn't feel the same way about him? But he continued on. Today he'd find out, one way or the other, how she felt, and it would be face to face.

As he neared Cedar Junction, he began to feel excited. First he would stop off at the horse trader's though.

A black mare immediately caught his eye in the corral. She was a little smaller than he liked, but she was well-built, with good bone and hooves. Her head was pretty, with just a hint of daintiness, her eyes wide and intelligent. A white star on her forehead shone through her forelock. Normally mares were used only for breeding and the geldings ridden. The Dalys planned on breeding their own horses soon, so she could be ridden until they found a quality stallion.

The man she belonged to went by the name of Hedge. He wanted a lot of money for her, and seemed confident he would get it. Matt agreed she was worth it, but he didn't tell Hedge that. He haggled with the man, knowing that making the deal was the horse trader's favorite part of selling horses.

Finally Matt agreed on a price. It was still more than he wanted to spend. "Throw in a halter so I can get her home and I'll take her off your hands." He knew it wasn't the smartest deal he ever made, especially with winter so close. They didn't need another horse to feed this time of year.

Matt turned down Hedge's offer of a hot meal and the chance to go inside and warm up. As good as it sounded, he wanted to get a move on, and hoped the man wasn't insulted. He mounted Easy and picked up a trot as he led the mare down the road towards town.

***

Lavina was helping her father that morning. Theodore Lavold hadn't stopped working since he had agreed to purchase the store. The previous owner had handed over the key to the front door, and left town within a week. There was something about a widow, but Theodore wasn't listening as the man told him his plans.

The Lavold family had settled into the cramped living quarters at the back of the store. There were only two rooms. The smaller one was a bedroom for Theodore and Elizabeth. The main room became a bedroom for the three children, besides being the kitchen and living area. There were beds in two corners. One the boys shared, and Lavina hung blankets around the other so she could have some privacy. There was room for a table and chairs, and a kitchen with counters and shelves. The cook stove provided the only heat. It was cozy, they all agreed.

Lavina washed the counter top and straightened the bolts of fabric. She then took the broom from the corner and swept the floor, reaching behind tables and barrels with the bristles the best she could. She swept towards the door, thinking how nothing had changed. This was exactly how she would have spent a morning helping her father back home. She swept the accumulated dirt through the doorway and out onto the wooden porch. The door closed behind her as she hurried to return the dirt to the street. It was chilly out and she had no coat.

As she reached for the doorknob, movement caught her eye. She turned to look down the street. It was a man, riding one horse and leading another, coming towards her. He seemed familiar, also the horse. She could barely make out his face between the upturned coat collar and the brim of his hat. She realized it was Matt when she saw his smile. She smiled back and waved.

He stopped at the hitch rail, dismounted, and tied the two

horses. Lavina waited up on the porch. Her breath caught as she once again looked at the incredibly handsome man coming towards her. Did he come here to see her?

"What are you doing here?" It was all she could think of to say.

"I had to see a man about a horse." He was still grinning as he repeated the line from the night before. "How have you been?"

"Fine, thank you. Did you get my letter?"

"Yes, but let's go inside."

Theodore was surprised when they came through the door together. He wore an apron over his black wool pants and vest. His white shirt had a collar, but he wore no tie. Those days were over. For him it was casual, working attire, but was still more formal than most people dressed in the frontier town.

"Papa, look who's come for a visit." Lavin tried to hide her excitement.

Lavold greeted Matt with a handshake. "Come in and warm up." As usual there was coffee on the stove. "Lavina, pour Mr. Daly a cup of coffee."

"I'll get it" Matt intercepted Lavina as she headed for the stove, mug in hand. He took the cup out of her hand and looked into her eyes as his hand grazed hers. Although she was still smiling, she met his gaze for only an instant before looking away.

Matt poured himself a cup of coffee. As he turned back from the stove, Lavold excused himself and went back into the kitchen. His wife had assumed it was a customer when she heard first the door, and then voices. Theodore closed the door and grinned mischievously at Elizabeth.

"That young Daly fellow is here. He came to see our daughter."

"Did she want to see him?"

"I believe so." They whispered together, happy for their daughter, but feeling protective also.

Out in the store, Matt said to Lavina, "Get your coat. I have something to show you." He spoke in a low, urgent voice that seemed to promise excitement and something wonderful. Lavina hurried towards the back of the store.

Matt stepped into the back, just through the doorway, after Lavina went through. He greeted Mrs. Lavold, and then followed Theodore back into the store. Lavina removed her apron before snatching her cape from a hook on the wall.

The two of them walked outside onto the wooden porch and Lavina took a deep breath of the fresh air. It was late fall, and the wind felt raw. A gray cloud covered the entire sky, but the weather didn't affect her. Suddenly she was too happy to care. They walked down the steps to where the horses were tied. Matt stopped in front of the mare. She had her head up, ears cocked forward, as she looked back at them. Easy, the gelding, stood with his head lowered, dozing. His ear flickered once, and he half opened one eye. The mare, being in strange surroundings, with strange people, danced a step to the side as Matt and Lavina approached.

Matt spoke softly to her and she stood. He reached his hand out slowly and stroked her face. She was beautiful and Lavina said so. Matt stood looking from Lavina to the mare, feeling happy in finding two such beautiful girls in one day.

"What do you think of my new mare? One day I'll find a stallion to breed her to." There was just the hint of brag in his voice.

"She's beautiful. May I pet her?"

"Sure, just be slow and easy." But the mare had been reassured. She sniffed Lavina's hand and allowed her to touch the silky softness of her black coat.

"What's her name?"

Matt had already thought about that. "I'm calling her Lucky." He didn't explain further, but he'd already decided this was his lucky day.

After admiring the mare, Lavina turned and petted the gelding also. She didn't want him to feel left out. Matt chuckled, imagining the entire D Rocking D string being spoiled by the beautiful woman at his side.

"Let's go have some dinner." Matt looked towards the

restaurant next door to the Lavold's store. Lavina was surprised. It was bold of him, asking her to walk into a public place with a stranger. She looked up at the restaurant also.

"You mean at Mother's?" Mother's Restaurant was owned by a woman named Sophie Larsen. She was a widow. Her husband had died out on their homestead when he fell off the roof he was shingling and broke his neck. Knowing she would lose the land, she drove the team to town with her two sons and as much as she could load into the wagon. It was a two-day trip to Cedar Junction, and she worried the whole way what would happen when they got to town.

By working hard and being smart, it wasn't long before she was successfully running Mother's Restaurant. Of the three establishments in Cedar Junction serving food, hers was the only one considered suitable for families. It wasn't where Matt had come with his buddies the few times he had been in town.

"Your father said he could do without you for a while." Matt was teasing, but Lavina liked that he was straightforward. Of course it would be all right. Mother's was just what the name implied. Besides, Mrs. Larsen had become a friend of the Lavolds.

"Lavina, welcome." Mrs. Larsen greeted her neighbor. She smiled at Matt as Lavina introduced them. Matt took Lavina's cape and hung it on a hook near the door next to his coat.

"There's room on the end here." The older woman guided the couple to the end of one of the long tables that filled the restaurant. There were no individual tables. Friends and strangers sat on benches, rubbing elbows and passing the bread.

The one meal on the menu that day was chicken pot pie. Mrs. Larsen brought out plates heaped high with scoops of the tasty chicken and gravy that had been baked with a flaky crust on top. Returning to the kitchen, she brought out another plate of fresh bread.

As they ate, Matt told Lavina about the roundup. She told him more about her move to Montana. "How's life here in Cedar Junction?" He asked.

"So far I've mainly been helping in the store. We've been busy, so there hasn't been time to get out much." She didn't want to complain, but she was getting bored.

"Well you're out now." Matt smiled at her. She felt a lot better as she tasted the bread pudding Mrs. Larson put in front of them.

They couldn't linger over their meal, as Matt had a long way to travel that afternoon. But they laughed, happy for the moment, and still incredulous that they were together again.

As Matt rode away he thought of Lavina's big brown eyes. He had only caught glimpses of them straight on because she never held his gaze for more than an instant before looking away. He wondered why, and thought she must be shy. But shyness didn't show in her words or actions. Maybe when she got to know him better she would be more direct.

Lavina watched Matt's back as he rode off. He sat straight and proud in the saddle, ready to take on life. It was something she had never seen in the men she had known back east. She didn't realize it until then, but that confidence was a trait the man she married had to have.

The little, black mare trotted a few steps to catch up with the gelding. Lavina shivered as she watched them. Matt turned and waved just before he disappeared into the mid afternoon gloom. He had seemed unconcerned about starting off this late in the day, knowing he would be riding for hours in the cold and dark.

"This isn't even woolly weather yet," he had said. What were woollies? She wondered. He had put his long johns on the month before, however. They would stay on until it warmed up in the spring.

\*\*\*

Living in Cedar Junction had already begun losing its charm for Lavina. Since the weather had turned colder she was forced inside. She wanted to challenge herself. At least there had been the library back home and her friends. Of course they were mostly married with children now. But here all she had was work. The store was shaping up nicely, becoming better organized, and with Lavina's help, cleaner. Now that they were caught up for the winter she was beginning to feel trapped.

She thought of Matt again. She'd asked him if he was coming back, and he said he would visit next month. Then he asked her if she would write to him. She smiled. Of course she would.

# Chapter 5

Big John saw the new mare standing out in the corral the next morning, waiting for her breakfast with the other horses. He was impressed as he looked her over. His son had spent his money wisely. He remembered the first time Matt had collected his pay.

It was on his first cattle drive when he was just sixteen. Big John was the trail boss and Matt was the youngest man helping bring a herd up from southern Texas to the rail yards near Ellsworth, Kansas. After eating dust for seven hundred miles, the cowboys were ready to celebrate. John counted out the ninety dollars for three months work and handed it to his son without a word.

"Hey, Kid, you coming?" One of the men yelled to Matt as he prepared to leave for town. John turned his back, pretending he hadn't heard, as Matt glanced his way. He knew his son thought himself grown up and he figured he wasn't able to tell him what to do any longer since he was making a man's wages.

"I'm coming." Matt rode off with the others. The next morning John found his son propped up against the side of a barn where he had passed out. His entire summer wages were gone, and he was left with only a bad hangover.

Matt remembered walking up to the bar, feeling like a man as he ordered whiskey in the noisy saloon. Sitting at a table with other cowboys he had his first taste. After a few burning sips, the alcohol had begun going down easily. A sweet smelling woman came over to him. One look at the top of her low cut dress and she'd had him. How he got to the barn, or where the rest of his money had gone, he had no idea.

The other, older men felt bad. They figured they should have taken better care of the kid. Big John knew it was a painful lesson, and one he had to learn. But from then on Matt was ready to listen to his father about responsibility with money. The following summers when he rode with his father, Matt stashed most of his wages in camp before
riding off to town at trail's end.

Big John looked at the mare one more time before going in to breakfast. This was a much better way to spend hard earned money he thought with approval.

*** 

Late fall became winter and the frontier settled into the routine of short, cold days. Morning chores were started as it began to get light, and evening chores ended in the twilight. In between, when the weather allowed, the addition at the D Rocking D headquarters began taking shape.

It was hard work. First the logs were peeled and the ends were shaped into dove tails so they would fit together tightly at the corners. Then, with the help of a pulley system the logs were lifted and placed one on top of another, one layer at a time. Once they were positioned they were held in place while spikes were driven through to secure them. Two windows were cut out and framed, and waited for the glass that had been ordered.

Christmas came to the D Rocking D. Usually there was a party to attend within a half day's ride, but this year it was a quiet affair. A snow storm left two feet of snow on December 24th, which made travel difficult. So a steer was butchered, and the Dalys and Bransons, plus Joe and Samuel sat down to fresh steaks for Christmas dinner. Afterward John opened a bottle of brandy he had brought from Miles City for special occasions. He poured it into tin cups and cracked china for a toast to another prosperous year on the D Rocking D.

A week later a chinook blew in and the snow began melting. Once the ground was bare, and the worst of the mud dried up, Matt announced that he was riding to Cedar Junction the following day.

"For goodness sakes, Matt! Tell us about her." Kirsten could hold it in no longer. They all knew he had visited a girl living there. Not wanting to pry, the men didn't ask about it. Matt had told his father a little bit about her, but no one else.

Matt smiled. He knew he wasn't getting out of it. "What's her name?" Kirsten knew she risked being called a busybody, but if Matt hadn't been ready to talk about her, he wouldn't have brought up the subject of visiting her in front of everyone.

"Lavina Lavold," Matt answered her. He told them about her family's move from Illinois, and that her father had bought the general store in Cedar Junction. Kirsten listened for a couple minutes, but she'd already heard all this from local gossip.

"But how much do you like her? Are you in love with her?"

"Kirsten..." Jesse couldn't believe his wife's directness. That just wasn't something you asked a man.

Matt had thought about it though. He was already wondering how soon he could ask her to marry him. "I like her a lot," he said quietly. It was all he needed to say.

The following morning his son's bunk was again empty when John awoke. He quickly dressed in the cold. It had to be love, he decided, leaving in the dark before a hot cup of coffee. Once again he thought about his wife.

\*\*\*

John Daly and his wife lived in Pike County, Missouri where Matt was born in 1859. Soon after that, the Civil War started.

Although John believed in state's rights, he tried to avoid becoming involved in the conflict since he had no quarrel with people to the north. He owned no slaves, and just wanted to live his life peacefully working his family's farm. That had changed as Union soldiers invaded the south. First his wife's family farm was destroyed, then his own, by a band of renegade Yankees. He joined the Confederate Army to help push them back.

Three years later, John was on the verge of becoming a bitter man. Fellow countrymen had turned against one another with a viciousness he couldn't have imagined. Libby, his wife, wanted to stay with what was left of their families and rebuild, but John wanted nothing more to do with the anger and betrayal that seemed to have become ingrained in that part of the country.

By 1867, there were trains to take them to Texas, and John finally persuaded his wife to bring eight year old Matt west. He immediately felt more at home there, while Libby complained about the dry climate. She never seemed to get over the fact that her comfortable life from before the war was gone, and that they had to create new ones. She had no sense of adventure and didn't understand her husband's enthusiasm for the west.

The feral longhorn cattle of Texas and northern Mexico had been increasing in numbers. When the war started there was no one to manage them, plus the market for beef collapsed. Their value had been in hides for leather, fat for rendering into tallow for making soap, candles, and lubricants, and the bones were in demand as fertilizer for the acidic soils in the east. There were an estimated six million of them running wild once the fighting stopped.

When the Dalys reached Texas, there was beginning to be

a market for beef to feed people in the east. Trails were scouted out to take the captured cattle to the growing cities. The first cattle drives took them all the way to the east coast, but as the rail lines expanded, it became much easier to trail them to points along the tracks and then ship them on boxcars.

John Daly could think of nothing he would rather do than spend summers riding across the open prairie. He hired on as a cowboy to trail the wild cattle from southern Texas into Kansas. It didn't matter that he knew nothing about moving large herds. Few men did. They learned as they went.

Within a couple of years, he had become trail boss on the drives he made, and was tagged with the name of Big John. He had learned well how to herd two thousand head of cattle seven hundred miles using only a handful of men.

It hadn't been an easy life though. As the boss, he was paid fifty dollars a month for the three month drives. That didn't begin to support his family. Plus he wanted to buy a ranch of his own. That meant that during the winters he took whatever jobs he could find. It was a tough way to make a living. Partly because his wife never quit complaining, he was gone more and more, sending money home. His son spent long periods of time without a father, but he felt it couldn't be helped.

Finally, when Matt was sixteen, he joined his father for a summer in the saddle. Libby disapproved, but knew it was a losing battle to keep her son home. She was adamant that he return for school in the fall however.

For five years father and son spent summers trailing cattle. By 1880 Texas and Kansas were filling with settlers. The cattle were trampling wheat fields on their way to the railroads, and John had to carry cash to pay damages to the farmers. More and more barb wire was being strung, which made it harder to find feed and water for the longhorns. There was talk of a national cattle trail, a fenced corridor specifically for moving cattle, but it never materialized.

The towns along the railroad were becoming civilized as well. The locals no longer allowed the cowboys their unbridled celebrating at trail's end. The cattle towns of Wichita, Abilene, Dodge City, and others sprang up as shipping points. One by one they shut down, or greatly restricted their stockyards. Finally the hundreds of thousands of cattle coming out of Texas were trailed to Ogallala, Nebraska and other points further north. The cattle drives took longer and longer, but Big John and Matt didn't care where they went, or how long it took. They had found their calling as cowboys.

By the early 1880's the herds weren't just steers being sent north to fatten before being sent to slaughter. Cows were also making the trip for breeding stock on the abundant grasslands of the northern prairie. The Daly's next to last trail drive took them all the way up into Montana Territory. Once across the Yellowstone River, they knew that this was where they wanted to make their home.

After the herd had been delivered and the cowboys paid off, the Daly father and son loaded up a packhorse and went exploring. They rode west along the Yellowstone to Compton Creek. A cowboy they met in a saloon in Miles City had told them there was rangeland north of there that wasn't being used. Following the freight route up the creek, they came to the tributary of Turkey Creek. Where the two streams met was the beginning of the town.

John Daly filed his homestead claim on a spot upstream where the creek widened to meander across a large meadow. Matt took land adjacent to it, and the father and son began planning. The next summer was their final cattle drive from Texas. Within the herd were five hundred head of cows John had bought as the start of their own herd. He had to borrow the money to purchase them, and it was the only time he or Matt ever went into debt.

It had been three years since Big John had seen his wife, not since he and Matt rode off to Montana with the intention of staying. He had wanted her to come join them, and she said she would. They both knew it was a lie, however. She went back to Missouri and stayed. A few letters were sent back and forth every year, but Libby Daly was content where she was.

Although he was still fond of her, John doubted he would ever see her again.

***

Lavina was expecting Matt this time when he rode into Cedar Junction. She had written him weekly. The week before she had received a note back telling her, weather permitting, when to expect him.

He came into the store and quickly shut the door behind him to keep the cold air out. The cold had stiffened his fingers inside thick gloves. His hat and slicker were crusted with ice. Lavina came over to greet him.

"Oh goodness, let me help you," she said when she got close enough to see his numb face. Matt couldn't remember the last time a woman had fussed over him.

He tried to smile. "It's so good to see you." The words were slightly garbled, and they both laughed at his attempt to talk through the numbness. "Is this woolly weather?" Lavina asked. Matt laughed even harder as he got the buttons on his slicker undone and pulled the sides apart to show off his wool chaps. He immediately wanted to grab Lavina and kiss her when he saw the surprised look on her face as she took in the thick chaps, made from long-haired, angora sheep hides, covering his legs. He contented himself with just looking at her.

Once again Matt had only a few hours to spend with Lavina. They went back into the kitchen, where she served him a plate of food. He let her do most the talking while he ate and warmed up.

Elizabeth and Theodore Lavold went into the store to sit on the bench by the stove. She carried her knitting; he brought a newspaper. They left the door to the kitchen open, but they were still out of sight, and out of hearing. Matt wanted to steer the conversation towards marriage, but worried it might be too soon. He and Lavina barely knew each other really. But how could he ever be more certain about wanting to marry her?

Finally he got up to put his coat on. It had been hanging

near the stove, and was toasty warm. Matt slid his arms through the sleeves and buttoned it up. He did the same with his slicker. Once his hat was on his head, they both began to feel sad.

"Can I come again next month?"

"That would be nice." Her voice trailed off. She had finally looked into Matt's eyes for more than an instant.

He took her into his arms, leaned down and gave her a long, lingering kiss. When he straightened up, her arms were around his waist. Reluctantly they stepped apart. "I'll see you next month," he said. For the second time that day, Matt slipped quickly through the door of the Cedar Creek Mercantile.

***

The short winter days became dreary for Lavina. After a heavy snowfall she wondered if Matt had a sleigh. She thought about the black mare he had shown her. And she thought about his blue eyes.

They were the deepest blue she had ever seen. The first time she looked into them, she could feel herself starting to fall into the deepness. She didn't know if she would be able to climb back out. So she only allowed herself quick glances. Finally, as Matt prepared to leave that day, she felt brave, or maybe desperate enough. She allowed herself to hold his gaze as he looked down at her. And she fell. Then Matt kissed her and when he left, she was still standing there.

She wrote him every week, not that there was much to say. She read a new book. New fabric arrived, and together she and her mother began measuring, cutting out, and sewing new clothes. There were the everyday chores to keep her busy. She also helped her father in the store.

There seemed to be a lot of single men coming in. Some traveled a good distance to shop at this particular store. News had traveled fast about the pretty storekeeper's daughter. Lavina made conversation with them, and listened to the news they brought. Living in such a sparsely populated area, they all knew of the D Rocking D, and some knew Matt and his father. None of them brought recent news of them that winter though.

She heard some men talk about how fast Montana was filling up with livestock. They seemed concerned. She wanted to ask Matt about it.

*** 

As Matt rode home after visiting Lavina on that cold winter day he was thinking and planning. He decided to ask Mr. Lavold for his daughter's hand in marriage. He'd write him a letter, and then he wouldn't be able to chicken out the next time he saw Lavina.

As he rode it became colder, and he finally had to get down and walk for a while to get the blood moving in his feet again. He didn't really mind traveling in the wintertime. It was part of his life. As he crested a hill, the wind caught him. He bowed his head and leaned into it. He would be traveling into it the whole way home. Stopping beside his horse, he remounted. The horse and rider set off at a lope to make good time while it was possible. It was going to be dark in an hour, and the wind could pick up even more. Life on the D Rocking D in the wintertime focused a lot on survival. Staying warm and fed was important, although their food selection narrowed when it got cold. A frozen steer hung in the barn, where chunks were hacked off as needed. Since it froze inside the cabin every night as well, a lot of things wouldn't keep. Dried goods weren't affected, but anything perishable they did without. And of course the milk cow was dry.

The walls on the new addition were chest high. Matt was anxious to work on it whenever possible so it would be finished in the spring. Not only did the snow slow their progress, but when more than a few inches covered the ground, the cattle were checked more frequently.

That was the main job of the two men kept on during the winter. Joe had spent the last two summers working at the D Rocking D. He was a happy young man who liked to socialize.

Once he reached the age of twenty-five he decided it was time to take life more seriously. He asked Big John if he could stay on for the winter, instead of living in town and drinking up his pay. For him the nearly empty bunkhouse was lonely, but he worked hard and didn't complain.

The other man was Samuel. Big John and Matt both liked him, even though he was so serious and seemed a little odd. But he said he preferred staying out at the ranch all winter through the short days and cold nights. He brought a stack of books with him, along with a small leather-bound book with blank pages where he recorded his life and thoughts.

When he first came to the ranch the summer before, it was obvious cowboying was new to Samuel. The first afternoon he was there, a couple of the other men put a saddle on a wild and dangerous horse that so far had bucked off all who attempted to ride him.

"Here's your horse." One of them handed the reins to the new man. Samuel guessed what was up, since everyone was watching. He also knew he had to prove himself in order to be accepted.

He took the reins with a determined look on his face. Before the horse could move, he grabbed the saddle horn and vaulted onto his back. The surprised horse hesitated for an instant, which was all the time Samuel needed to shove both feet into the stirrups and settle deep in the saddle. The horse took to bucking hard, grunting each time his feet hit the ground, and bellowing each time he went airborne. He added twists and turns as the rider stayed with him, much to everyone's amazement.

Samuel rode the horse to a standstill, and then flapped his legs, driving him forward. The gelding took off at a gallop across the creek and out onto the prairie. An hour later they returned. The big dun was dripping sweat, his lathered sides heaving. Samuel dismounted and looked at the others.

"What's next?" His expression was still serious, but inside he felt triumphant as he saw the amazed looks on the faces staring at him. Just because he was new to being a cowboy didn't mean he had never sat a horse before.

Big John started over from the barn when Samuel was handed the reins. He had seen the same thing happen many times before. It was a joke played on inexperienced men, and he wasn't going to allow it. He had seen more than one of them hit the ground hard; one kid had been crippled permanently.

But he never had the chance to stop the prank. Big John watched with the rest as the slight young man not only stayed on the bucking horse, but took him for a ride afterward. He did make it clear however, that the cowboys were never to play that particular trick again. Samuel earned respect that day.

During the winter the five men rode out frequently. Matt, Big John and Jesse left only for the day. Joe and Samuel frequently were sent out with a packhorse for as long as a week. They stayed in line shacks as they searched the country for both cattle wearing the D Rocking D brand, and for areas where grass still stood for them to graze.

The line shacks were tiny, crude cabins, or sometimes dugouts, built on the borders of the grazing districts for cowboys to stay in while riding the range. A few of them had stoves inside for cooking and heat, but some only provided shelter from the wind and snow. Anyone who needed a place to stay for the night was welcome to use them.

When the cattle drifted they had to be brought back and put in a spot that had feed and open water. Some days the cowboys spent every daylight minute in the saddle, riding through wind and snow, or with the blinding glare of the sun reflecting off the snow in the frigid cold. Meals were spaced far apart, as there was no way to prepare a midday meal out in the open.

One evening Matt came home later than usual. Kirsten poured him a hot cup of coffee. "Supper's in the oven. It's still warm."

"Is Big John back?"

"No. Isn't he with you?"

"He went around through Bog Flat" This was a sub-irrigated meadow surrounded by willows. This time of year the ground was frozen, and the cattle holed up in the thick bushes when the wind blew. "He should have been back before me. Are Sam Yule and Joe back?"

"They're in the bunkhouse." Matt re-buttoned his coat and hurried back out into the cold. Jesse quickly pulled on his boots and outer clothing and ran after him. After getting Joe and Samuel from the bunkhouse, they went and caught horses. Ten minutes later, the four men rode out into the night.

Matt tried not to worry as they rode the route his father should have taken to return home. Although the wind still blew the snow around on the ground, the clouds had lifted, revealing the moon overhead. The clearing sky meant it was easier to see where they were going, but it also meant the temperature was dropping. His father could freeze to death by morning if he lay on the ground hurt. There was also the possibility that they would miss seeing him. Every couple hundred yards, one of them shouted out into the darkness. They all listened intently for an answer.

After Matt shut the cabin door, Kirsten went over to the stove and fed it more wood. Normally she let the fire go out after supper was cooked, but the men would be cold when they returned. Using precious wood just for heat was a waste, so she pulled a bowl and spoon, plus flour and sugar off the shelves while she thought about what she could quickly bake in the heating oven.

Big John had reached Bog Flat hours before. He searched the thickets, and sure enough there were at least a couple hundred head of cattle hunkered down out of the wind. They seemed content though. Most were chewing their cud as they lay there waiting out the storm. He didn't want to disturb them, so rode past with enough distance that they resembled strange, dark mounds in the deepening gloom.

He turned his horse towards home, and as he reached the other side of the snow covered meadow he searched with his eyes to find the best way up the hillside. At the edge, his horse suddenly broke through a deep drift that hadn't been visible. The horse floundered in the chest deep snow while John hung on, trying to get him to stand. Finally they got back out onto the meadow. He dismounted and grimaced as he saw the horse refusing to stand on one hind leg.

He stroked the horse's rump to calm him, and then rubbed down the leg. When he got to the hock, the horse jumped sideways at the pressure of his hand.

Son of a bitch, John thought. There was no way the horse was rideable. He might even be ruined. Slowly he started making his way home, leading the limping horse.

It was hard to stay warm walking at such a slow pace, and John felt his feet going numb. He debated about whether to keep going, or if finding shelter for the night was smarter. The moon poked through the clouds, so he decided to keep walking. He knew he was less than ten few miles from home. If only his horse could keep hobbling along. He spoke to him softly for encouragement.

Two hours later he heard a voice call out. He answered and was found by the others. He stiffly mounted behind Samuel and they rode for home. Matt stayed behind and led the lame horse the rest of the way.

# Chapter 6

M att composed a letter in his head. It was short and to the point. Would Theodore Lavold object to him asking for Lavina's hand in marriage? That should work, he thought. After hemming and hawing for a couple of weeks, he finally sat down with a sheet of paper and a pencil. He wrote the short note and addressed it to Lavina's father.

Wanting to be sure the letter got to town, he made the ride one sunny day. There was snow on the ground, but the air was still, and the sun felt warm on his back. He was tempted to turn his horse east, towards Cedar Junction.

Once he had given the letter to Silas Riggs and was assured it would safely reach its destination, Matt breathed easier. The wheels were in motion. He visited with Silas while sitting on a bench soaking up warmth from the stove, but felt too restless to stay long.

Thanking the store owner for the coffee, he rose to leave and walked outside. The temperature had risen only slightly. He wanted to get going,  but decided that a drink would warm him up for the ride home. Inside the Blue Bear the fire was roaring to compensate for the cold air coming in through the cracks in the walls. Matt walked through the smoke to the bar and Bobby took down a bottle of whiskey.

"How're you wintering there, Young Daly?" The bartender greeted Matt.

"Just fine. How's business?" The bar was empty except for the two of them, and Matt realized it might not have been the best question to ask, even though he meant it as a greeting.

"Take a look around."

"They'll be back once it warms up."

"Nah, the town is dying. Has been since the train came through."

The man was partly right, but Matt believed the increasing number of settlers would keep the town alive. He left the bar shortly after. There were other things, like a marriage proposal, to think about.

Silas sent the letter out with the next trust worthy rider on his way to Compton. From there it was only a couple hours by train to Cedar Junction. Theodore Lavold received the letter two days later. Lavina saw it when the mail arrived that day, since it was the only envelope in the box at the post office. She had just mailed a letter to Matt. How strange, she thought when she recognized the handwriting.

"There's mail for you here," she called to her father from the door.

"Put it on the counter." Theodore was cleaning ashes from the wood stove. Lavina put it down and went back to the kitchen. She kept her curiosity in check. Her father would read it in his own time.

Two days later Lavina decided the letter must not concern her. Finally, after dinner, when her brothers had gone back to school for the afternoon, Theodore spoke to her.

"Come sit down for a minute." Lavina sat at the table with her mother and father. "Matt Daly has asked for your hand in marriage." Her father got right to the point. "The question is, do you want to marry him?"

Lavina was momentarily speechless while her wide eyes stared at her father. "Yes, yes I do." She sounded calmer than she felt.

"Well, there is one condition." Her mother spoke up. Lavina looked over at her.

"What is it?" She couldn't imagine what her mother would say.

"I want to get to know my future son-in-law. We must invite him to come stay here and visit for a week."

Lavina was all for it. "But there's no room for him here."

"He can rent a room and take his meals with us."

"I don't know if he'll want to." They discussed it for a while, and Lavold ended the conversation by saying, "I'll write him back and tell him what we decided.

\*\*\*

Just over a month later, Matt left again for Cedar Junction. It was late winter, but it felt like the worst of the cold weather was over. He told everyone his plans one evening over supper. Samuel and Joe were off staying in a line shack sixty miles east of the D Rocking D headquarters. There was a report of cattle with their brand over that way. They had to be checked on, and brought closer to home.

Suppers had begun to get boring, but at least they were plentiful. They ate a lot of beans, beef and baking powder biscuits. The sourdough starter had frozen, which killed it. It gave a stronger flavor to baked goods, which they preferred. Kirsten would make a new batch when it warmed up, or wait until Curly came in the spring and ask for more of his. For now she used baking powder.

"I asked Theodore Lavold if I could marry Lavina." Matt stated, seemingly out of the blue. His father stopped chewing and looked at him.

Kirsten let out an excited laugh. "Finally, some female company!"

"He and Mrs. Lavold want me to visit for a week. I'm

69

leaving Thursday." Since it was already Monday, he didn't give them much warning.

"Well okay, if that's what you want," Big John was smiling. He stood up from the table and took the bottle of whiskey off the shelf. "I guess it's time for a celebration." Soon there was more laughter coming from inside the cabin as Matt took the brunt of their jokes on matrimony.

As the train pulled into the station at Cedar Junction, Matt felt nervous. He had planned on riding over from Turkey Creek, but his father had talked him out of it. "You need to arrive looking like at least half a gentleman. You're lucky they let you in the door, grubby as you are."

He had a bath the night before. It wasn't something he normally did in the winter. It was too cold, and the water took a long time to heat. It was much easier to wait for summer and find a body of water to splash around in. But Matt hunkered down in the tepid water he'd poured in the washtub and scrubbed up. Kirsten trimmed his hair, and John even had him clean and oil his boots, things that needed doing anyway.

Lavina was the only person standing on the platform. It had begun to snow lightly as she stood there waiting. Matt picked up a small bag. He felt awkward carrying it, but John had discouraged him from bringing his saddlebags also. They met on the platform. Matt gave Lavina a big hug as he greeted her. They walked the few blocks over to the store, unsure of what to say to one another.

The store was quiet, and the light dim except where it came through the open doorway in the back. "They're here!" James yelled out as they entered the store.

Matt knew it was now or never. If he waited, he was afraid they would get swept up in the excitement and he would miss his chance to ask Lavina the all important question. He stopped behind the big stove in the center of the store and pulled Lavina to him. "Will you marry me?" He used that same low, expectant voice.

She felt goose bumps rise on her skin. Shivering, she said, "Yes," as the door burst open and voices filled the room.

Matt had to admit he enjoyed the week he spent with the Lavolds. He spent nights in a hotel down the street. Around six o'clock every morning Lavina opened the back door into the kitchen for him. He and Mr. Lavold sat at the table as Lavina and her mother served breakfast. He wasn't used to the division of labor, or of sitting idle. At home, if not helping with the cooking, he would have been out feeding the horses, or hauling water or wood for the kitchen.

As they finished breakfast the first morning of his visit, Matt stood up to help with dishes. "Come with me," Theodore said to him. The two men went out into the store. After feeding the wood stove, they opened up crates, pulled out canned goods and stacked them neatly on the store shelves.

Matt settled into a routine with the Lavold family. In the mornings he helped Theodore in the store. After the noon meal, he and Lavina had time to themselves. They took walks, exploring the growing town of Cedar Junction, ran errands, and went next door to Mother's Restaurant for pie. When it was quiet in the store, they sat on the bench and read or talked.

Matt told Lavina about his childhood down in Texas. There were long periods of time when his father was absent, and he and his mother were on their own. He earned spending money by running errands and doing odd jobs for the neighbors.

\*\*\*

One day, when he was eleven, he was returning home and he walked past a small house on the edge of town that always intrigued him. The rumor was that the man who lived there was a gunman. Matt didn't know exactly what that meant, but he always hoped to catch sight of the inhabitant.

"Hello there, young man," a voice called to him from the covered porch.

Matt stopped and looked hard. It took a moment to locate the voice amongst the junk stored there. "Hello," he called back.

"How would you like to earn a nickel?"

"Yes, sir."

"Well come on up here. I need help moving some things." Matt went up onto the porch as the man stood up and stuck out his hand. "My name's Dan Morgan. They call me Dapper Dan, I guess 'cause I like nice clothes." It was true. The man was wearing a black, silk vest over a purple shirt.

"Matt Daly." Matt also stuck out his hand, feeling grown up.

"Nice to meet you, Matt. First thing is, we need to get this sofa inside." He set a bottle down on the porch railing. They lifted, pushed and pulled, and finally had the heavy piece of furniture inside the door.

When Matt's eyes adjusted to the dim light, he saw it looked like an ordinary home. There was a living area with a doorway leading to the kitchen. Narrow, steep stairs went up through the ceiling on one side.

"Up alongside this wall." They slid the sofa over to the wall. "Much better. Now, let's get this thing out of here." Dan indicated an old, broken down, easy chair with stuffing coming out of the seat.

Once it was out on the porch, Dan picked the bottle up and sat down. "Much better," he repeated. He took a swig of the amber liquid in the bottle. "Now, young Matt, tell me about yourself."

Matt sat on the step and told him where he lived and about his father being gone. Dan listened as he sipped from the bottle. They talked for a while, and then Dan looked up at the sky. The sun was getting close to the horizon.

"You better be gettin' home 'fore your Ma starts worrying." He stood up and fished a nickel out of his pocket. He tossed it to Matt before turning to go inside.

After that Matt took every opportunity to go past the house, hoping to see Dapper Dan sitting outside on the old, gray chair. If he was there, Matt stopped to visit.

One day he finally brought up the subject he really wanted to know about. "They say you're a gunman."

Dan laughed. "Yeah, I've been called a lot of things."

"Are you?"

"Well, I've never shot anyone, so no. But I used to shoot for a living." Dan was well into a bottle and started talking about his days as a trick shooter. He told Matt he traveled around showing off his prowess with a pistol, and said he made a good living. Matt was fascinated. He asked questions, helping the man relive the days of his former life.

One day Dan took a shiny wooden box down off a shelf and opened it. Inside was a pair of .36 caliber Navy Colts with ivory grips. He took the pistols out of the box and began spinning them around his index fingers in exact precision before flipping them in the air and catching them as if ready to shoot when they came down.

Matt was spellbound as Dapper Dan showed off. "Can I watch you shoot them?" He asked excitedly.

"Maybe someday." Dan touched the polished steel fondly before once again closing the box. He thought for a moment and came to a decision "You better scoot along now. Come back in the morning and I'll show you some shooting." Matt went home wishing he had a pair of fancy pistols.

The next day was Saturday. That morning Matt walked up onto the porch and knocked on the door. Dan was inside sipping coffee. They chatted for a few minutes before Dan stood up. "I guess you came to see a show." Matt nodded eagerly.

Dan took the pistols from their box and put them on the kitchen table. Then he took his powder horn and cap box down and carefully loaded each pistol, measuring powder into each chamber. That was tamped down before a patch and ball was placed on top. Once the guns were loaded, he reached for a holster hanging on the wall. He buckled it around his waist and slid the pistols in, one on either side.

Matt watched fascinated. His father had guns of course, but when John was home they hung on the wall. He had not yet taken the time to teach his son to shoot.

When Dan had the pistols ready, he led Matt out back.

There were targets set up, mainly tin cans. Those and broken bottles littered the back yard. They walked over to a fresh pile of empty bottles, which Matt realized, were never in short supply. Once there were twelve of them lined up along the ditch bank, Dan said, "Well I guess we're ready. You stand over here," indicating he wanted Matt up against the back of the house.

He then proceeded to put on a display of shooting that was astonishing. Both guns seemed to be in the middle of a spin when suddenly one was back in the holster as Dapper Dan palmed the hammer back on the other one. Matt heard a shot as a bottle exploded, and then both guns were twirling through the air. Again, one pistol would drop in the holster as another bottle exploded. The dozen shots were off in a couple of minutes. Dan never missed as the bottles disappeared one by one down the line. It was an act designed to bedazzle an audience and it worked. Once more Matt went home wishing he could shoot like that.

After that Matt visited the small house on the edge of town as often as he could. He soon figured out why it was best to visit Dapper Dan in the morning. Since the showman hadn't yet begun drinking, he was still able to shoot accurately.

One day Dan said, "I have something for you." He pulled out a Remington Rider's .36 caliber double action pistol. It was rusty and none of the parts worked. "I found this in a creek after a shootout down south. This gun used to be a gunfighter's weapon of choice. It's useless now, but you can use it to practice." He had seen how much Matt liked his fancy pistol work, and figured it wouldn't do any harm to let the kid play with a gun that would never fire.

Matt snuck the pistol home and whenever he had the chance, he'd play with it, imitating Dan's moves. At first the heavy gun was awkward, but after a while Matt got used to it. He used a scarf for a holster and practiced drawing, pretending to shoot once the gun was out.

One day his mother found the gun. She was horrified that her little boy had such a thing and she wouldn't give it back.

When John returned home after being away, Libby showed it to him. Big John just laughed when he saw what his wife was so upset about. "It's only a toy. This gun will never fire again."

"But it's still a real gun."

"There's no harm in it. He'll have to learn to shoot soon anyway."

Libby couldn't understand when John tried to explain about living out west and the need to know how to handle a firearm. He gave the gun back to his son, but made him promise never to point the gun at anyone and to keep it out of his mother's sight.

Matt kept practicing handling the pistol while Dapper Dan gave him pointers. Finally one day Dan let him actually fire one of his pistols. It was a thrill for Matt and he decided he was going to save his money and buy a gun of his own, one that worked.

He discussed it with Dapper Dan. "Do you want a single action, or a double action pistol?"

"I don't know."

"Well, do you want to shoot fast or accurately?" Dan's guns were single action, meaning the hammer had to be pulled back before they could be fired. Double action pistols could be shot without pulling the hammer back, which meant it was easier to shoot yourself in the foot.

Matt didn't know any of this. He just wanted to shoot fast and never miss, like Dan.

Dan decided a single action pistol that used cartridges would be best for the boy. The newer guns that used ready-made cartridges made loading much easier, although Dan preferred the old way because when he loaded his pistols, he knew for sure what he had when he fired.

It took him a year to save the money, but finally, with Dan's help Matt purchased his own pistol with a holster. It was an old Smith and Wesson .41 with a short five and a half inch barrel. Dan got it from a friend, and figured the shorter barrel would be easier for Matt to draw. The boy never told his mother about it and kept it well hidden in the wood shed out behind their house.

Matt was obsessed with being the fastest draw around. Dan teased him about it. "What, you want to be a gunfighter when you grow up? You won't live very long in that profession."

"No, I just like shooting. I never want to kill anybody." So he kept on practicing drawing and twirling out behind the shed. Any firing of the gun had to be done over at Dan's.

Matt got incredibly good at handling the pistol by the time he was sixteen. When he took off with his father to herd cattle, he brought the gun along, but Big John made sure he knew how to handle it, and told his son that it wasn't to be fired unless absolutely necessary.

*** 

Matt didn't tell Lavina about his fondness for guns as a boy. He had gotten over his obsession with drawing fast and showing off. Although he still admired a well-made firearm, it was simply another tool.

Instead he told her about being without his father for long periods and about his schooling. His mother had been adamant that he finish high school, which worked for Matt. There were no cattle drives during the winter. He still liked to read, and it was something he and Lavina had in common.

He also told her about trailing cattle up from Texas. The first time he went with his father, he'd barely been able to stay on a horse and he'd never handled a rope before. He and Big John rode south from the small community they lived in near Dallas, almost all the way to Mexico. There the herd of wild longhorns had been captured and waited their arrival.

The animals needed a road brand before they could be driven north. That was where Matt got his first education about cattle. Although a chute was used, the wild cattle had to be persuaded to enter it. It seemed like it took forever to run the two thousand head through, especially to a sixteen year old eager to travel.

Nothing about it had been easy as Matt remembered. He was saddle sore for the first couple weeks and he remembered always being hungry. It was hard work, but it was also exciting.

Being the newest and youngest man on the trip, he rode drag the entire trip. He ate a lot of dust as he constantly urged any steers that lagged to keep moving. After a full day on horseback, he still had to ride a two hour shift each night, circling the sleeping cattle with another cowboy to help keep them quiet. It seemed he was always tired.

His father became Big John to him also. The trail boss told his son, when the youngster had a hard time getting up one morning, that he could sleep next winter, but right now he had a job to do. That summer Matt learned how to get by on little sleep.

The next year when he joined his father, he was no longer the kid, and was assigned the position of riding flank. That was the year they met Curly. The cook hired on for the trail drive and had worked for the Dalys ever since.

*** 

One night before Matt returned to the hotel, he and Lavina slipped into the dark, silent store. He held her hand as they sat on the bench talking. There was one thing he had to be sure of. He explained to her what their living conditions would be like as husband and wife. Even though the new room on the cabin would make it seem spacious to Matt, it would still be tight. Also, she would be living among a bunch of cowboys, and their manners weren't the best.

Mainly he wanted to warn her of the solitude. There were no close neighbors, and few women. Instead of walking out the door and being in the midst of streets and buildings and people, when she walked out the door on the D Rocking D, she would see a lot of emptiness.

Lavina wasn't worried. There seemed to be enough people around, and she was anxious to meet Kirsten and Jesse and Big John. She would miss her family, but they weren't that far away.

"Can you see the mountains from your ranch?" She was thinking more about what her new life would bring than what she would lose. The first time she saw the rugged peaks, rising up into the sky while coming west on the train, was something she would never forget. What could be more beautiful? When she and her family had moved farther east, to Cedar Junction, she was disappointed at the flatness of the view.

Matt smiled at her. "We can see them."

"How far away are they?"

"A long day by wagon." The only times Matt had been up into the mountains was when they went to cut down fir trees to haul home for building with, or when cutting standing dead for firewood. He remembered long days on the end of a saw, pushing and pulling for hours on end, the dust sticking to his sweaty skin. It was the hardest he had ever worked, which made it difficult for him to appreciate the beauty of his surroundings.

Matt always remembered courting Lavina amongst the bolts of calico and muslin, with tin cans shining dimly on shelves lining the wall. They set a tentative date during the first part of May for the wedding.

Afterwards he stopped at a saloon to have a drink and a smoke on his way to sleep at the hotel. Settled in a chair at an empty table, he leisurely rolled and then lit the cigarette as he sipped a glass of whiskey, planning the future with Lavina as his wife.

Matt made two more trips to Cedar Junction, one during the first week of March, when the last big storm of the season hit. He made it there with no problem, as he wouldn't have left home if the weather hadn't been favorable.

Coming home was a different story. He put off beginning the return trip an hour longer than he should have, as leaving Lavina was becoming harder. He realized his predicament a couple hours out. The wind picked up and it became difficult to keep moving forward. It started snowing and the wind blew the flakes horizontally, stinging his face. His horse knew the way, but it was impossible to stay on the road. Finally Matt gave up, and spent a long, cold night huddled under a cedar. Both he and Easy were protected from the wind, but not from the cold.

Late the following day they made it home. The storm had passed, but both horse and rider were exhausted, cold and hungry from struggling through the deep drifts it had left. The experience made Matt even more determined to have the addition finished, and Lavina as his wife before spring roundup.

He and Jesse and Big John finished the new room with time to spare. Just over six feet high inside, it had a low, packed dirt roof like the rest of the cabin and two windows. The last task before the room was completed was the chinking. They mixed ground-up hay with mud to fill the cracks in between the logs. It was a crude, but cheap and convenient way to make the cabin snug.

There was room for a real bed, which John had ordered as a wedding present for his son. Jesse made a cabinet out of the last of the milled boards for the newly weds to use as a clothes closet. There wasn't room for much more, but it seemed almost extravagant to Matt after the years of sleeping on a bunk in the main room.

# Chapter 7

O n his last trip to Cedar Junction, Matt again rode the train. The following day was his wedding day. He and Lavina were getting married in the morning, then taking the train back to Compton that afternoon. A team waited with the wagon at Gust's livery to take them home in the evening.

It was a beautiful spring day in the middle of May, one of those magical days Matt could feel the earth coming alive when he set out for town. The songs of the meadowlarks filled the air, helping bring the prairie to life. Blue birds darted in front of the wagon, brilliant blue against the green of spring. In the cottonwoods along the creek, robins searched out nesting sites, pausing to let loose with their own songs. The new leaves shimmered in the breeze, catching the sunlight. Breathing in the fresh air, Matt thought a perfect day like this only comes along once in a long while.

Lavina was standing on the platform waiting to meet him once again, as excited as he was. What was taking so long?

Slowly the train pulled in and stopped. The conductor seemed to take his time placing the wooden steps beneath the door. Matt was right behind him. He flew down the steps and over to her, grabbed her up off the ground, and swung her around. She squealed with delight, causing people around them to turn and stare. But it didn't matter if they made a scene. The man she loved was here and was taking her home tomorrow.

In the morning the Lavolds walked over to the church and met Matt there. The couple stood in front of the minister, said vows, and was pronounced man and wife. John had wanted to come, as well as Kirsten and Jesse, but Matt decided he didn't want them there. Maybe he was being selfish, but he wanted his new bride all to himself for as long as possible. There was plenty of time for meeting and visiting when they arrived at the ranch.

Afterwards they had an early supper at Mother's Restaurant. Finally they rushed to get Lavina's belongings to the station and say goodbye so they wouldn't miss the train. There was only one trunk. She would send for the rest once she was settled in at the D Rocking D.

It helped that the goodbyes were hurried so no one felt too sad. Her parents already missed her. As happy as they were for their daughter, part of them also dreaded this day. They were confident it was a good match though, as they were both fond of their new son in law. Theodore hadn't found anyone who spoke badly of Matt, and he had asked around.

The train ride home was a blur. Gust had the wagon waiting at the station in Compton when the train pulled in. He was the first one to address the new Mrs. Daly. They visited for a few minutes, but Gust didn't want to keep them. Besides he didn't know how much of those two beaming faces he could stomach. They were just a little too cute for his taste. He tried to think back on what it had been like to be young and in love. He shook his head and spit out a stream of tobacco juice as he turned back towards the barn after he and Matt hitched the wagon.

Matt helped his bride onto the wagon seat. He climbed up

beside her, pushed his hat down further on his head out of habit and spoke to the team. That was what Lavina remembered most about the trip to her new home. He handled the team as easily as he rode. And he had tossed her trunk in the back of the wagon as if it were a bag of feathers. It would have taken two of the other men she had known before to lift the trunk, and they would have complained about not having someone to do it for them. At that moment she felt safe. With Matt at her side, nothing could hurt her.

***

The following morning Lavina stirred, then sat up with a start. She had no idea what time it was, except it was full light. She suddenly became aware of her naked body. Self-consciously she pulled the covers up, but Matt wasn't there. She thought about the night before.

No one was around when they arrived. A lantern hung outside the door. Lavina stepped into her new home and looked around as Matt held the light. The cabin was smaller than the larger room in the back of her father's store, only sixteen by eighteen feet. To the left was the kitchen area, really only a counter that ran from the door to the corner and along the back side. Above it were shelves. She saw a stack of mismatched plates and cups. A tin of baking powder sat next to a jar of salt. To her right was a row of wooden pegs for hanging coats and hats and a washstand with a small mirror hanging above it for shaving. A cook stove, and the table and benches sat clustered in the middle of the dirt floor. Two bunks in the other corners filled the remainder of the cabin. Opposite the outer door was another one. The newness of the wood of both the door and the frame stood out against the log walls, which were gray from wood smoke.

Matt touched the stove. It was still warm. There was a pot of food on top, and he knew there would be biscuits in the oven. He felt relieved, as he half expected everyone to be waiting, facing the door, anxious to see his bride.

"Where is everyone?"

"I don't know. They're around here somewhere." His father must have bedded down in the barn. "Are you hungry?" It wasn't the question he wanted to ask.

"No, thank you."

"I'll get your trunk."

"Let me hold the light."

It seemed to Matt an awkward beginning to his marriage. They went out for the trunk and he suddenly remembered. He set the trunk inside and took the lantern from Lavina's hand. He pulled her back outside, quickly scooped her up in his arms and carried her through the door. She shrieked with laughter, loud enough to wake the dead, Matt thought. He laughed with her as he closed the door, relieved the ice was broken.

Lavina sat in bed in the morning light, blushing as she thought about her wedding night, of Matt's passion and the way his hands had felt on her body. She pulled her thoughts back to the present, jumped up and began dressing. Before she left the bedroom, she put her hair up, and then made the bed and straightened up the room.

She opened the bedroom door and stuck her head through, feeling bashful. To her relief, she saw only one person in the other room, a tall woman about her own age. So this was Kirsten. Her long, golden hair hung in a braid down her back.

"Good morning. We let you sleep." Kirsten smiled as she turned and saw Lavina looking at her. It was obvious breakfast was over. "I saved you some food. Coffee?"

The next thing Lavina noticed about the woman in front of her was that she was wearing men's pants. Lavina was shocked. And was she just offered coffee? She didn't know any women who drank coffee. Women sipped tea, and they certainly didn't wear men's clothing.

"Yes, please." She felt a sense of adventure. The coffee was strong and bitter. She couldn't help making a face.

"This will help." Kirsten stirred in sugar. "When Eva freshens, we'll have cream."

When who does what? Lavina realized she had a lot to

learn. She was already becoming confused. But the sweetened coffee went down easier, and she immediately felt more comfortable in her new home. She took another sip.

"Sit down." Kirsten came to the table with a plate of food, fresh sourdough biscuits, covered with gravy. Bits of meat floated on top. The meat, left over from last night's supper, had been turned into breakfast. It smelled good. Lavina couldn't recall eating since the meal at Mother's Restaurant the day before.

"Where is everyone?" she asked as she sat down.

"They're around yet. Big John wants to meet you. Go ahead and eat first." As she ate, Lavina watched the graceful way Kirsten continued her chores. There were no wasted movements as she took a metal tub from a hook underneath the counter and placed it on the stove. Then she filled it from a pail of water. Leaning over, Kirsten opened the smaller door on the stove, to the left of the oven. She gave the embers in the firebox a stir before placing more wood inside.

She sat down opposite Lavina and began telling her about the ranch and the people the new bride was now living with. As she listened, Lavina was also thinking. Unrestrained, that's what her new friend was. From her movements and her speech, even the way she dressed. She had never seen such freedom in a woman.

Matt walked in shortly after. Kirsten was telling her about when she and Jesse had first met Matt and his father. Kirsten saw the door opening and stopped what she was saying. "Hey there! Are your ears burning?" She didn't seem to care what he might think. Lavina looked over at Matt. They had been caught talking about him. She tried to stop laughing.

Matt didn't care what story Kirsten had been telling. The sight of his wife thoroughly enjoying herself made his day perfect. He walked over to her, bent over and kissed her on the mouth. He would give almost anything to spend the day in bed with her. He straightened up, looking into her eyes.

"Some cattle strayed. We're going to bring them back. We'll be home later."

Lavina was surprised. He was leaving already. "I'll be here." She smiled to hide her disappointment. "Where's your father?"

"Oh, yeah." Matt acted as if he had forgotten that she hadn't yet met her new father-in-law. "I'll get him." He turned around and went back through the door.

Big John woke up before light that morning as usual. He stretched, feeling the bed of hay beneath him. It was as comfortable here in the barn as in the cabin and he was more than happy to give his son some privacy on his wedding night. He rose, then shook out and folded the blankets before stepping outside to check the weather. The stars were beginning to fade and a crescent moon hung low in the sky. It was chilly out, but not unseasonable for May.

He went around to the corral to pitch hay to the horses, already thinking about the day ahead. He was a little worried. For once he wasn't thinking about the neighbor to the north. His men had seen three strangers on a ridge a few miles to the west the day before. They had sat their horses, watching the cattle below for a couple minutes, and then disappeared. They were too far away to make out their features, but if they had been there for honest reasons, they would have ridden down to say hello.

Finally he had smelled smoke coming from the pipe above the cabin roof. As if it were a signal, Kirsten and Jesse appeared out of the dim light. They joined Big John outside the barn.

"Did I hear screaming last night?" Kirsten asked smiling. The two men looked down, chuckling. "Yeah, I heard it too," Big John answered. "They must have had a good time." A couple minutes later they decided it was safe to enter the cabin.

Inside, Matt had the coffee water on, and he practically waltzed as he reached for the coffee beans and grinder.

Lavina met John Daly and Jesse Branson as she finished her breakfast. Big John and Matt resembled each other in many ways, she observed. Their strong chins and broad smiles were the most obvious features.

"Call me John or Big John, but I don't answer to Mr. Daly." John looked at his new daughter-in-law and decided his son had found himself a beautiful wife. He couldn't help feeling a little envious. She was small though. He hoped this life wouldn't prove too difficult for her. But Matt loved her, and that's what mattered.

The three men left after only a few minutes. They went towards the barn where they already had horses saddled. Lavina heard the sound of horse's hooves trotting past, heading north. She walked over to the window and watched the men ride off, easily sitting the horse's trots, while sitting tall.

"What can I help you with?" She turned back towards Kirsten.

"You should just relax today. There's nothing I can't do."

"No, I want to help."

So Kirsten put her to work. Lavina Daly's first day as a married woman was spent doing the everyday chores of a frontier ranch wife. If anything she tried too hard, but she was determined to prove herself.

Once the morning chores were completed, Kirsten said, "Let's go across the creek. I have something to show you." She led the way across the footbridge and over to the other cabin.

Lavina stepped inside and liked what she saw. The building was about the same size as the main room in the Daly's cabin and was cheerfully decorated. Calico curtains in shades of purple and yellow hung from the two windows. There was a shelf holding a few knickknacks, mainly remnant pieces of china. The quilt covering the bed was a double wedding ring design. It was made by Kirsten's mother and had been carried from Nebraska packed in the wagon.

"Here, by the stove," Kirsten walked over and set the bowl she was carrying down into a box in which six baby chicks huddled. A neighbor's hen had hatched them out and the woman had sold them to Kirsten.

"I paid a whole dollar for them, but at least half should be pullets, so we'll have eggs." She was excited at the prospect. Lavina had never thought about eggs being a luxury before.

Her family had always been able to buy fresh eggs. She started realizing just how remote her new home was.

***

The first weeks of married life seemed bizarre to Lavina. Matt was gone all day. When he returned in the evening, the main topic of conversation was spring roundup preparations. She didn't really know where he went, and there was some mystery in the air. Many nights she was asleep when he quietly came into the bedroom. She awoke to his kisses. Because she saw him so little, their lovemaking seemed surreal. It was sometimes hard to connect the passionate man she felt in the night with the handsome cowboy she watched ride off in the early morning light.

Try as she might, she wasn't able to catch him before he was up and out of the house that first summer. One time she got a quick goodbye as he finished his coffee. She tried to get him to wake her, but all he said was, "You just sleep."

"Is this how it is around here all the time?" Lavina and Kirsten were alone in the cabin.

"Well, this time of year." Kirsten had hesitated before answering her. It was the hesitation Lavina wondered about.

One evening Matt and his father were finally home. Matt looked exhausted. John looked at him, amused. He doubted his son was getting any sleep. No one made a move to go to bed. "Matt, go lie down for a minute. I'll be here."

Be here for what? Lavina had no idea. Matt pulled her into the bedroom and down onto the bed with him. "Why don't you just go to bed?" she asked.

"Because I have to go out again."

"Why?"

Matt pulled her close and shut his eyes. "Just lay with me here for a minute.

She had almost dozed off when she heard hoof beats outside. Matt was already on his feet when his father knocked on the door. He told her to go to bed, and that he'd be back soon.

After he left she went out into the other room and watched the two men walk to the barn. A lantern swung between them. They had both strapped on pistols, and she could see the glint of a rifle barrel. A minute later, horses were led from underneath the shed. The light was extinguished and hoof beats faded into the night.

Lavina slept little. She was up and dressed when Kirsten showed up in the morning. "Matt and Big John aren't here?" She glanced around. Jesse was gone also.

"No. Kirsten, where is everyone?"

"Let's find out."

The two women walked over to the bunkhouse. Kirsten banged on the door. No one answered. They looked around. Samuel was coming from the barn.

"Good morning," he called out politely.

"What's going on?" Kirsten got right to the point.

"I believe they have them surrounded a few miles down the creek."

"Who's surrounded?" Lavina's frustration at these tight-lipped people was suddenly unbearable.

"The rustlers."

"Rustlers?"

Kirsten and Samuel looked at one another. She answered. "They're some men stealing cattle. A couple of ranches formed a posse to catch them." All the men were gone except Samuel. He had been left to stay with the two women. Lavina stared at Kirsten, furious that no one had told her. "Matt didn't want to worry you."

"Are they in danger?"

"They're smart, and they know the country." Samuel wanted to make it easy on Lavina, but he knew anything could happen.

She turned and walked back towards the cabin. She didn't know if she was more scared or mad. Kirsten followed her. "Breakfast might be a little late," she said over her shoulder to Samuel.

They waited all day, with no word. Lavina's fear turned to anger, then back to fear. She stayed busy, both women did, in an effort to keep their minds off the situation. She pounded, rather than kneaded bread dough, then went out and split a large pile of kindling all by herself. Normally she wasn't much good at managing the heavy axe, but today her anger gave her strength.

It was late when Kirsten finally said good night and left. Lavina watched in the doorway as the lantern wobbled down the path and across the creek. She shut the door, feeling exhausted. Maybe she could sleep.

It was hours later when Matt woke her. She sat up, ready to give him a piece of her mind. She heard Big John in the next room. He was sound asleep in just a few minutes.

"Where have you been?" Her voice was a harsh whisper.

"Taking care of business." She knew he was smiling.

"Don't I have a right to know when you are in danger?" Matt sat down next to her to pull off his boots. Someone had spilled the beans to his wife.

"I'm not in any danger. We took care of it." Matt wondered if Jesse and Kirsten were having the same conversation.

He put his arm around Lavina. "Everything is all right." He wanted to comfort her further, but her moonlit hair framing the curve of her neck was the most beautiful thing he had ever seen. He felt her body relax and fill with relief as he kissed her. She believed he would never let anything hurt her.

There had been reports all spring of strange men lurking. These were the first ones to actually be caught stealing. Ranchers were keeping as close an eye on their herds as possible, given the vastness of the range.

John had advised Matt against speaking about the trouble with the cattle thieves. He believed in protecting women from problems he felt didn't concern them. He also believed in taking care of matters himself. So they rode after the thieves with the intention of ending it. Luckily it hadn't turned into anything nasty.

That wasn't the case in many areas of the open range. Cattle and horse rustling had become rampant. In April, 1883, the first annual Montana Stock Grower's Association met in Miles City for the purpose of addressing the issue. The cattlemen had organized and since then there had been numerous hangings and shootouts as thieves were run down by vigilantes, both in Montana and down in Wyoming.

Unfortunately innocent men were also executed. Maybe one had filed a homestead claim near a spring that a rancher wanted. It was easy to plant a few calves in his corral as proof he was stealing. It was a definite end to the problem for the rancher.

\*\*\*

The following week the spring roundup began. Curly showed up and was surprised by the latest addition to the D Rocking D household. He was happy for Matt and a bit sad for his bride. He knew she had some hard days ahead of her as a ranch wife.

Spring roundups had a different focus than the fall ones. They were organized the same way, with large circles made by riders to gather the cattle into the middle. In the center, fires held hot branding irons, since the main purpose was to mark the calves and establish ownership. Men on horseback had the job of determining which calf belonged to which cow. The pairs were separated from the herd, and then the calves from their mothers, one at a time.

Once by itself, the calf was roped by and drug over to the fire, with the rider calling out the brand to be used. There, a ground crew held it down while the appropriate brand was applied. A couple quick slashes with a knife and the males became steers.

Big John and Matt, as ranch owners, worked horseback, their ropes never still. Newly hired men had the job of wrestling with the calves on the ground. All worked quickly. As one calf was released, there was another to take its place, with one more on the way. Men ran back and forth from the fire carrying red hot irons. They had to be certain that the correct brand was applied. It was tough, noisy and sometimes confusing work, with the cows calling after their calves, and the bawling of the calves as their hides were burned. The stench of singed hair never left the air.

They D Rocking D crew set out early one morning. The cowboys went on ahead, followed by the wagon and the horse herd. Kirsten and Lavina were on their own for the next month. Normally Jesse would have stayed behind also, but they needed him out riding. One of the men they hired was in jail over in Miles City for disturbing the peace, meaning he had gotten drunk and shot up a saloon. For the second time, Matt would be anxious to return from a roundup.

Matt and Big John relished setting out in the spring. After spending so many dark winter hours cooped up in their small home, they enjoyed the freedom, and the sunshine.

Many years the weather became warmer as May turned to June, but this was a year when it was rainy and cold the entire time. While the D Rocking D's crew was sliding down steep hillsides chasing suspicious bovines and struggling to keep a fire hot enough to heat branding irons, Lavina and Kirsten were slogging through the mud between the creek and the cabin.

"We need rain barrels," Lavina commented as she hauled buckets of water up from the raging creek. The buckets had to sit to let the sediment settle out before the water was fit to drink.

"We need a roof first." The packed earth roof soaked up the moisture instead of letting it run off. Once it became saturated, the water leaked through into the cabin. There was coarse muslin draped across the ceiling to stop dirt from falling on them, but it didn't stop the water from dripping. The two women brought in armloads of wood and dropped it on the floor to dry. "We need a woodshed." Lavina hoped it didn't sound like she was complaining.

"Put it on the list."

Eva, the milk cow, was ready to calve. Kirsten began

putting her in the barn at night, and one morning they heard the bawl of the new calf when they went out. Now there would be fresh milk and cream.

Nothing more was said of the cattle rustling incident until Lavina finally asked about it one day. "It's just one of the things that happen out here from time to time." Kirsten was down-playing the incident, but it worried her also. "It had to be dealt with."

Lavina felt a chill. She lifted a plate from the soapy water and gave it a scrub. She dipped it in the next tub to rinse it, and handed it to Kirsten to dry. "How many were there? What happened to them?"

"Three or four. They were run off. Big John went easy on them."

Lavina blinked, staring at the soapy water. Matt hadn't told her any of this. She remembered how well armed he and his father had been that night.     "Will they come back?"

"Not if they're smart." Kirsten saw her worried look. "Our men can take care of themselves." She hoped she sounded reassuring.

Some thought the thieves hadn't been dealt with firmly enough. It would have been considered the ranchers' right to hang them out there on the creek where the posse had run them down. Way up in a nearby coulee they had found a newly built corral holding close to a hundred head of steers, along with a bunch of young calves. Using a running iron, the outlaws had already changed the brand on the steers from a D Rocking D to a D Circle D.

Legally, branded animals belonged to whoever owned the brand. The rustlers intended to register it before they sold the cattle. It was obvious who the newborn calves belonged to though. They ran bawling to their tight-bagged mothers when reunited. The cows had never stopped calling to their babies the two days they were gone. That was how the cowboys were first alerted that something was wrong within the herd; content cattle are quiet.

How stupid, Kirsten thought, taking those calves. How

were they going to keep them alive? They were much too young to be without their mothers. Another day or so and they would have begun dying. It was obviously the gang's first job. Maybe that was why Big John had insisted on going easy on them.

The dishes were done. Kirsten untied her apron, hung it on a nail and turned towards Lavina. "Didn't you say you wanted to learn how to ride?" Lavina nodded. "Well, you're going to need something to ride in."

Kirsten had tried riding sidesaddle once. The horse had been flighty, and although she was a good rider, it was hard to keep both her balance, and the horse under control. From then on she had continued riding astride. Her parents hadn't approved, but it was hard to tell their daughter about being proper. She was too practical. Wearing tight, fashionable clothing was not, nor was sitting sideways on a horse when it was misbehaving. Besides, there was no room for her rope.

She first began fashioning riding skirts. They worked, except the legs were too full and the material bunched at her knees as she rode. The chafing got worse as the day wore on. She finally started buying men's wool pants at the ready-made clothing store in Compton. She pretended they were for her husband, which was plausible, since the couple were about the same height.

The two women went through Lavina's clothes, pulling skirts and blouses out of the trunk, along with the green, silk dress Lavina had been married in. "This is pretty," Kirsten remarked. "Did you make it?"

"My mother helped."

"This is good work." Kirsten examined the hand stitching closely. Lavina felt proud. At least there was one thing she was better at than Kirsten.

"You might have to alter these blouses if you want to work in them." She indicated the full mutton sleeves that were in fashion. Since they were continually getting in the way, Lavina couldn't agree more.

At the very bottom of the trunk were a corset and a

bustle. Her mother had insisted Lavina take them, even though she never wanted to see them, much less wear them again. Her hoop skirt was only a dim memory, as she had refused to even pack it. Before leaving Illinois, she had given it to a friend, stating she didn't have room for it. She didn't object to fashion, except where her comfort and movement were restricted. Besides, where would she wear such things out here?

Kirsten laughed as she pulled the two figure enhancing items out. "What are you going to do with these?"

"Burn them." Lavina still remembered trying to sit on an upholstered couch with the bustle tied around her waist underneath the skirt of her dress. For an hour she had sat there, pushing with her feet so that she wouldn't slide off the slippery fabric onto the floor. Her legs started cramping as she sat there politely drinking tea, but wanting to jump up and scream.

She looked at the corset and remembered the wooden stays digging into her ribs as she tried to take a deep breath. No wonder women always seemed to be fainting. She felt relieved that Matt had never looked at her as if her figure needed improvement. She put the fashion accessories back in the bottom of the trunk where she could forget about them.

They decided on a brown, wool skirt. "It's easy. Just cut down the middle, then sew a seam on either side," Kirsten explained. Lavina took out her scissors and a needle and thread and went to work. "Perfect," Kirsten declared when she saw the finished result a couple hours later. "Tomorrow you can have your first riding lesson." Lavina felt daring as she tried on the altered skirt.

They decided to surprise Matt. Kirsten would teach Lavina to ride while he was gone. Lavina couldn't wait to see the look on his face. She wore her riding skirt the rest of the day, and put it on again the next morning.

It had finally stopped raining, although the sky remained overcast. Lavina looked down towards the creek when she opened the door. The leaves on the cottonwoods and willows were now full size. Beyond them the hillsides were bright green.

Learning to ride was harder than she thought it would be. First she had to get the horse saddled. Kirsten led her horse, a brown and white paint with one blue eye, named Jack, over to the barn. Luckily the horse was amenable to the clumsy fumbling of the inexperienced person at his side.

The saddles most people used in the west were bigger and heavier than the English saddles used back east. Kirsten showed her how to swing it up onto the horse. With her height and strength, she made it look easy. When Lavina tried, it was all she could do to lift the unwieldy mass of leather, where it landed with a thud on the horse's back. Jack flinched, but stood still. Then Kirsten showed her how to wrap the latigo around the cinch ring and then back up to the saddle ring, using a flat knot to secure it and hold the saddle in place.

Lavina stroked Jack's coat, anxious to actually begin riding. Kirsten demonstrated how to mount. She lifted her left foot up and stuck it in the stirrup while grabbing hold of the saddle horn. Then she bounced once on her right foot before pushing off and up into the air. She made it look easy. Lavina pictured Matt effortlessly swinging up onto his horse.

When she tried, it was anything but easy. Kirsten stood at the horse's head, keeping him still as the smaller woman gouged his ribs with the toe of her boot, struggling to grab the saddle horn to help pull herself up. "It'll get easier," Kirsten encouraged her student. Finally she led the horse over to the stump used for splitting wood. "Stand on this." She hoped her horse would remain patient.

From the stump, Lavina easily stepped up into the saddle. The stirrups were too long, so she did without. Kirsten led the gelding around the yard, instructing Lavina to sit up and let her legs hang straight. Lavina looked down at her, beaming. This is where she wanted to be, riding alongside Matt, loping across the prairie.

While Lavina was having the time of her life up on the horse, slogging through the mud got old fast for Kirsten. She decided to turn the pair loose in the corral. After giving instructions on how to guide Jack, she let go of the bridle. As they splashed around in the mud, she shouted out instructions from the side.

"Sit up," she repeated "Give him some rein." Lavina grabbed hold of the horn and shrieked with delight as the horse began trotting. Kirsten stood at the side laughing. At least she wasn't afraid. Every afternoon for the rest of the month Lavina spent as much time as the weather permitted on the back of the horse.

***

The remuda returned to the ranch late one afternoon at the end of June. Big John led the way. Matt, Jesse, and the other cowboys followed behind. Lavina and Kirsten hustled into the house after greeting the men. They suddenly had a crew to cook for. That evening Curly drove the chuckwagon into the yard.

The evening was warm. It felt good after all the rain and cold weather. "Come on outside," Matt said to his wife once supper was eaten and the evening chores completed. There was still an hour of sunlight left. He set two stumps next to one another for them to sit on. "We need a porch," he commented as he rolled a smoke. The two of them sat side by side, enjoying each other's company. Far off they heard coyotes yipping, as they too enjoyed the evening.

Lavina inched closer to her husband. Matt smiled at her. "You don't have anything to worry about," he reassured her. He was concerned for the livestock though. It wasn't the coyotes as much as the wolves that were a problem. The buffalo had been killed off before the Dalys arrived. Not only were the Indians going hungry, but the predators as well. Now the white men were hunting the deer, elk and antelope that still roamed the prairie. Matt and his father were no different. They carried rifles and relied on game for fresh meat instead of butchering one of their own steers whenever possible. The wolves had to find a new food source, which meant they were starting to go after cattle.

Big John and the Bransons came out and joined them. "We did well with calves this year, close to seventy-five percent, near as I can figure." Big John looked down at the piece of paper he had been figuring on. Both he and Matt became animated when they talked about cattle. "Those shorthorn bulls we bought last year were worth the money. And with all the rain this spring, the steers should fatten up nicely this summer."

The talk turned from cattle to a discussion of what was needed most as far as improvements on the ranch. The hired cowboys would do most of the riding, freeing the Dalys to work at ranch headquarters. Besides cutting the grass in the meadow to put up as hay for next winter, the remainder of the summer they would focus on building. Matt promised Lavina they would spend a lot more time together.

# Chapter 8

There was a new home being built to the northeast of the D Rocking D, about twelve miles distant. The goal was to have the roof on by the Fourth of July, and then before the owners moved in, they planned on hosting a dance to celebrate Independence Day. Since the house had a wood floor, it was the perfect place for the socially deprived people in the area to gather.

The night before, Lavina took out the box of dried apples and put a large pile of the withered slices in a bowl. She covered them with water to soak overnight. Dried apples, for pies and other baked goods were a staple since they were easy to ship and kept for long periods of time. Their use was limited only by the creativity of the cook. The morning of the Fourth there was a hint of excitement in the air. Lavina began making pie crust early. She rolled out the dough and transferred it to the pie plates. She then added the apples, plus sugar and cinnamon before adding a top crust. There was room in the oven to bake two at a time and she intended to have four of them to take to the party.

The men rode out after breakfast as usual, but were back by mid-day. Kirsten milked early and the team was hitched to the buckboard. By late afternoon they were off, piled into the wagon with the pies carefully stashed under the seat. They considered bringing a saddle horse or two, but Big John declared he was sleeping on the way home, so Matt drove, with Lavina sitting next to him and the Bransons and John sat on blankets in the back. The hired cowboys rode horseback.

Arriving at the new house as the shadows lengthened, they were greeted by two brothers. The new neighbors were bachelors eager to meet any young ladies living in the area. When they spied a wagon pull up carrying two young women, they hurried over.

"Howdy, there!" one of them called out. "I'm Robert Jenkins and this is my brother Dave." Their faces fell somewhat as introductions were made and they realized neither Lavina nor Kirsten were single.

It didn't dampen their spirits though. The two brothers escorted the Dalys and Bransons over to the house to show it off. Although it consisted of only one story, the two bedrooms, plus a living area and kitchen, made it one of the more extravagant homes in the area.

Another wagon pulled up and the brothers hurried over to meet the people it carried. They were again disappointed. By the time all the neighbors arrived, the men outnumbered the women four to one. It didn't matter though. With two fiddles and a guitar there was live music, and more than enough food to feed the festive crowd.

Around sunset the musicians began tuning their instruments. Everyone gathered in the main room of the house, ready to dance. One of the fiddlers struck a tune and the two other musicians joined in. Immediately the floor filled with swaying couples.

Lavina wore her green, silk dress and Kirsten had put on a yellow one. Everyone was dressed in their good clothes, including the men who wore brightly colored shirts and scarves. The couples twirled in the dim light, the colors flashing with the movement to the lively songs. Anyone not fortunate to have a partner stood and watched with tapping toes. Kirsten and Lavina were in demand as dance partners and the only way they got any rest was to escape outside occasionally.

At midnight the music stopped and the food was brought out and put on a long table made from planks of wood set on barrels. Everyone dug into the feast, which included a steer that had been roasting covered in coals in a fire pit outside.

"Are you having fun?" Matt asked his wife, although looking at her rosy cheeks and smile, it was obvious.

"Oh, yes." The two of them piled food onto their plates and went looking for Big John.

They found him outside talking to a couple of other men. Matt introduced them to Lavina as neighboring ranchers. She knew they had been talking about all the rustling going on in the area, but when they saw her, the subject of conversation changed.

"Hey, I heard Von Tyler found himself a wife."

"Yeah, a squaw from over in the Bitteroot."

"He needs the help." The man they were speaking of had come west with his family, a wife and two small children, the year before. His wife had gotten sick and died almost as soon as they reached Montana. He didn't come to the dance because some people didn't approve of his recent marriage.

Lavina didn't understand why men would never talk about serious things in front of their wives. Women needed to know what was going on, but she kept the thought to herself and didn't ask questions. Instead the group stood and chatted about trivial things as they ate. Lavina was the only one sitting as Matt had insisted she take the only seat, which was a stump.

When she was done, Lavina excused herself and went to find Kirsten. She had seen a bottle sticking out of a coat pocket and knew it wouldn't be brought out until she was gone. Then the real business at hand that summer would be discussed over whiskey and cigarettes.

Kirsten was talking to a group of women, some of them neighbors Lavina had met only that evening. "How do you like living all the way out here?" one of them asked her.

Lavina smiled. It took her a second to remember the woman's name. "Edna, right? I love it," she answered.

"The new will wear off pretty quick." The woman wasn't old, but stress wrinkles already lines her face. Her expression was one of contempt. She wanted nothing more than to return to civilization, and spent her days waiting until her husband made enough money ranching so they could leave.

"Dolores, that was a wonderful Brown Betty you brought. Tell me how you made it." Kirsten changed the subject.

"I found some currants the last time we were in Bozeman. They did add a nice flavor, didn't they."

The women continued their socializing, exchanging recipes and other household tips. Eventually even Edna smiled when Lavina complimented her on the blouse she was wearing.

Once everyone had eaten their full and rested, the music resumed and didn't let up until there was daylight showing in the east. Finally the men went out to saddle and harness horses for the trip home. People were still laughing and enjoying the party atmosphere and called out goodbyes as they departed.

The Bransons and Dalys arrived home and Kirsten immediately went out to milk Eva, still humming one of the tunes. Lavina went inside to start breakfast. They all agreed it had been one of the best dances they had been to.

*** 

The next big event of the summer was when the Lavolds came to visit for a week. It had been planned the winter before. Lavina was excited, but also a little nervous. Her parents weren't used to the primitive living conditions on the D Rocking D, and even though she was a married woman, Lavina still wanted their approval.

Theodore and Elizabeth Lavold arrived with their two

sons in a wagon rented from the livery in Compton. When Theodore's eyes lit up at the sight of her, Lavina realized how much her family had missed her. Their eyes also showed astonishment when they saw the tiny cabin on the remote ranch. They looked at Lavina carefully, wanting to see that she was happy living seemingly out in the middle of nowhere. They soon realized that the ranch was actually a small community and were reassured.

Lavina and Matt gave up their bed for Theodore and Elizabeth, and slept in the two bunks in the main room of the cabin. Big John and the boys slept out in the barn. They joked about staying out in the spare bedroom.

Elizabeth was also shocked when she first saw Kirsten wearing men's pants. She said nothing, deciding her daughter's friend was probably too poor to afford proper clothing. But when she saw Lavina with a cup of coffee, she couldn't help exclaiming, "Lavina Lavold! What have you become?" The three women were alone in the cabin and they burst into laughter. Elizabeth realized she had no more say over her daughter's life, and it sounded so funny, speaking to her as if she were still a girl.

Matt and his father started talking much more politely when the in-laws arrived. "Yes sir" and "No sir" were added to the conversation. But everyone got along, despite Mrs. Lavold's fear about her daughter's corruption.

Lavina's two brothers, Teddy and James seemed grown up. They were both taller than she was, and at thirteen and fourteen, they were expected to put in a day's work. They went out in the field with the men every day and helped fence the remaining homesteaded acres. Jesse was finally adding a porch onto the cabin, and with Theodore assisting, it went quickly.

Lavina talked to her brothers about life out on the prairie, and about raising cattle, and although they helped without complaining, she could tell neither was interested. They preferred the busyness of living in town, and Teddy talked of going back east to school.

Elizabeth was proud that he was interested in his

education. She wanted both of her sons to attend college. She had the view, like many, that making a living off the land was an inferior way to live. That was her concern about Lavina living in such isolation. The closest school was in Compton. She didn't know how Lavina's children would receive a proper education. The main reason she had insisted on getting to know Matt before she approved of his marrying Lavina was because she was concerned that he was illiterate. She was pleasantly surprised to find he was at least somewhat educated, and enjoyed reading.

The evening after the company left it seemed quiet. Big John rose from his chair once supper was finished and walked over to the shelf where the whiskey bottle sat. "Surviving the in-laws deserves celebration." They all knew he was kidding, but they agreed on the celebrating part. He sat back down and poured whiskey into a cup. Then he passed the bottle to Matt. Matt poured himself a drink. He passed the bottle to Kirsten.

"What about me?"

Matt looked at Lavina and said, "No, you don't need any."

"Why not?"

John, Kirsten and Jesse looked amused, but said nothing. Lavina persisted, and finally Matt shrugged and handed her the bottle. "Go easy."

She poured the alcohol into a cup that had held coffee and took a sip. If she thought coffee was harsh the first time she tried it, this was worse. It burned her throat and all the way to her stomach. She gasped and then coughed. The others laughed, all remembering having a similar first experience drinking hard liquor.

Lavina immediately felt a warm glow. She took another, tinier sip. A deck of cards had appeared on the table.

"What are we playing, gin?" She asked.

Matt turned to his wife with an amused look on his face. "Poker."

Lavina laughed. "You waited until my family left before you really corrupted me." They all laughed again. Matt began explaining the game, while Jesse passed out matchsticks for betting. Like most ranch owners, Big John didn't allow real betting on his place.

They played late into the night. Lavina couldn't remember having so much fun. Matt's leg pressed against hers under the table, as they sat next to one another on the bench. Of course he saw her cards, so she lost early. It didn't matter. Everyone gave her some of their matchsticks so she could continue.

Matt watched that she drank only a small amount from the whiskey bottle. Finally, after she lost everything for the third time, they decided it was time for bed. Kirsten and Jesse left and John sat down on his bunk to remove his boots.

Matt and Lavina went into their bedroom, where Matt pulled her to him and kissed her. "I love you," he whispered.

Lavina looked at him. Like a lot of men, he wasn't good at expressing his emotions. She knew he loved her, but his words surprised her. "I love you too." She fell asleep in his arms, feeling a glow from the whiskey, but also the glow of knowing her husband loved her.

\*\*\*

Going to town, even to tiny Turkey Creek was a welcome outing for Kirsten and Lavina. They dressed in longer, fuller skirts before setting off in the buckboard with Jesse. At home they wore skirts that were six or so inches from the ground, which made them easier to keep clean, as well as to move around in.

Most western towns didn't allow women on the streets unescorted, or improperly dressed. They also weren't allowed in saloons. As rebellious as Kirsten was, she wasn't ornery enough to create a scene and risk being locked up. She didn't hesitate to voice her objection in private however.

Climbing down off of a wagon or buggy in a long restrictive skirt was not only awkward for women, it was dangerous. The skirts could and did get caught on the wagon.

The least inconvenience was a torn garment. But worse things also happened. There was the embarrassment of landing on their faces. Injuries and even deaths also occurred, because if the horses spooked the helpless woman could be run over or drug. The two women hitched their skirts up out of the way as much as was proper. Jesse came around to help them land on the ground safely.

Silas Riggs greeted the three of them as they entered his store. "Hello, Mrs. Branson, Mrs. Daly, Jesse. Nice day out." He welcomed the chance to socialize with people he considered neighbors. "What can I help you with?"

"Did you get fabric in?" Lavina asked.

"I got some wool and some nice prints." He led them over to a table stacked with bolts of cloth.

While Kirsten and Lavina looked through the fabric, Jesse loaded the wagon with other supplies. As he was finishing, a man unknown to them walked in. Instead of greeting the other people in the store, he ignored them as he walked to the counter. He demanded a bag of tobacco and abruptly walked out after throwing a coin on the counter.

"Who was that?" Jesse asked, finding it strange that the man seemed so unfriendly.

"One of Buehler's men." That seemed to explain it to all of them except Lavina. She knew nothing of the bad blood that was brewing between the D Rocking D and the Spade ranches.

"Why was that man so rude?" She asked Kirsten when they were alone outside.

"I'm not sure." She didn't know what to say. There was no reason for their neighbor to dislike them, since there was plenty of room on the range for all their cattle. None of them gave the incident much more thought.

A few weeks before fall roundup Lavina decided it was time to surprise Matt. She ran out one afternoon just after dinner to saddle Jack. When Matt walked out a few minutes later, she was riding the horse up from the barn. She tried to sit as tall and confident as Matt and his father when they rode. Matt grinned as he admired his wife's achievement. She rode around the yard, showing off, wearing her riding pants. He was proud of her as she trotted the horse past him, determined to keep the gelding moving in a straight line, despite bouncing around. She never grabbed for the horn.

"When can we go for a ride together?"

"What about right now?" He walked down to the corral and caught a horse to saddle.

They spent the afternoon riding through the hills. Loping up a long incline, the mountains came into view as they neared the top of the ridge. Stopping at the top, the horses caught their breath and the breeze cooled them, as they admired the view. Lavina stared in awe at the landscape in front of her. The ridges below had a slight haze to them in the late afternoon sun. In the distance the mountain peaks looked purple against the sky. It was one of her most memorable experiences yet. She hoped there would be a lot more like it.

Shortly after the couple returned home, Matt called to her from outside. "I've got something for you," he said as she came to the door. He was holding the end of a lead rope. Behind him stood Lucky, the black mare he had bought the year before. "I want you to have her."

He was giving her Lucky! "Oh thank you, thank you, thank you!" She was acting like Kirsten, but she couldn't help herself. Finally she forced herself to calm down before approaching the mare. She reached her hand up slowly, as she had seen Matt do, and stroked the mare's face.

"I'll keep riding her for a while," Matt said. "But you'll be able to handle her soon."

Lucky went on the fall roundup as part of Matt's string. After that she stayed in the corral eating hay for winter use. By spring Matt hoped to have the mare broke well enough so that Lavina could start riding her. She was willing and intelligent and was already becoming one of his favorite horses. But now she was Lavina's. He was happy to have such a wonderful gift for his wife.

\*\*\*

Just before fall roundup, another trip to Miles City was planned to meet with cattle buyers. Big John encouraged Matt to go in his place once again, and to take Lavina. He was content to stay home and tend to the ranch. Matt had learned the business well, so there was no reason for him not to go.

Lavina was excited. It was a rare opportunity to leave the ranch and her longest trip away since being married. They took the train from Compton and stayed in the Cattleman's Hotel. They were gone for three days which seemed a regular vacation.

Walking down the main street in Miles City, Matt and Lavina passed a photographer's studio. "Come on, let's have our picture taken," Matt said. He had just insisted on buying Lavina a new hat to match her green silk dress, which she was wearing. The hat was quite stylish, with dyed feathers that matched the dress perfectly.

Neither of them had ever had their picture taken before. Sitting in front of a cloth backdrop, on an ornate sofa, they felt unsure of themselves. But the photographer told them they looked fine and to sit still. As they paid him, he assured them he would mail the photograph to them once he developed the glass negatives.

Leaving the shop, they heard, "Why, Matt Daly! I haven't seen you in ages!" Lavina had paused in the doorway to look at the photographs on display in the window, so the woman calling out hadn't seen her. Matt immediately looked back at his wife, thinking, uh oh.

Miles City was a rare town where prostitutes were allowed to walk around in broad daylight. For the most part they were treated as regular citizens. In fact some of the bolder ones didn't hesitate to be seen with their clients. This particular woman Matt had known for years, as she followed the cattle trails from towns in Kansas to points further north. Now she was making a decent living from the cowboys in Montana.

Matt tried to ignore her as she walked towards him, but Lavina had heard the greeting and stuck her head out to see who was calling her husband. An attractive, respectable looking, young woman stopped in her tracks, looking at Lavina and then back to Matt. She started to turn away,

Lavina stepped out into the street and said, "How do you do? I'm Mrs. Daly." Looking closer, she noticed the woman's features were enhanced by carefully applied makeup.

Matt began stuttering, and turning to Lavina, finally got out, "This is Lily." He realized he didn't know the woman's last name, and probably not even her real name.

Lily smiled. "It's nice to meet you Mrs. Daly." She turned to Matt. "Congratulations. I was wondering why I never see you around anymore." In fact it had been over a year, since before he had met Lavina, that he had last seen her. Now he understood why his father had insisted Lavina accompany him. There wouldn't be any opportunity for the temptation of other women.

Matt and Lavina said goodbye to Lily and continued down the street. He was worried, but although she had a slight frown on her face, Lavina said nothing about the woman, even though it was obvious how he knew her.

The following day, they rode the train back to Compton. For the most part, it had been an enjoyable trip. When the photograph arrived a couple weeks later, Jesse made a wooden frame for it and Matt hung it on the cabin wall.

# Chapter 9

Kirsten Roberts was the oldest child in a large family. Since the next three children born to her parents were girls, she ended up doing a lot of the outside chores on the family farm in eastern Nebraska. She preferred the outdoors anyway, and being strong and hardy, didn't mind the physical labor. Of course she also had to take on big responsibilities when still young. That included helping her mother give birth to her fifth child when she was nine years old.

When she went into labor that day, her mother became worried. "You have to find help."

"Where?" The little girl stood looking up at her mother, sizing up the situation.

"Go get your father!" Kirsten took control. "Come lie down." She led the anxious woman into the bedroom and helped her onto the bed. Then she stuffed fuel into the cook stove and put on water to heat. Finally she went outside and looked around. Go for help where? By the time she reached her father way out in the field, and returned with him, the baby could already have come. And she already knew her father wasn't much help delivering human babies anyway. There was no one closer.

She went back inside the house and checked the stove before going in to see how her mother was doing. "I'll help you," she said with determination.

"What." A single word came out of her mother's mouth before her face twisted into a grimace as another labor pain hit her. The smaller children began crying.

Kirsten gathered her siblings around her and explained to them what was happening. "You have to be brave. And soon we'll have a new baby." Then she sent them outside. "But stay close." She pulled a clean pinafore on over her dress before going back to her mother, praying the delivery went easy.

Mrs. Roberts delivered the infant with only her small daughter's help. By the time her father returned that evening, tired from walking behind a plow pulled by their mule since sunup, Kirsten had not only cleaned up, but was putting supper on the table.

That was the beginning of her reputation, and she realized that she enjoyed assisting births. When she got older she became the midwife women wanted when a baby was on the way. The irony was that after six years of marriage to Jesse Branson, she was still childless.

*** 

Kirsten studied her friend's face. Lavina had almost collapsed as she reached the house with the heavy pails of water from the creek below. She caught herself on the table and pretended she had tripped, but Kirsten was concerned. Lavina had seemed tired lately and now there were dark circles under her eyes. She had also lost weight over the summer.

Suddenly Kirsten smiled at her. "You're going to have a baby!" She made the declaration confidently, recognizing the subtle signs. "And here we are working you to death.

The smile turned back to concern, but the truth was that Lavina was the one driving herself, as if needing to prove something. "You're going to sit here and rest a while." She wouldn't hear Lavina's protests. When the men came in at mid day they all noticed that Lavina was sitting in Big John's chair. She had never sat there before.

"Take a look at your wife," Kirsten told Matt. She was trying to be stern, but her excitement allowed a smile to show. He looked at Lavina again. He also noticed that she looked tired. Was something wrong? Before he could ask, Kirsten said, "Go ahead and tell him." She herded the others out the door and followed behind.

The realization finally hit Lavina, and she smiled up at Matt. "I, I'm with child."

Kirsten was persistent about Lavina taking it easy, and didn't allow her to haul water or wood. Lavina felt she was being treated like a child as Kirsten had her lie down and rest every afternoon. At mealtimes Kirsten piled the food on her plate. Within a couple of months the expectant mother's cheeks were once again rosy as her belly grew.

Eight months later Matt was pacing outside the door to the bedroom. On the other side Kirsten was helping Lavina birth their baby. He heard her cry out in pain, but only once. When Kirsten came out and poured herself a cup of coffee, she seemed unconcerned. "Everything is fine," she assured Matt as she disappeared back into the bedroom.

He tried to follow her, but was sternly told by Kirsten, "I'll let you know if I need your help." She could see him competently helping deliver any baby but his own. It was no different with anyone. Being too close to the one in pain made most people freeze.

It was late. The lantern had been re-filled and the fire in the stove still burned. Big John and Jesse sat with Matt, drinking coffee. At last they heard the unmistakable cry. They watched the bedroom door expectantly. Finally Kirsten opened it and beckoned Matt. He glanced at his father. "Well, go ahead," the older man smiled. Matt went into the bedroom to meet his new son. They named the infant John after his grandfather, and he quickly became Little John.

\*\*\*

That summer the men built two new corrals adjoining one another. One was round, to be used for breaking horses. They sunk a thick post deep in the center for snubbing. The gate led into the other corral where the horses would be held. The following week they brought home a dozen unbroke horses they had bought sight unseen from a herd that had been trailed up from Kansas. It was risky buying horses that way, but they always needed fresh mounts, and there were few to be found in the area. The only time these geldings had felt the hand of a man was when they were roped and thrown, then branded and castrated, as two year-olds. Now they were four and five years old, wild as mustangs and scared to death of people.

A bronc buster was hired to break them. His name was Pete and he had a good reputation. It was so good that he asked for, and got, five dollars a horse for his work. It was good pay for a couple weeks of work. Of course he was expected to have them all rideable in that time. And he had to agree to sleep in the barn as there was no room in the bunkhouse. That didn't bother him. As long as the food was good, he wasn't picky about where he slept.

Big John was picky about who broke his horses though, and about how they were treated in general. If a new hand showed up wearing spurs with sharp rowels, they had to be changed out or ground down. Spurs were a tool of the trade, and no cowboy would be caught without them. But John demanded they be humane. He also didn't allow the men to carry quirts. He didn't believe in whipping horses, or in bloodying their sides.

The day Pete arrived he walked down to the corral, where the new horses were being held, to size them up. Even though they were in with the older ones, it wasn't hard to tell which the new ones were. Most of the broke horses had marks on their backs. A lot of miles under saddle wore the hair off, and now many of them had spots where the hair had grown back in white.

"Not a bad set," Pete decided, as he studied the milling horses.

He checked out the round corral next. It was stout, with thick rails spaced only inches apart, six feet high. Nodding his approval he went back to the horse corral. Studying the unbroken horses, he determined, by the look in their eyes and the way they watched him, which ones he thought would make his job harder. Mentally he divided the horses into two groups. The first group he would begin working with in the morning. The second group would wait until the first was considered rideable, meaning he had most the buck out of them and that they were learning to follow directions from the reins.

The following morning the excitement began. The first horse, a bay with white stockings on both hind legs was hazed into the round corral. Pete stood in the center of the pen with his rope and shook out a loop as the frightened horse galloped in a circle around him. He swung the rope a few times overhead before letting loose, and caught the animal around the neck on the first try. Quickly he wrapped the rope around the post in the center and scrambled out of the way as the horse realized he was caught. He fought hard, rearing up and pulling back before plunging forward, trying to free himself.

Once the horse stopped and stood still because he was out of air from the rope around his neck choking him, Pete came in with another rope. He laid a loop on the ground and tricked the unhappy horse into stepping into it with his front feet. Quickly Pete took the slack and jerked the horse's feet out from under him. The horse went down hard and while he was down, the bronc buster wrapped a set of hobbles around his front legs. Then he replaced the rope around his neck with a bridle.

When the horse scrambled back to his feet, Pete hung on tight to the reins in one hand, and with a saddle blanket in the other, sacked him out. This meant he flapped the blanket all over the terrified horse. The hobbles helped to keep the jumping to a minimum as the gelding fell down every time he tried to escape. Finally he just stood and trembled as the blanket smacked him.

Next the saddle was put on and cinched, which took a while as the horse fought again, bucking each time it was placed on his back. When the saddle was finally cinched tight and the horse stood still once again, the hobbles were removed and it was time for Pete to mount. Twisting hard on an ear with one hand so the horse's attention was on the pain, Pete had time to slip a foot in the stirrup and quickly hop aboard. All hell broke loose as the animal bucked for all he was worth, trying to dislodge the man on top of him. The first day he was ridden to a standstill, and then Pete jumped off, considering it a good first lesson. After a few days of this, once the horse stopped bucking, the gate was opened, and Pete urged the horse out into the open where he went for a ride. Usually it was a mad dash for freedom, and another horse and rider ran alongside to haze the out of control pair away from dangerous obstacles such as large rocks and steep ravines, and to lead them home again.

It was exciting to watch. Matt and Big John kept an eye out in case Pete got hung up or injured, so they could come to his rescue. And the other cowboys watched the show whenever possible, sitting on the top rail of the fence, whooping and yelling encouragement as Pete rode. From a distance he seemed to bounce through the air above the rails of the corral.

Lavina could hear the excitement from the cabin as she worked. She wished she could go down and watch with the rest, but Little John was waking up from his nap, and she had the noon meal to prepare. It seemed that was always the case. She missed out on a lot of activities because there was always work to be done. Even Kirsten slipped off to spectate. She'd return to the cabin laughing as she told Lavina what the young mother had missed.

\*\*\*

In May, the following year, Lavina was expecting their second child. She and Matt hoped it would come before spring round up. As it turned out the little girl was born with weeks to spare. A dry spring set the roundup well back as the ranchers waited for the grass to grow up out on the prairie so the cattle would come out of the creek bottoms and coulees to graze out in the open.

The drought continued into the summer of 1886. The Dalys knew not to increase their herd. It might turn out to be a year where, as Big John put it, "Sometimes you just have to tighten your belt a notch." Drought and falling cattle prices, both periodic, were the two main reasons to start watching cash flow.

Still the longhorns kept coming up from the south. Herd after herd made the long trip and were turned out onto the parched prairie.

It seemed that every time a dry storm blew through, lightening strikes sparked fires, and the air was filled with a smoky haze all summer long. Everyone kept an eye on the horizon for bellowing clouds of smoke. The upwind direction was especially watched. Not only did the fires burn off vegetation, but cattle and buildings were also at risk from the fast moving prairie fires.

Both Matt and his father were concerned about the increasing number of cattle filling the range. More speculators were investing in cattle as the price for them continued to climb. The neighbor to the north, Bully Buehler had found two other men, wealthy foreigners, to invest in his ranch, and they added thousands more steers to the Spade herd.

Buehler was also becoming bolder in his efforts to expand onto neighboring ranges. The D Rocking D cowboys never rode out without being armed. Although nothing was said in their presence, the women felt the tension, and Matt and his father were preoccupied. With two young children to care for, Lavina didn't pay as much attention to their moods, but she still worried. There had already been trouble. One day in town, Matt and Big John had stopped in at the Blue Bear for a snort of whiskey before heading home. Three of the Spade men were there. They had hinted that the Dalys had better stay out of their way, that they needed more grazing space, and that they were going to take what they wanted.

"We'll be waiting." Big John's voice was calm, but the look in his father's eye told Matt his father would do whatever it took to keep his land.

They left the bar and headed home. Neither man wanted trouble. They rode home in silence, each keeping his thoughts private.

They knew that Buehler already controlled hundreds of thousands of acres of rangeland, which his many riders guarded zealously. Matt and his father tried to keep their cattle on one side of the ridge, and the Spade cattle on the other, but with the scarcity of grass, the bovines wandered. The two herds started mixing.

On the D Rocking D roundup, Buehler, instead of sending one of his cowboys to rep, came himself, along with two of his men. He watched over the entire operation as if expecting the other ranchers would try to steal from him. He tried to claim all mavericks as his own, when there was no telling who the unbranded cattle belonged to. The other ranchers, wanting to get along with their neighbors had worked out a system years before. They drew straws, and the man who pulled the longest claimed the first one. After that they took turns as to who got to burn their brand on the next one that was found and so on. They all overruled Buehler and made him wait his turn.

None of the other outfits invited the Spade men to eat with them. Usually men from other outfits were welcome at neighboring fires. It gave them a chance to socialize and share news.

Buehler came over to the D Rocking D chuckwagon the first night out, expecting a meal. Curly saw him coming, and since his men had all eaten, dumped the remainder of the pot of stew on the ground in front of him. The plucky cook had no reservations about letting his feelings known.

\*\*\*

116

With five of them living there, the cabin became even more crowded. Big John spent more time out in the bunkhouse, when there was an empty bed, to give his son's growing family more room.

Lavina found out, as did other women, that her time was no longer her own once she had children. Lucky stood idle out in the pasture. She had been able to ride the mare only a few times after Little John was born. Then she had become pregnant again and that was the end of riding. Her horse became part of Matt's string once again.

Early one morning Kirsten stepped out with the milk bucket in one hand. She looked around, appreciating the new day. Except for the birds singing in the trees down by the creek, anticipating the sunrise, it was calm and still. She walked to the barn where Eva and her calf waited.

The pair were put in separate pens at night and then reunited in the morning and let out into the pasture once the cow was milked. Kirsten released Eva from the small pen and the cow walked into one of the stalls. She waited while Kirsten poured a can of oats into the manger. The calf got some oats as well to keep it quiet.

Kirsten sat down on the milking stool and placed the bucket underneath the cow's udder. With a rhythmic motion she began squeezing the milk out of the teats, working her way around the four of them. She leaned her head against the cow's warm side, listening to the inner rumblings of the rumen. It was a peaceful way to begin the day.

The flock of chickens had increased to eight. They roosted in the barn at night and Jesse had built nesting boxes in a back corner for egg laying. But one of the hens was hiding her nest. That morning Lavina left the two children sleeping on Big John's bunk and went out looking for the nest. She wanted to find the eggs before they spoiled in the summer heat. She walked past the open barn door where she heard the rhythmical sshew, sshew of milk hitting the pail as Kirsten milked Eva before breakfast. Outside the barn, Matt was bent over underneath a horse's belly as he held up a front leg, replacing a shoe that had been lost. She heard tapping as he pounded a nail into the hoof.

Continuing around to the back of the barn, her eyes searched for hidden eggs. What she saw was completely unexpected. There was a body laying there. Her mind seemed to work in slow motion as she took in the scene. She could tell it was a man, but only by the clothing. One side of his face had been bashed in, and it was swollen and hideously misshapen. Dried blood crusted the face and hair.

Lavina's scream destroyed the morning tranquility. Eva, stomped her hind leg, knocking over the milk pail. The horse jerked his leg out from where it was wedged between Matt's knees. Matt dropped the hammer and ran to where Lavina stood frozen, unable to take her eyes off the grizzly sight. He took one look and grabbed her, quickly positioning himself between her and the body. The others came running as Matt steered her away.

Jesse grabbed Kirsten and followed Matt and Lavina up to the house. Both men made their wives promise to stay there and refused to answer any questions. They rushed back out to where Big John stood over the body.

None of them knew why the man was there, but they could see from the fresh horse tracks that he had been dumped off the night before. John insisted they take the body to town immediately. He told the other two that if they covered it up, it would turn them into liars.

"Hitch the team," John instructed. The three of them heaved the dead man into the back of the wagon. While Matt stayed with the two women and the children, Big John and Jesse climbed onto the wagon. They each had a rifle within reach as they set off for town.

The sheriff of Turkey Creek wasn't really a sheriff since there was no organized county. The local businessmen had hired him because it made them feel safer since they were so far away from any real law.

In fact, the man, Hiram Booker, wasn't even sure what

his duties were. Someone had found an old badge for him to wear. He could have been accused of impersonating an officer, but the badge was old and rusty, and no one took it too seriously. He'd never arrested anybody. Some questioned why they needed him. But it didn't cost them much. The owner of The Palace let him sleep in a back room and fed him two meals a day. The saloon owners donated whiskey to keep him content and the man who ran the way station fed his horse. His other needs were taken care of as they arose.

Sheriff Booker chuckled about it almost every day. The joke was on the townspeople of Turkey Creek. He had been down in Wyoming Territory running with a gang of petty thieves. They had gotten bolder and decided to go after big money. It hadn't lasted long, as a posse went after them with a vengeance after they robbed their first bank. Booker's cohorts had all been shot out of the saddle as they fled. He had almost run his horse to death escaping. As luck would have it, he was carrying most of the money they'd stolen.

When he rode into Miles city he was looking for a place to lay low. He traded his worn out horse for a healthy one. Then he bought new clothes. With his mustache shaved and his trimmed hair showing underneath a new hat, his looks were somewhat altered, and he looked respectable. He headed west, watching his back the whole way. By chance he rode into Turkey Creek and came up with a plan.

He had always been a fast talker, and he buddied up to the people in the remote town, acting like a genuinely honest and caring man. It had worked. He found the best disguise ever. A few wondered why the stranger would take a job as sheriff without pay, but he didn't plan on staying long enough for anyone to figure it out. As soon as he decided it was safe, he'd move on without any goodbyes.

When Big John and Jesse brought the dead man to town, the first thing they needed to do was find Sheriff Booker. They asked around and finally located him down by the creek. He had a fishing line in the water and was leaning up against a tree, sipping from a bottle. "Hey, Booker." He stood up as John called to him. The two men in the wagon immediately noticed a cockiness they hadn't seen in him before.

"Mornin'. What can I help you with?" He eyed the two men carefully.

"Something we need to show you." John motioned towards the back of the wagon. He handed Jesse the lines before jumping down. As usual, Jesse didn't speak. He watched the sheriff walk over. There's something funny going on, he thought.

Booker's eyes widened as he saw the gruesome sight in the back of the wagon. He hadn't counted on actually having to act as sheriff. "What happened?"

"We found him like this. Someone dumped him off behind my barn."

Booker arched his eyebrows. "Dumped him off? That's a likely story, but it don't hardly make sense." Besides the sneer in his voice, both Jesse and John noticed that his polite way of speaking had vanished.

"We found him lying out there this morning, just like this." "Well, I don't know if I believe you." He looked from Big John to Jesse.

"I don't care if you believe me or not. Now you need to see that he gets buried." John's voice had an edge to it. He had no tolerance for any man, and especially this little rat, questioning his honesty.

Booker backed down. "What's his name?"

"No idea. We'll leave him back behind Curtis' barn." John back climbed onto the buckboard, settled into the seat and took the lines back from Jesse. He urged the horses forward and never looked back, making the sheriff walk back to town.

When Big John returned home he went to the house. He opened the door and looked inside. Lavina was inside, peeling potatoes. Little John played at her feet. The baby, Annie, slept on his bunk.

"Are you okay?" he asked. She nodded and he left to find his son. Jesse had driven the team into the shed and began pulling the harness off of them. Matt came over to help.

"What did Booker say?" he asked.

"What could he say?" Matt heard the anger in his father's voice. All three of them knew who the dead man was. He was one of the thieves they had caught stealing their cattle and let go two years earlier. Big John hadn't lied to the sheriff though. He didn't know the man's name.

There was nothing more they could do, except go on living their lives. Sooner or later they would discover who had set them up. They all had a bad feeling because they were pretty sure they knew who it was, and why.

"Where's Kirsten?" Jesse asked Matt. They were all feeling protective.

"She went across the creek." He motioned towards their cabin with his head. Jesse crossed over the bridge to check on his wife.

That night Matt held Lavina tight. He kept assuring her everything would be all right, but it was as if a chill had taken hold of her. A dark cloud had suddenly descended over the D Rocking D.

A couple days later a lone horseman rode into the yard. It was the manager of the way station in Turkey Creek. "Good morning, anybody home?" he called out while still on his horse.

Lavina came outside. "Good morning, Mr. Hicks."

"Is your husband home?"

Jesse came out of the barn when he heard the man call out.

"Howdy, Curtis. What brings you out this way?"

Curtis looked at Lavina, then back to Jesse. "I need to talk to Big John." He obviously didn't want to talk in front of Lavina.

"He and Matt won't be back until later. Stick around and have something to eat."

"Can't. I have to meet the stage this afternoon." Curtis decided it would be all right to tell Jesse what he had to say. He dismounted and Lavina watched them walk off together. She wished she knew what was going on.

121

That evening Jesse went out to the barn when Matt and Big John rode in. It was late and they were tired. Jesse knew they weren't going to like what he had to tell them "Curtis was out today."

"Oh?" Matt and John looked at him. They figured he had taken a look at the body they had dumped out in back of his barn.

"He said the other night a bunch of Buehler's men rode into town. They put their horses in the barn, like they didn't want anyone to know they were there. Bobby heard them talking in the Blue Bear. He said it sounded like they were planning to run someone off. He didn't know who or where." Jesse paused. It was a lot of words for him. "Curtis said the dead man was one of them, one of Buehler's thugs."

Matt and his father looked at one another, their suspicions confirmed.

"There's one more thing," Jesse continued. "He said as soon as we left the other day," he looked at John, "The sheriff came and got his horse. He rode out in a hurry, headed north."

"I knew that fool was up to no good the minute I laid eyes on him."

The tension at the D Rocking D didn't lessen as summer progressed. At least one man stayed at the ranch headquarters at all times with the women and children. Lavina couldn't get used to the clunking sounds of guns knocking against wood when the men came in to supper. She was adamant they remove guns and spurs and hang them on the wall with their hats while they ate.

One day Matt was out riding on the northern part of their range with Joe, when they came across a spring that had been fenced off. Besides the fact that it was the only water for a mile in either direction, which was crucial for their cattle, the fence was against the law. In 1885 the illegal fencing of public lands had been prohibited by an act of congress. There was no one around and the two men tore the barb wire down before riding on.

A week later Bully Buehler came riding into the yard at

the D Rocking D. He had four men with him. "Hey Daly!" he yelled as he jerked his horse to a stop outside the cabin. The only one inside was Lavina. She didn't know who the men were, or what they wanted. Kirsten and Jesse had gone to town, and Matt and John were out riding, but Samuel was around someplace. She didn't believe anyone would hurt her, so she came to the door.

"I'm Mrs. Daly," she said evenly, after opening the door.

"I have business with your husband."

"He's not here."

"Are you sure he's not in there hiding?" One of the other men called out, and then snickered. Where was Samuel? For a moment Lavina almost panicked. Had they done something to him?

"You all need to leave, NOW!" The voice came from behind them. The riders turned to see the hired cowboy standing with a rifle leveled at Buehler's head. Samuel looked like a crazy man. His eyes were bulging out of his head. He had no hat, and his black hair stuck out from his head in all directions.

No one said another word. The riders turned their horses around and left. Samuel kept the rifle on them until they were out of sight. Then he collapsed to his knees, his face pale. Lavina ran over to him.

"Are you all right?" She helped him to his feet and guided him towards the house.

"I think I drank some bad water." He had been behind the bunkhouse retching when Buehler and his men rode up. Lavina had him lie down on Big John's bed. Then she went outside to reassure herself that nothing was out of place.

Matt was furious when he heard what happened. His father agreed with him that they couldn't let this go. The next day the two of them rode for the Spade Ranch.

It was a half day's ride, which meant a wasted day. That put the Dalys in an even worse mood. They rode up to the cabin that served as the headquarters. There was a corral with a few horses and a crude open-sided shed. Saddles and other gear lay strewn around inside. The cabin was tiny, with no windows that they could see, just cracks large enough to peer out of without being seen.

"Buehler! Get out here!" Big John yelled. Matt looked around, watching for a trap.

A man came to the door. He looked drunk. "Mr. Buehler aint here, but I'll be sure to let him know you called." The man had a defiant smile on his face. "By the way, Mr. Buehler don't like it when you mess with his water holes."

Big John was ready to jump off his horse and strangle the man, but he held his anger in. The kind of cockiness the man showed meant he had plenty of backup. "You tell your boss I don't scare easy."

Matt was afraid it would escalate. There were obviously more men inside, and he and his father were sitting out in the open. "Leave the water holes alone. They belong to everyone."

The man just laughed, but Matt wasn't finished yet. "If anyone scares my family again, I'll kill 'em." He turned to his father. "Come on, this was a waste of time."

As they rode over the ridge Buehler and two other men walked outside and watched them disappear. The man who had done the talking said, "You heard him threaten me."

"Yes, he certainly did." Matt and John didn't know it, but they had played right into Buehler's hand.

A week later they found twenty of their steers shot dead, and the water hole had another fence around it. Matt rode a horse to town the next day. He was looking for trouble. He couldn't help feeling helpless and frustrated. His father didn't want him to go, but they needed ammunition, and he was out of tobacco.

They had all been staying close to home, wondering what Buehler's next move would be, and had discussed the situation. It seemed certain Buehler had bought off the sheriff, or maybe he had threatened him. Asking a lawman for help would have been their last choice anyway. The independent ranchers preferred taking care of problems their own way, quickly and permanently. But something had to be done. They had alerted their neighbors as to what was going on, and everyone was keeping an eye on the situation.

Matt rode his bay gelding, Easy, mostly because he was his fastest horse. He wanted to be able to escape trouble if needed, and to get home fast. Trotting into town, Matt didn't notice anything suspicious, but he felt nervous. He went straight to the general store.

"Boy am I glad to see you!" Silas exclaimed as he walked in the door. "People are talking about how you threatened one of Buehler's men. Some are even saying that you killed that fellow you found. And Bobby heard one of Buehler's men say something about a fire out at your place."

"I need cartridges and a bag of tobacco!" Matt was alarmed. Silas hesitated as he watched Matt's face. "I have to get home!" Silas turned back to the shelf and began grabbing boxes of ammunition. He knew what caliber Matt needed for the guns he used. Matt carried a Colt Frontier Model double action pistol because it chambered the same cartridge as his Winchester rifle.

Matt stuffed the tobacco in his pocket, and then scooped up as many boxes of ammunition as he could carry and hurried out the door. He stuffed the boxes into his saddlebags, vaulted onto his horse's back, and had him at a gallop before they reached the edge of town.

Matt ran Easy harder than he had ever pushed a horse, anxious for the safety of his family. When he was a mile from the house he finally slowed to a walk. He scanned the sky in front of him, searching for smoke. The only thing he could hear was the sound of his horse's labored breathing. Just as he was starting to feel relief, a shot rang out. The gelding leaped off the road and into the brush as a bullet splintered a tree in back of them. They trotted through the thick willows as fast as they were able, with Matt hunched over to avoid overhanging branches. He tried to get as close to the house as possible without being seen again.

But someone else was waiting for him. There another shot and a sharp ping as the bullet hit nearby. Matt broke for open country, urging the tired horse to run for their lives. There were a couple more shots, but none came close. The shooters stayed hidden down in the trees.

He reached the top of the closest ridge before pausing to look around. He saw no one, but he wasn't high enough to see the ranch buildings. The horse and rider continued climbing until they reached the rimrock. There Matt dismounted to lead Easy up through a rock-filled crack to the top of the cliff. Mounting, he hurried along the edge to a spot where he could look down onto the D Rocking D headquarters. He squint his eyes, straining to see. There was movement, two specks that he decided must be people, but he couldn't make out who it was, or what they were doing. He kept watching. The two tiny figures disappeared into the cabin. At least nothing was burning.

He stood there, his eyes never still as he searched for movement, not only at the ranch headquarters, but also along the creek and on top of the ridge lines. Fear turned to anger, and then to worry. He tried to believe his eyes, that nothing was wrong, but his gut said differently.

It remained quiet and after an hour, Matt convinced himself it must be safe to return. Besides, he was too anxious to wait any longer. Easy's breathing was back to normal and the sweat had dried to a crust on his coat. He led the horse back down through the crack in the cliff, mounted, and set off at a lope.

As he got closer to the buildings he became wary. He paused for a moment, listening and studying the ridge line around him. Then he moved on.    As he entered the trees along the creek, a branch caught in his stirrup and broke off. He bent over to pull it loose, and the move saved his life. This time the shooter had been patient and waited until he was sure of a clear shot before firing. The whine of the bullet startled his horse. He took off running while Matt struggled to regain his balance. He turned the horse down the creek, avoiding branches as he frantically tried to look around to see if he was being chased. Finally he stopped again and listened.

Matt decided that, as worried as he was about his family, he had to find a safe place to hide out until Buehler and his men got tired of waiting and left. There was a spot across the creek, up in the hills, where he could remain hidden, and yet see anyone coming. He urged his tired horse into a lope once he was again out of the trees on the opposite creek bank, not knowing if anyone spotted him or not.

An hour later he reached the place, a hollow in the side of a hill surrounded by cedars and ponderosas. He stopped a final time to listen and study the landscape. As he entered the trees, a voice called out.

"Been waiting for you, Daly." It was Bully Buehler and he had a rifle pointed at Matt. His face wore a triumphant smirk. Matt grabbed his pistol out of the holster, raised it and fired. It was pure instinct, exactly what he had practiced for years as a boy. The speed and ease with which he drew his gun surprised him. Buehler fell to the ground with a grunt. Matt looked up. There were two more men in the trees. They were holding their horses, keeping them quiet as they watched Matt approach. Startled at seeing their boss go down, they began retreating back into the forest. Matt didn't go after them, but started back down the hillside.

As he rode, his mind thawed and he realized what he had done. He knew the sheriff would come after him. He also knew that the only witnesses would tell a diffcrent story about what had happened. He decided he had to leave the area for a while to protect his family.

# Chapter 10

T wo days later, after swimming the river in the early morning darkness, Matt rode into the town of Compton. He snuck into Gust's barn and waited, shivering, knowing his friend would help him. An hour later the livery owner opened the door to the barn. Quietly, Matt called out to him. Gust recognized the voice.

He hung the lantern on the wall before turning to face his friend. "Matt." He paused. The dim light showed the sadness on his face.

"I have to get word to my family." Matt assumed the livery owner knew what had happened.

Gust didn't let him get any further. "Matt," he said again. He couldn't seem to get any other word out. Matt was suddenly very scared. He waited for the other man to continue. "They're all dead, your wife, your father, the Bransons."

"No! They can't be!" Matt refused to even try and comprehend what he was being told. Gust hurried on, repeating the story that was going around. "They say you killed Buehler and resisted arrest. There was a shootout. Guess some were caught in the crossfire." He paused again, hating to be the one telling Matt this news. "They also say you killed that man you found out at your place."

Matt couldn't breathe. He thought he was going to fall down. It just couldn't be. Lavina, Big John, plus Kirsten and Jesse, all dead. He couldn't speak to explain what had really happened. He had killed a man, and in retaliation his family had been gunned down.

"You need to get out of here." But Matt wasn't listening. As the dawn dimly illuminated the buildings, he led his horse out of the barn and staggered down the street. Finally he mounted. Gust watched him disappear into the gray light, feeling helpless.

Matt headed east. It wasn't planned. That just happened to be the direction his horse headed. His mind tried to work. He should be preparing for fall roundup. Everyone at home would be waiting for him.

Two hours later, Gust was on his way out to a new home site. The wagon had been loaded the day before and now he was delivering the building materials. He sat atop the wagon, thinking about what he had told Matt earlier, hating that he'd had to pass on such devastating news. Besides feeling sad, he had a hard time believing that Matt's father and wife, plus his neighbors, had been gunned down. The peacefulness of the entire region had been shattered. He looked around, half expecting to see a change in the landscape to match the brutality of the killings. Since it was all anyone was talking about, it must be true.

As the wagon, pulled by an experienced team, began descending a steep hill, the horses sat back hard on their brichens to hold it back. Gust helped by leaning on the brake. Suddenly the well-worn tongue snapped where it attached to the wagon. Instantly Gust lost control. The tongue hit the ground as the wagon rammed the horses, pushing them downhill as they frantically tried to get out of the way. The vehicle gained speed even as Gust continued pushing down on the brake handle. It skidded sideways as the horses, still attached by the harness managed to jump out of the way. The old teamster was flung off the side where he flew through the air and landed on the rocks below.

The team continued running, finally becoming completely free of the wagon as the harness and wagon broke apart. Still hitched together, they ran until exhausted before finally stopping. A cowboy happened upon them where they stood, heads hanging. He quickly cut them loose before following their tracks back to where he knew he would find a wreck.

Gust lay where he had landed, dead from internal injuries. He'd never had the chance to tell anyone that Matt Daly had been in his barn that morning.

*** 

A couple days later Matt rode into Miles City. He stopped in front of the bank and looked around. He was still trying to get used to being a wanted man with nowhere to go and no one to go home to. Part of him wanted to just lie down and never get up again. Another part wanted to keep on living. The compromise was to stay numb.

He stepped down off Easy and tied him to the hitch rail. Entering the bank, he looked around to see if anyone acted wary of him. The teller was a stranger to him, and he asked to withdraw money from the ranch account. He continued watching the few men conducting business in the dimly lit building. Once the transaction was completed, Matt turned and walked out, finally taking a deep breath when he got outside. Now if he could get out of town without seeing anyone he knew.

A month later, Matt was still riding aimlessly. He thought about his children, and figured they would have been taken to live with the Lavolds in Cedar Junction. If he was wanted for killing two men, it was no use trying to see them. Besides, he felt a complete failure, unable to protect his family. They were better off with their grandparents.

He drifted south into Wyoming Territory, staying hidden as much as possible. Once in a while a cowboy would spot him riding through the hills. Strange riders were suspicious because of all the cattle and horse rustling. Also Matt knew that news of the shootings near Turkey Creek would have spread by now. He kept moving, stopping to camp where he was well hidden. The only things he ate were what he shot, usually rabbits or prairie chickens. Some days he went hungry.

Finally the loneliness became unbearable. He came across a road and began following it, still heading south. He passed a couple of men on horseback, but just nodded and lowered his chin so no one could study his face. A day later he entered the town of Sandy Flats. There was nothing remarkable about it. It was just another stage stop in the middle of the windswept prairie between Sheridan and Cheyenne.

Outside a saloon he dismounted and tied his horse. As usual he looked over at the two other horses standing tied there. He walked around to where he could study the brands on their hips. He didn't want to risk running into someone he knew.

Inside, he walked up to the bar and ordered whiskey. It went down easy, and he began to relax. Taking a deep breath, he turned around. There was a man sitting at a table looking at him. Matt didn't recognize him, but the man was studying his face. He eased to the side of the room, acting more casual than he felt.

Once outside he walked down the wooden sidewalk, looking for a store that sold tobacco. After making his purchase, he paused outside on the wooden boardwalk and looked down the street, intending to find a room for the night after a hot meal and a bath. Instead he found himself face to face with the stranger from the saloon.

"Thought I recognized you." The stranger seemed to be taunting him. Matt studied the man's face. He couldn't remember ever seeing him before.

It was Monty Harris, one of the gunmen Bully Buehler had hired to kill Matt and his father. He had been on his way back to Arizona and had run into Matt by chance. He couldn't believe his luck. The opportunity to finish the job had just fallen into his lap.

His anger at missing his mark the first time resurfaced as the man responsible for a wasted trip north stood in front of him. He preferred to finish any job he started since he had a reputation to uphold, and now there was a reward out for Matt Daly. He wouldn't be cheated twice.

Matt didn't know any of this. "I'm just passing through. I don't know you."

"But I know you, and last I heard you're worth as much dead as alive.

Matt's blood ran cold. "You're making a mistake."

The stranger drew Matt out into the street. Matt glanced down at the pistol the man wore on his hip, then back to the man's face. He was too confident he decided. But that didn't make him any less lethal. Obviously he had experience killing.

"Let's just pretend we never met." Matt still wanted to avoid a violent conflict.

"That aint gonna happen." Harris stared Matt down. The problem for him was that he thought it was going to be easy. Matt waited, desperately hoping for a way out of the situation, but he wasn't going to back down.

After what seemed an eternity, the man got bored and decided to end the showdown. He reached for his pistol. As soon as he moved, Matt drew his own gun, aimed and fired in one quick movement. It seemed to be slow motion, until the gunmen hit the ground. And it was way too easy. Once again, it felt just like when he practiced as a boy.

Matt snapped out of his trance-like state and headed for his horse. He still held his pistol, and he looked around, making sure there was no one else wanting to take a shot at him. He vaulted onto his horse's back and fled the town at a gallop.

The few people watching were amazed. Matt had moved so fast. One went out to the fallen man. He had a hole in the middle of his chest. It didn't appear he would live.

"Do you know who this is?" The bartender had come out

into the street. He looked around at the small crowd that was forming. "This is Mean Monty Harris. He's beaten a dozen men to the draw." The group of men continued staring at the man lying there. A puddle of blood was spreading out around him.

"Better get the doctor for him," someone suggested.

Matt's reputation began to spread. No one knew the actual number of men Mean Monty had killed, but those who knew him stayed out of his way. Some were relieved when he died.

A federal marshal from Cheyenne was sent up to investigate. The matter was dropped when the witnesses all told the same story. The dead man had drawn first.

Matt ran Easy hard until they were well out of town. Then he left the road, crossed a stream and headed up into the hills to find a spot where he could watch to see if anyone came after him. After a sleepless night he headed south again. Avoiding the skyline, he rode down in the coulees and along the base of the hills, always watching.

Matt wanted to believe the shooting had been more of a bad dream, a continuation of the one he'd been having since he had left the D Rocking D that fateful day. But the smell of gunpowder and the red on the man's chest had been too real.

He continued riding south, still wandering, feeling more and more lost. Finally his urge for whiskey to help him forget made him desperate enough to find another town. Also, he was hungry. His mouth watered at the thought of a real meal. Once again he followed a road he came upon to the town it led to. This time he was very cautious. There was one less man after him, but there might be more.

He rode Easy into town at a walk, watching men and horses, and hoping no one would notice him. It was a bigger town, with a couple of side streets, and the main street was busy. He found the local livery stable and had the man in charge feed his horse. Then he asked about a farrier to give the gelding a new set of shoes. The man looked him over, but noticed nothing unusual. Matt appeared to be just another cowboy passing through.

Next he headed for a doorway with batwing doors through which piano playing could be heard. He drank a couple shots of the rotgut that passed for whiskey. He wanted more, enough to become completely numb, to drown the thoughts of his dead wife and father, and also of the two men he had killed. Later, he decided. First he had to eat.

The next morning Matt rode out of town, well-fed. He would have been content except for the memories he couldn't let go of. He was still wandering aimlessly, his mind incapable of focusing on a plan.

From Wyoming, Matt passed into eastern Colorado, and then followed the South Platte River down to Ogallala, Nebraska. He hadn't been to the cow town since he and his father had trailed cattle up from Texas. It had grown considerably, and become much more civilized. Farmers were moving in, plowing up the prairie and stringing barb wire fences. Matt began to feel homesick for the open range of Montana. But he didn't allow himself to think about his old home for long. It was too painful. He wanted to forget that life.

He stayed in Ogallala for a week, hanging out in the saloons, drinking every night until he couldn't think or feel. Then he staggered back to the livery to pass out in the barn. The owner found him there more than once when he arrived in the morning. But it wasn't unusual. As long as they caused no trouble and didn't smoke, cowboys were welcome to sleep off a night of drinking.

The only difference was that most of them were in town to celebrate, happy to be off the lonesome prairie for a few days. This stranger was quiet and sad. He kept to himself and didn't say much.

Finally Matt decided he had better move on. From talk in a bar the night before, he found out he had a reputation as a gunfighter after killing the hired gunman in Wyoming. He thought the man was after him because of a wanted poster with his likeness on it. No one had yet recognized him in Nebraska, but after sitting next to the cowboy at the bar, and hearing the story about himself, he decided it wasn't safe to stay in one place for long. He paid the livery bill for Easy and rode out.

It was mid fall and beginning to get cold. The cottonwoods along the creeks were turning gold, and the morning he left town there was frost on the ground. Once again he went south. He was prepared to travel. He had bought a thick, sheepskin lined coat and a couple of wool blankets. Easy had put on a couple of pounds standing in the barn, as Matt had made sure he had plenty to eat.

The horse and rider drifted down into Kansas. It was practically unrecognizable from what Matt remembered from only a few years before. The prairie was gold, the color of the ripened wheat that covered it as far as the eye could see. Most of it had already been reduced to stubble, but a few farmers hurried to finish harvesting their fields. Teams of huge work horses pulled mowers, while men on foot followed behind binding the stalks into bundles. Then the bundles were stacked on a wagon to be hauled to the thresher.

He passed farmers driving heavy teams pulling wagons full of grain. They glared at him with hostility, remembering the rowdy cowboys who had shot up their towns when they hit trail's end. Matt ignored them and kept moving.

Matt didn't know it, but someone had recognized him in Nebraska and he was being followed. The man was dressed neither as a farmer nor a cowboy, and was careful to attract no attention as he followed a safe distance behind. His only distinguishing feature was his large nose that protruded from his face like a giant beak. Big Nose Newcomb wasn't going to let the same thing happen to him that had happened to his partner back in Wyoming.

\*\*\*

The first blizzard of the season greeted Matt as he crossed the Red River into Texas. He holed up in a cave he found up a coulee a few miles from the river. There was feed for his horse, water for both of them, and he was out of the wind enough to keep a fire burning. He considered going on down to Fort

Worth, but once the weather cleared he decided to go west towards the less populated panhandle. There was no reason except for wanting to stay away from people as much as possible. He stopped in towns long enough to get drunk, and for a few hours at least, leave behind the thoughts that continued to torment him.

Something else had begun worrying him. He was almost out of money, and his appetite for alcohol was growing. One night he stopped at a saloon and considered his options. He looked over at the poker tables. It was too risky, and he had never been good at cards anyway. He might have to find work somewhere. That would be risky also. He didn't know if anyone knew of him this far south, but he might have to take a chance and stay in one place for a while.

One night he stopped in a small town. Normally he did his drinking in the quieter places, but tonight he was drawn to what sounded like a noisy celebration. He entered the two story saloon through the half doors and looked around. There were women wooing the male patrons, prostitutes dressed in frilly and revealing clothing. The piano player was staying warm pounding out the rowdy requests from the crowd.

Matt got a bottle and sat down at a table. He used a glass, pouring into it from the bottle and drinking quickly. When it was a third gone, a girl with flaming red hair approached. One whiff of her perfume and a look at the curls cascading down onto her breasts, only partly hidden by a low cut dress, and she had Matt's attention.

"Buy me a drink?" she asked as she sat down next to him. Her skin was smooth and fair.

Matt poured more alcohol from the bottle. They shared the glass as she looked him over. He was dirty, which meant he hadn't been in town long. At least he was nice looking and seemed polite. She hadn't seen him around. Her thoughts weren't really about Matt. Her concern was whether he would pay for her services. He watched her, saying little, loneliness overwhelming him.

Twenty minutes later they were on their way upstairs. It

was dark so Matt followed the woman closely. She told him her name, but he paid no attention. She never asked his name. He would be gone in an hour or so.

After rolling around together on the bed in a drunken haze, Matt fell asleep. It was getting late and the noise downstairs had lessened. Instead of getting dressed and kicking him out, the girl decided to stay with the lonely cowboy while he slept off the alcohol.

Downstairs the gunman waited. He had followed Matt into the saloon and watched the pair climb the stairs. He noted the amount still left in the bottle Matt was carrying.

Big Nose preferred doing his killing away from town where there was less likely to be witnesses, but since Matt never drank except in town, he never had the chance. When sober, Matt remained vigilant as he rode. When he slept, he woke at every sound, however slight. His horse also became restless and alerted him to strange noises. Besides, the killer was becoming impatient to reach southern Arizona before really cold weather hit.

He made a decision. It was time to end it so he could collect the reward and be on his way. Exiting the bar, he led his horse around back where he left him tied to a tree near the back staircase. He came around the front again and waited to see if Matt came back downstairs. Besides being sober he had another advantage. He had visited the upper floor of this particular establishment and knew his way around.

After sitting in on a poker game for an hour, he went out back again. He climbed the staircase, opened the door, and listened before entering. It was dark inside. No one had bothered to refill and light the coal oil lamp at the top of the front staircase. Big Nose started quietly down the dark hallway. He knew which room the girl had taken Matt to, since he had also spent time with her. His heels made little sound on the wooden floor as he crept past the closed door. He paused and listened again. There was no sound coming from the room. That the girl could be hurt didn't occur to him. As far as he was concerned, she was just a whore. He turned back to the door, opened it and quickly fired four rounds at the bed.

Matt had been asleep next to the girl when he heard the slightest clump of a heel outside the door. He dove for the floor behind the bed as the gunmen threw open the door and fired. The girl screamed as Matt hit the floor. The man hesitated, not knowing what he had hit. If Matt were still alive he'd have to shoot again.

The pause was long enough for Matt to raise up high enough to peer over the bed. He fired twice into the darkness, unable to see if the man still stood in the doorway. His pistol, as well as his clothing had been stashed in this particular spot for a reason. He had not been as drunk and careless as he seemed.

The impact of the bullet slammed the gunman into the wall opposite the doorway with a loud crash, and his gun clattered to the floor as it was dropped. The scream coming from the bed turned to a gurgle as blood filled the girl's lungs. There was one last gasp for air, then silence. Scooping up his clothing and boots, Matt leaped over the bed and ran for the door. He stepped over the body, straining to see in the dark. Once through the doorway he hurried as fast as he could down the hallway, running one hand along the wall as he felt his way, hoping there was a back exit. A lantern was cautiously being carried up the front stairs.

"What's going on up here?" Matt heard a man behind him yell. "Get the sheriff!" By now Matt was halfway down the stairs. The dead gunman's horse was still tied to the tree. He quickly pulled his pants and boots on, listening and looking back up the stairs. The only thing he heard was his own heart pounding as he held his breath. He wanted to breathe after his frantic sprint, but first he needed to listen.

He untied the horse and mounted awkwardly while clutching the remainder of his clothing under one arm. He steered the horse around the back of the buildings, away from any light and towards the livery. Once at the barn, he jumped down, pulled the barn door open and led him inside. Quickly, he swung the door shut again. He dropped the rein and groped in the darkness, trying to find the stall Easy was in. After a minute he found his horse and then his gear. He threw the blanket onto Easy's back, quickly followed by the saddle, doing everything by feel. Out on the street three horses galloped by. Matt felt for his rifle, and finished dressing.

Two minutes later he led Easy out into the night, mounted him, and rode off in the opposite direction the other horses had gone. He looked around, wishing there was a moon. He tried to follow the road, but wasn't sure where Easy was going.

As the adrenaline wore off, Matt's mind went back to what had just happened. He was horrified. Not only had he killed another man, he had caused an innocent woman to be killed. He pushed the thoughts aside and focused once more on staying alive.

Matt cursed himself for giving into temptation, not only because of the trouble he caused once again, but now he was completely broke. Winter was coming on and he had nowhere to go and no money.

Since the men who had ridden after him went east, he continued west, leaving the Red River and cutting across the Texas Panhandle. He watched carefully all around, avoiding places where he could be trapped or snuck up on.

The three men who took off after him didn't get very far. The only reason they headed east was because the road was better in that direction. At the edge of town they slowed to a walk, unable to see in the darkness. They continued on for a while, but it was useless trying to find and follow tracks. By dawn they were back in town.

The sheriff knew of the hired gunman. When he was found dead, he figured the outlaw had it coming. The bartender had seen Matt go upstairs with the dead prostitute and it didn't seem likely that he had shot her. Although no one knew who Matt was, the lawman decided it was a personal matter. It wasn't pursued further since it seemed obvious Matt had killed in self-defense.

Another storm hit the plains as Matt rode on. He camped

where he found shelter, thankful for the bad weather. It would slow anyone searching for him. A week later he rode into the town of Amarillo. Being cautious as usual any time he was in a town, he stopped at the local livery. His horse had lost weight from long days of traveling in the cold, and his hooves needed attention once again.

"I need my horse grained and re-shod." The man in charge was an old cowboy who had fallen off of one too many horses. Now his activity was limited to caring for the horses of traveling men such as Matt. He sized up both the stranger in front of him and his horse.

"I'll have to see cash before I can take your horse." He'd been burned by too many cash-poor drifters, which was how the scruffy man in front of him appeared.

Matt had no money. "Do you have any work for me so I can pay off some feed?"

The man indicated a fence he had been repairing after a team had run a wagon through it. "You any good at fencing?" He knew many cowboys were too proud to get down off their horses for manual labor.

"I've done it."

"Well let's get at it then." After watering Easy and tying him under a tree, where he dozed, Matt and the livery operator spent the remainder of the afternoon nailing up rails. Matt was glad the posts were already planted since that was the hardest part. It felt good to be doing honest, constructive work once again.

Finally the two men stopped for a drink of water. Matt hadn't eaten in a day and a half, but he wasn't going to let on that he was hungry. He'd work until dark, and then figure out how he was going to feed himself. His horse was taken care of, which was most important.

"My name's Cliff Wilkins." The stable owner stuck out his hand for Matt to shake. He wasn't an old man, but his hair was mostly gray and there was the beginning of a crook in his back. He had judged a lot of men in his day, and reserved politeness until he had sized a man up. After seeing Matt go after fence building with competence and a determination to get the job done, he made up his mind. Deciding the stranger was a good man down on his luck, he would help him all he could.

Matt hesitated at the out-stretched hand. "Bill," he answered as he shook Cliff's hand.

Just then two riders arrived. They wanted to leave their horses over night. Matt helped to unsaddle the two geldings. Cliff grained them while Matt climbed the ladder into the hayloft to pitch hay down into the mangers below.

As the two men chatted with Cliff, they rolled cigarettes. Matt watched as the three of them moved away from the barn before a match was struck. They stood talking and smoking, then tossed the butts out into the street as they walked off. Cliff turned towards the barn and once his back was turned, Matt hurried over to where the end of one cigarette still burned. He picked it up and took a drag.

Cliff caught the movement out of the corner of his eye. He didn't want to embarrass Matt, but a man shouldn't have to resort to stooping in the street for a smoke. He walked over and said, "Here," tossing over a bag of tobacco. Matt rolled a cigarette and handed the pouch back. After rolling his own, Cliff walked over to a wagon, and leaning against it, struck a match on the metal rim of the wagon wheel. He lit both cigarettes.

"Thanks." The two men leaned back and smoked in silence.

"Come on over to the house for some supper. My wife always cooks enough for one more."

Matt considered declining. He wasn't used to being reduced to such neediness and his pride almost got the best of him. But his stomach spoke louder. He accepted Cliff's invitation, and that evening, for the first time in four months, he ate home cooking. The smell of potatoes and steaks frying brought back memories of the D Rocking D. When Cliff's wife put a wedge of apple pie in front of him he became so homesick he had to eat quickly and excuse himself as soon as possible.

He slept in the barn, up in the hayloft, wrapped in his blankets. The hay was soft and warm, and with a full belly, he slept the best he had in a long while. The next morning he woke early. He had satisfied his immediate needs, and was unsure what to do next.

Cliff showed up shortly after. Matt helped him feed the three horses in the barn, and then went out and tossed hay to the ones waiting out in the corral. He hauled water back to the barn from the creek flowing through the corral. The livery owner watched him and made a decision.

"You want to stay and work the winter I'll pay you five dollars a week. It's not much, but you can sleep in the barn and eat with me and the wife."

Matt considered. He didn't think anyone would look for him hanging around a livery barn. As long as he kept a low profile it should be fairly safe.

Cliff continued. "The truth is, it's getting hard to get around in the winter. The cold makes my bones ache. You sure would be helping me out." Matt agreed. It wasn't much money, but it would do until it warmed up next spring.

Cliff owned a few horses that he hired out and Easy was turned out into the corral with them. Only the horses staying the night, or ones that would be needed soon were kept in the barn. Cliff also had a buggy and a wagon that he rented out. They weren't needed much in the winter, but occasionally someone needed the team and wagon to haul supplies out to a ranch and paid for Matt's labor.

He showed up at the house for two meals a day. Cliff and his wife liked having the younger man around even if he didn't say much, and usually ate quickly and left. Occasionally he talked of some of the places he had been, but he never mentioned Montana, or that he'd been married. Cliff never questioned Matt, as he considered the man's past none of his business. That he worked hard and was honest was enough for him. Plus the missus couldn't complain about his manners at the table.

The livery owner knew Matt was drinking heavily. Word got around about how he spent his nights. Usually he bought a bottle from a nearby saloon and took it back to the barn. He rarely socialized and watched everyone around him. Matt began to look haggard despite the regular meals and sleeping hours. Cliff supposed it was from all the alcohol he was consuming.

The truth was that Matt wasn't sleeping much at night and hadn't since the night of the shootings in the upstairs of the saloon. He would pass out drunk, only to awaken a couple hours later, his heart pounding. He would listen for the sound, real or imaginary, that had startled him. It turned out to be nothing, a mouse scurrying across the floor, or a horse and rider going by. But Matt would lay awake, sometimes for hours, only to doze off again and have the same thing happen. He tossed and turned, trying to remember the girl he'd been with. What did she say her name was? He was tormented by her memory.

There was a restaurant down the street. The baker was an Italian named Alberto who arrived early in the morning to bake for the day's meals. Matt saw the light in the window as he stared out of the barn early one morning. He went to the back door and introduced himself. The cook let him into the kitchen, where he sat and drank coffee in the warm kitchen. After that he showed up almost daily. It was nice for the baker to have someone to talk to during the lonely time of his day. He spoke with a thick accent and it didn't matter that Matt didn't talk much. He had enough to say for the two of them. The cowboy didn't hesitate to help out, and hauled water and bags of flour, or brought in armloads of firewood when needed. Matt would stay until the sky began turning gray in the east, and then head back over to the barn to feed the horses. Sometimes he accepted a cookie or a biscuit as a parting gift.

One evening Matt went to a saloon after supper. He paused at the door, glancing around the room before entering. Walking to the bar he examined every face. He paid for a bottle of whiskey and turned around. A man was looking back at him. He was younger than Matt, and had a cocky air about him.

After he looked away, Matt walked past where he sat, through the swinging doors and out onto the sidewalk. He started back to the barn, listening behind him.

The back of his neck tingled. He heard footsteps, the clump of boot heels out of sync with his own. The spurs jingled too loudly. Matt didn't have to look at them to know that they were way too large, more for show than to cue a horse. But he wasn't thinking of that just then.

The man in the bar had recognized him. He had been in Wyoming and saw Matt out-draw the hired gunfighter. It had impressed him. He had recently visited the barn when no one was around to study the brand on Easy's left hip. It was still visible in spite of the horse's long winter coat.

The man considered himself quick with a pistol and wanted to make a name for himself. The last he heard there was a hundred dollar reward for killing or capturing Matt Daly. Killing was easier.

Matt stopped and turned around. He positioned himself so that he was in the shadows and the other man had a light from an upstairs window shining down on his face. "What do you want?"

"I'm just out for a stroll. Nice evening."

"Well then stroll on ahead of me." Matt's voice was low and sinister sounding. Wanting to avoid suspicion, the man continued down the sidewalk in front. He felt his own neck hairs stand on end. He quickly turned. Matt had vanished. The stranger headed back to the bar. Oh well, he thought. Maybe his chance would come tomorrow.

By the next day Matt was long gone. He rushed back to the barn, caught his horse, saddled him and left. Who were all these men gunning for him? If they were lawmen he could understand since he was wanted for killing Bully Buehler. But the men coming after him seemed to be outlaws.

Matt didn't know his own reputation. There were men who wanted to kill him just to say they had done it. Avoiding most people, and not hearing the gossip going around the frontier towns, he didn't realize how famous he was becoming in the outlaw world. There was no wanted poster out on him however. Everyone around Turkey Creek knew he'd been set up when the dead man appeared behind the barn at the D Rocking D.

One of Buehler's hands, who was really just a scared boy, decided to stick around and get the truth out. He told the marshal from Miles City that Buehler had become angry when the dead man refused to kill D Rocking D cattle. He was apparently grateful that John Daly had let him go with only a stern warning after he stole from the rancher. His boss picked up an axe and swung, striking the side of his face from behind, and killing him with one blow from the blunt edge.

The kid also admitted that it was self-defense when Matt shot the owner of the Spade ranch. He told the marshal that Buehler was hiding in the trees, waiting to kill any member of the Daly ranch who came that way, and had a rifle on Matt before the cowboy ever saw Buehler or his men. He didn't know much about the hired gunmen, except that there were two of them, that they rode out early the morning after the killings, and that they were angry at not getting paid. But their names and destinations were unknown. He gave a description of the pair and their horses.

\*\*\*

Matt headed north. Again, there was no reason except that he was tired of Texas. Every plant on the southern plains seemed to have thorns growing on it. The winter seemed as cold as the ones he'd spent further north. Since his leather chaps had holes worn in them, he no longer had much protection from the cold or the thorns.

The chaps weren't the only things worn thin. His boots had holes in the soles. His hat no longer shed water. Since he was wearing the only clothes he had, his shirt, vest, and pants were caked with grime. He couldn't remember the last time he'd worn socks.

His hair hung to his shoulders in a tangled mess. He

hadn't shaved since leaving Amarillo. His appearance was one of a desperate man. There was a hardness about him from no longer trusting anyone. He was not a man to sneak up on.

There was only one thing he knew of to calm his frayed nerves, and that was alcohol. At least when he was drunk he could sleep for a few hours before he jerked awake and spent the remainder of the night listening in the dark. He could also forget the three men he had killed, and the face of the dead prostitute.

Matt went back into Kansas. It was now spring, what used to be his favorite time of the year. He followed a different route, one further west than the road he had traveled on while riding south the previous fall. Some of the land was still unfenced. But instead of seeing the prairie greening up around him, he saw only destruction.

The blizzards of the winter of 1886-87 were severe. Hundreds of thousands, maybe a million head of cattle died across the western prairies, from Montana all the way down into Kansas. Entire herds were wiped out. The coulees and gulches were filled with their carcasses, where they froze to death, driven by the wind and snow.

Matt rode mile after mile, not believing what he saw. He had been in such a drunken stupor the entire winter that he missed what was going on.

But it didn't matter. None of it mattered anymore. He tried to hire on at different ranches, but there were no jobs to be had. There were a lot of men out of work. The rich investors packed up and left, leaving the smaller ranches to pick up the pieces of the ranching industry in the west.

Matt kept moving, living as he had been for almost a year now, doing what it took to survive. He rode into the town of Cheyenne, in Wyoming Territory. He and Easy walked past the Cheyenne Club just after it was shut down. Matt had been to Cheyenne once before. He and his father had been welcomed into the fancy club where wealthy, cattle speculators and ranchers told tall tales after counting their money. Now he wouldn't have been allowed inside given his present appearance. But the building was locked up tight, one more casualty of what came to be known as *The Big Die-Off.*

In desperation Matt hired on as a sheep herder for the summer. Self-respecting cowboys would never go near the wooly buggers. Some blamed the sheep for eating all the grass. And there was an untrue story that the sheep's hooves emitted a smell that fouled the earth so that cattle refused to graze where sheep had walked.

Matt just wanted some peace. No one would be looking for him to be tending sheep. He could spend the summer in the mountains, away from the alcohol that had dulled his brain, and away from the guns that so often seemed to have their barrel ends pointed in his direction.

The band of ewes, with their lambs, grazed high in the Snowy Mountains during the summer, above the death and destruction that changed ranching in the west. The sheep fared better than the longhorns in the cold, but it was the first time in years that the range was understocked.

Even in the quiet peacefulness of the mountain valleys, Matt was seldom at ease. He thought he heard men coming for him. He imagined their shapes hiding behind trees and rocks. Slight sounds spooked him. Both his pistol and rifle were always within reach. He thought he must be going crazy.

One afternoon he was ready to abandon the band of sheep and head for the nearest town to tame the demons in his head the only way he knew how. He saddled Easy and mounted, ready to ride away. Down below where he was camped, he saw a wagon, pulled by a team of horses, coming towards him. He got down off his horse and waited.

It was supplies from ranch headquarters. They arrived none too soon as Matt was getting low on food. But it ruined his plan. He stayed and helped move a bag of flour, and beans and cans of coffee from the buckboard into the sheep wagon.

The ranch foreman was a happy man named Ed. He was planning on spending the night and returning home the following day. It sounded good to hear another human voice. Matt threw out the cold coffee and started supper for the two of them.

Ed had brought potatoes and onions, a rare treat. Matt fried up a skillet of them, and baked biscuits in a dutch oven hung over the fire. There was no meat, but the meal was satisfying. As dusk settled in, Ed threw a couple more pieces of wood on the fire and then pulled out a bottle from underneath the wagon seat.

"Thought you might like some refreshment."

"Thanks." Matt took the bottle, pulled the cork out and took a swig. He passed the whiskey back. Ed swallowed a sip.

After a couple minutes, Ed started talking again. He told about all that happened around the ranch that summer. Gossip from town was more interesting. A couple of times he asked Matt his opinion, as the bottle went back and forth, but never got much of an answer.

Ed was on the ranch when the previous herder quit. The man, another out of work cowboy, had changed his mind about lowering himself to tending sheep, and left the band along the trail, halfway to the mountains. Needing a replacement quickly, Ed and Jake, the ranch owner, headed to town.

It was hard to tell by listening to the two of them who was the boss and who the foreman. They thought alike, and were best friends and partners. It didn't matter that one of them had ultimate control of the purse strings. Both were frugal, spending money only when they figured it would bring a good return.

Jake and Ed stopped their horses at one of the saloons, hoping to find a man who wasn't yet drunk this early in the day, and that they could convince to take the job. Since they lived in primarily cattle country, it might be hard. If they had been running a cattle outfit, there would have been a line of men all the way down the street seeking work.

Matt rode up just then. The sheep men quickly looked him over before the foreman asked him, "You ever tend sheep before?"

"Nope, and I'm not lookin' to."

"Fifty dollars a month and keep." The ranch owner knew

his only chance of replacing the deserter was to offer the next guy more than he could make on a cattle ranch. It was a lot of money, something Matt needed.

"Will you stake me to new clothes?"

The old ranch owner looked Matt up and down again. Glancing at his boots, he could see the cowboy in front of him needed more than clothing. This fellow was definitely down on his luck. "Okay, I'll give you a month's wages in advance, and I expect you out at the Circle J headquarters by this evening. We'll need to head out first thing tomorrow."

As Matt agreed, Jake nodded to Ed. The foreman took out a wallet and handed Matt fifty dollars cash. "I'm Jake Judson and this here's Ed Markus."

Matt took the money. It was more than he'd seen in quite a while. "Thank you. My name's Bill." The men shook hands before Matt headed once more for the saloon door.

"Let's see if we can't find you a pair of boots." Jake and Ed got on either side of him and steered him towards a ready-made clothing store down the street. Matt was going to get a drink first, but the two sheep men were smarter than that. Jake wasn't going to just hand over his hard earned money to a stranger. As usual, they both wanted to see that they got their money's worth.

At daylight the following morning Matt rode his horse out to find his woolly charges. Besides a new hat, boots and clothing, a fresh haircut and shave improved his appearance. He was also sober.

Jake and Ed were two of a kind. They were almost always happy and things usually turned out for them. They considered looking out for their fellow man a worthwhile investment.

When Jake decided to go into the sheep business, many predicted he'd have trouble in the predominately cattle area where he and Ed lived. But the two men were well liked by all who knew them and cowboys refused to kill their sheep when ordered to "Clean up the range," by their bosses.

Now they could have the last laugh, if they'd wanted to,

as sheep fared much better through the blizzards of the winter before. There was still a great demand for wool, and not being over-extended at the bank, Jake was able to cover his losses.

Both men were concerned about their new sheep herder's well being. They could see something was bothering him. So when he loaded up provisions for Matt, Ed took along a bottle. He wanted to see if he could get Matt to open up a little.

Ed's good nature was infectious and, sitting in front of the fire, Matt found himself smiling. It had been a long time. He told Ed how grateful he was for the job. And he spoke a little bit about the places he'd been. Once again, Montana and a family were never mentioned.

The bottle continued back and forth as it got later. Finally Ed brought up a subject that had been going around the local saloons. "Seems there's this gunfighter, been putting holes in a lot of men. Some say he's killed a dozen already. They say he's faster than anyone around. Daly, his name is. Came from up north."

Suddenly Matt's life started making sense. He had been turned into someone he wasn't. But he felt a chill. How many more men were out there waiting for him? He said goodnight and bedded down in his usual spot underneath the wagon. Ed sat gazing into the fire a while longer.

The next morning Matt found himself even more on edge. He was craving more alcohol, but the bottle was not to be seen. Ed knew better than to leave whiskey out with his sheep herders.

Having another person around had started out as a good thing, until Matt found out about his own reputation. He didn't if know Ed was oblivious to his real identity as he seemed, or if he just didn't care. But he couldn't stay in the mountains forever.

Even with his worries, the summer went along smoothly. Ed showed up in the wagon once a month with more food and to see how his sheep were faring. At the same time they moved Matt's camp. The only horse up there was Easy, and they needed a team to pull the heavy sheep wagon. So they unhitched the horses from the buckboard and backed them up to the sheep wagon. Ed drove it, while Matt encouraged the sheep from behind. The animals knew to follow the wagon. It was their source of safety, plus they were headed to fresh feed. Once at the new spot, the team was unhitched. Then Ed rode one horse, still hooked to his teammate, back to where the buckboard had been left, re-hitched the team and headed home.

It was getting cold when Matt brought the sheep back out of the mountains. After he had been snowed on twice, he decided to wait no longer for orders from headquarters. He left the wagon where it sat, since he had no way to move it. Someone would have to retrieve it later, maybe in the spring. It took two weeks to get the two thousand head safely home. He didn't push them, as they needed to keep weight on for the winter. Plus there was still an abundance of grass along the route they traveled. The empty range had grown plenty of feed that summer from all the moisture it received the winter before.

The foreman was happy to see the sheep safely home. Another band of sheep belonging to the Circle J was being harassed by some frustrated cowboys. The conflict never amounted to anything, but both Jake and Ed went over to defuse the situation. They had just returned home and were making plans to bring the rest of the sheep out of the mountains when Matt arrived. Jake was so happy to see them safely home that he gave Matt a fifty dollar bonus on top of the four months wages he was owed.

Matt rode off with a pocket full of cash. Ed watched him go and shook his head. He was concerned Matt would be broke in a week. He told him to come back if he wanted a job for the winter. But Matt was done with sheep. It just wasn't the same. His heart was in raising cattle, at least it had been.

# Chapter 11

Matt rode into the town of Laramie. In years past it would have been a lot livelier, with cowboys just off the range been drinking up their summer wages. Now there was a grimness. It was the same feeling that encompassed the entire western prairie.

Matt tied his horse to the hitch rail in front of the first saloon he found. As usual he checked brands on the other horses standing there and looked at the faces inside before entering the bar. After purchasing a bottle of the cheapest whiskey, Matt walked past a table where a couple of men sat. One of them looked at him and sniffed loudly.

"Smells like we got one of them prairie lice in here." He was too drunk to know if Matt really smelled like sheep or not. He just wanted to pick a fight. Matt set the bottle down on a table, picked the man up by neck and threw him to the floor. He glared at the shocked man lying at his feet, then at his companion. "Who are you insulting, you dirty sack of shit?" "Just be on your way!" The bartender yelled at Matt. He knew the two were trouble makers, but they were also regulars, something he was short of these days. Matt grabbed the bottle, shaking from the rage that had engulfed him. It scared him. Never had he felt out of control like that. He had wanted to kill the man with his bare hands.

He decided he was going to have to keep moving. But first he was going to have a bath and buy new clothes to get the stink of sheep, real or imaginary off of him. It was cold out, late fall. Matt wondered if he should risk getting a hotel room. There was one that offered baths. That would feel good. Maybe he would stay just a couple of days. Matt let his guard down as whiskey saturated his consciousness.

He had also been recognized. A cowboy who had once worked for Bully Buehler saw him on the street. He was sitting in on a poker game at another saloon that evening.

"Hey Red." He knew the man sitting across from wanted a reputation with a gun, so he decided to bait him. "There's a man in town you oughta' meet, name of Matt Daly."

Red knew the name. He practically drooled. "He's here now?" The other smiled. The trap had been set. He had no feelings towards Matt one way or another. He just wanted to cause trouble.

The man named Red called Matt out the next evening, after he knew Matt had spent the afternoon drinking. "Hey Daly!" Matt turned and faced a tall redheaded man showing off the new Colt Peacemaker that hung from his hip.

"I know I don't have a quarrel with you because I don't know you." Matt first wanted to talk his way out of a gunfight, but once again he felt his rage bubbling close to the surface.

The other man was way too cocky. He sneered. "I hear you think you're pretty fast with a gun. I also hear you're yellow."

There was no way Matt was going to back down. He seemed to become another man as his rage turned to cool anger. He would wait all night for the scum to draw first, and then he would blow the asshole's face off. His determination grew, taking over any other thoughts. His eyes narrowed as he stared the man down. Red faltered slightly by blinking. He had expected Matt to be scared of his large presence. It had always worked before.

A sheriff's deputy came running up the sidewalk. "What's the problem here? There's no shooting allowed." Neither man backed down. "You'll wind up in jail if the sheriff comes."

Matt turned and walked off as he saw relief enter the other man's eyes. It was time to move on. Within ten minutes, his horse was saddled and he was gone.

As he rode north, he was still shaking. The meanness seemed to come out of him from nowhere. He didn't know if he could have stopped himself from killing again if the deputy hadn't intervened. Matt kept looking over his shoulder as he rode into the November night. He hunched his shoulders against the cold wind. It was a week since he hit town, but he still had half his pay in his pocket.

It didn't take Matt long to realize he'd have to find somewhere to hole up. Surviving on the plains in the winter without shelter would be impossible. Still he continued north. The few riders he passed eyed him suspiciously. He was headed the wrong direction for this time of year. Matt just nodded and lowered his head after a quick glance. Once they were past, he listened to hear that they kept traveling, as they did the same.

A week later it started snowing. Matt hit the North Platte River. Easy, his horse, naturally took the easier route, downstream and with the wind. They headed southeast following the river, and stayed in the more protected bottomlands.

Matt wondered if Ogallala would be safe. He needed to find a town where he could stay the winter. His horse needed a rest. Fortunately he'd had an easy summer, with plenty of lush grass to eat, and he'd put on weight. But since bringing the sheep home, the two had covered a lot of country.

Easy had a thick winter coat, but there were places on his back being rubbed raw from the many miles under a saddle. And traveling in the cold melted the weight off of him. Matt was beginning to feel ribs when he slid his hand across the gelding's side.

The closer Matt got to town, the more nervous he became. In the past year and a half he had been around few people. It was becoming harder to be around anyone at all. He made the best barrier he knew how. Meanness oozed off of him. People were repelled from his vicinity. The violence in his eyes told everyone to stay away.

Inside he was worried. How was he going to survive the cold? The only thing he really wanted to do was get drunk, which was his first intention. He rode Easy to the local livery, where the grizzled man in charge looked Matt up and down.

"Twenty-five cents a day, a dime extra for grain." The man neither greeted him nor introduced himself.

Matt nodded. "See to it that he gets well taken care of." He stared at the other man until he looked away.

"How long you plan on bein' here?"

"I don't know yet." He gave the man a couple days board for his horse in advance, and walked down the street to a saloon he had spotted while riding in.

The next morning Matt woke up slowly. His head hurt and he couldn't remember where he was. As the light hit him, he realized what had disturbed him. It was the harsh creaking and banging of the heavy barn door as it was pulled open. He pulled his face up out of the dirt and looked around. The livery owner was staring at him. His alarm turned to irritation when Matt moved.

"You can't sleep here. The last guy almost burned the place down."

Matt got to his feet, still dazed. He tottered a second, wanting to sit down. "Where am I?"

"Scott's Bluff." He eyed Matt. The desperate look from the day before was gone. In its place was confusion.

"Where?"

"Nebraska."

Matt's mind began working again. He remembered walking into the bar the evening before and not much else.

155

"Where can I get some coffee?"

"Round the corner to the right."

Matt turned towards the open door, squinting at the light. Suddenly he felt cold. Where was his coat? He went over to where his saddle sat in the corner. He pulled his slicker off the back and put it on, not that the oiled canvas offered much insulation. Then he walked out the door without giving the other man another glance.

After sitting in the warm restaurant, drinking coffee and thawing out, Matt found the bar he had been drinking in the night before. He looked around before entering. The bartender was the only one there. He reached behind the bar and picked up Matt's coat when he saw him enter. He tossed it over.

"Thanks." The bartender turned away and Matt felt relieved. There must not have been any trouble. There hadn't been. Matt had made it through the better part of a bottle, and then left, leaving his coat.

"If you're who everyone says you are I wouldn't be causing any trouble here."

"And who is it they say I am?" Matt turned back towards the bar.

"That outlaw fellow. Daly"

"How many men do they say this outlaw killed?"

"Well, eight or ten, at least. They say he's a born killer."

"Well that man aint me, and I don't want trouble." Matt's voice was low, but clear. He walked out of the bar. It had to be a case of mistaken identity and somehow his name had become mixed up in it. He wondered who the outlaw was. He didn't realize there was only one man. The story was embellished upon each time it was told. Now Matt had a reputation to match the worst gunmen.

He walked back to the barn to check on his horse. Years of habit hadn't left him. The old man running the place was still there. The horses in his care were contentedly munching hay. After putting on his coat, he tied the slicker back onto his saddle. The thermometer was still dropping.

"I see you found your coat." The man tried to make

conversation, but Matt didn't feel like talking just then. He walked over to the stall where Easy stood eating and looked the horse over. He turned to the man, who was still watching him.

"See that he gets plenty to eat," he repeated. Matt was just another cowboy seeing to the well-being of his horse.

That afternoon, he got himself a room in a hotel for the night. He knew his talk about not wanting trouble had spread around town. Hopefully he would be left alone. Sitting in the hotel room, Matt began thinking. Maybe he could get on with a cattle outfit next spring. It would be nice to be riding the range looking after cattle again.

The next morning he again woke out of a haze with a throbbing headache. It took a moment to recognize his surroundings, and he was immediately alarmed. He had once again let his guard down. He rolled out of bed and pulled on his boots.

As he sat sipping coffee, he watched other people come and go, and thought about what to do next. He began asking about jobs. It wasn't unusual. There were a lot of hungry cowboys around. Many of them had already left for good. Cattle ranches had either gone broke, or weren't hiring.

Discouraged Matt walked towards the saloon. A man stepped out in front of him. "I hear you're pretty good with a gun." The man challenged him.

The first thought through Matt's mind was, where are these men coming from? He felt like a trapped animal with only one way out. His rage surfaced and his lip curled. "You want to just stand there, or do you want to find out?" He was surprised at the coolness of his words. Inside he wanted to tear the man's head off. His challenger wavered at the intensity in Matt's voice. The sound was low, but a snarl could be heard underneath.

The man mumbled, "I was just playin'," as he began backing up. Matt watched him go. The power he felt was exhilarating. He smiled slightly as the man turned and ran once he reached the corner of the building.

Then the sadness returned. And with it was despair, and a

feeling of desperation. There was only one cure for it, and that was temporary. Matt located a saloon he hadn't been in before. He looked around the room, checking each face before entering.

\*\*\*

It was the coldest winter Matt could remember. He slept where he found shelter. Most people didn't hesitate to help the cowboy. Even though he was a stranger, people out on the desolate prairie opened their doors and invited him in to eat. He slept in haystacks, and in barns. In exchange he helped out with any chores that needed doing. One night a store owner let him roll up in his blankets on the floor near the stove. Somehow he and his horse stayed alive, but he was afraid to stop moving.

He had no idea where he was going. It seemed he was on an endless road. The towns, with their sleazy saloons, blended together. He felt like he was going in circles, and that there was no stopping, and no way out. He began truly believing that he was going crazy.

One evening he was standing outside another saloon in another town. It was March, and there was just the hint of spring in the air. But Matt wasn't feeling the air. He was once again trying to figure out how to get drunk with no money. Walking inside, he saw a bottle on a table. The men sitting at the table were leaning towards an adjacent table listening to a story coming from an animated voice. It must be a good one, as most of the bar patrons listened with fascination. He glanced behind the bar. The bartender's attention was on him. Realizing he was being suspicious, he left.

Outside he went around back. There was a door part way open. He could see crates just inside the door. He began easing through. "Go on out the way you came." The bartender had a shotgun aimed in Matt's direction.

He shrank against the outside wall, and was about to give up, when his anger surfaced. He pulled his pistol from the holster and reappeared in the doorway. The other man had turned back towards the front room. He ducked as he heard the hammer on Matt's pistol pulled back.

"Just lay there." Matt's voice was a threatening whisper. The bartender didn't move as Matt pulled two bottles from the open crate. The man knew that losing a couple bottles of rotgut was cheaper and better for his health than if the bum shot the place up.

Matt hurried around front and untied his horse. After a quick look around while stuffing the bottles in his saddlebags, he mounted and rode off at a walk, so as not to be noticed. He felt himself slipping into depression when he thought about what he had done.

He rode for a few hours through the frosty night air until he came to a creek bottom that was sheltered from the breeze that had come up. But he had something other than the cold on his mind. He dismounted and wrapped the bridle reins around the closest tree. Then he pulled one of the stolen bottles from the saddlebag. Matt sat down underneath another tree, and leaning back against it, pulled the cork from the bottle.

When he woke the following morning, he was numb from the cold. He tried to focus his eyes to look around. He finally realized the white on the ground was from a heavy frost and not snow. He staggered to his feet as the bottle rolled to the side. He looked over at his horse. Easy stood saddled and unfed where he had been tied the night before. The horse waited patiently for his owner to notice him.

Why was he so cold? Matt shivered as he looked around for wood to start a fire. Finally he realized where the cold was coming from. He had pissed himself. His upper pant legs were frozen stiff against his skin. He cursed as he realized how low he had sunk. He walked over to Easy and looked into the horse's eyes. They were sunken into his head. He patted the thin neck, noticing the dull coat.

Matt felt thoroughly humiliated. He remembered stealing the whiskey while threatening a man. He struggled to think clearly, to find a way out of his present life. But all he saw was a dark engulfing fog that was too thick to see through. It took all his strength to fight it, and he was losing. Finally he leaned against his horse and cried. He sobbed into the horse's neck, unable to control it. Easy just stood there. Matt's shame grew, but he couldn't stop the outpouring of sadness that threatened to choke him.

At last he stopped, feeling exhausted. He looked around carefully before unsaddling his horse. They both drank deeply from the stream. Matt staked the horse out, using his rope to allow him to graze the new grass that was still less than an inch high. Luckily there was plenty of fallen wood for a fire. He would have to dry the clothes he was wearing as he had nothing else to put on.

As the days gradually became warmer and longer, the horse and rider traveled back into Wyoming. Off in the distance Matt could see the dust from a herd of cattle as a spring roundup was held. Easy lifted his head and smelled the air, looking towards the cloud of dust, his ears forward. He knew what was going on and wanted to go help, as that was a job he knew. But Matt kept his distance. He wanted nothing to remind him of happy times from his former life.

As he rode, he came up with a plan. It was the only way he could figure out to stop the nightmare that had become his life. Eventually he entered a small frontier town, looking around to see if it had any distinguishing features. It was nameless, at least to him. Since he planned on staying a while, his first stop was the livery. He wanted to make sure his horse was taken care of.

He had no money, so asked the stable owner if he would buy his saddle. The man looked it over and agreed. "I'll give you twenty dollars for it."

Matt took the cash the man handed him and gave some of it back. "Take good care of my horse." His tone had an urgency to it that the man found odd.

"All right." He didn't think Matt selling his saddle was strange. Since it was well worn, maybe the cowboy was buying a new one.

Now Matt would wait. He walked down the street.

Six days later, after spending most of his time in the

liveliest saloon in town, and with the saddle money almost gone, he was finally recognized. An ugly man who was missing part of one ear approached him.

"So you're Matt Daly. You don't seem so tough to me." The man grinned slightly, sizing him up.

Matt could feel his anger rising, but his voice was cool. "You want to find out?"

But the other man just chuckled. He wasn't about to piss off the desperado in front of him. "I got a friend who wants a piece of you real bad. I'll wait for him."

"Where's he at? I'll take you both on." But the ugly man wasn't stupid, and he wasn't a gunfighter. He knew Matt's reputation. He had also promised a buddy of his that if he ever came across the notorious Matt Daly, he'd let him know. The big, red-haired man wasn't about to back away from Matt again.

"Red'll be here in a couple of days." The man threw his head back and laughed, causing his partial ear to look even more hideous.

"I'll be here," Matt stated quietly. The waiting seemed an eternity. He didn't sleep. Whiskey seemed to have no effect on him. He knew what he had to do.

There was an unused cabin behind one of the saloons. Matt sat in it, alone in the dark. It would be light soon. The man who hunted him was on his way. He still couldn't figure out what he'd done that made Red want to take him on. But it didn't matter. His thoughts went back to his wife and family, back to happy times on the D Rocking D.

One afternoon, shortly after he and Lavina had been married, Matt and Jesse rode into the yard. There was no one around. Matt dismounted and glanced inside the cabin, but it was much too hot to be indoors. Outside, the sun glared down. Jesse checked the barn. Kirsten and Lavina weren't around.

Suddenly the two men heard shrieks. They turned to look. The two women were horseback, galloping up the creek. They screamed with delight as the cold water splashed them. The horses were having as much fun as their riders. Their nostrils flared as they ran.

Kirsten led the way, her blond braid streaming out behind her as she urged her horse on. Lavina was right behind her, holding on tight. She didn't have a lot of riding skill, but she wasn't hanging back as the water drenched her. Matt remembered her hair had come loose and followed her in shiny, brown waves. He and Jesse turned to look at one another, then back to their beautiful wives, their grins matching the delight on the women's faces. Right then they knew they were the luckiest men in the world.

The sky was turning gray. Matt looked out the small window. He could barely make out the corner of the saloon and the tree next to it. It wouldn't be long now, he thought.

The sun rose on a beautiful spring day. The air was cool, but the blue sky promised it would warm up in the afternoon. Matt still sat, not feeling the chill of the cabin. He leaned back so the sun wouldn't hit his face.

It wasn't until afternoon that he heard the words he was waiting for. "Hey Daly, there's someone here to see you." There was an ominous tone to the voice. Matt slowly got to his feet and put his hat on. He never checked his pistol, just buckled the holster on.

Opening the door, he stepped out. The man with half an ear stood waiting.

"Come meet my friend." He laughed.

Matt still felt nothing, not even the rage he usually felt when challenged. He followed Half Ear out to the street. The big, red-haired man was waiting. He felt more confident than the last time he had taunted Matt. It was rumored that he'd been practicing on others, and now thought he could easily take on the best.

The two of them faced off, slowly stepping out into the middle of the street. Bystanders backed off to the sides of buildings, out of the way of either man's gun.

Red wanted to show off. He was facing down a notorious gun slinger and he hoped the whole town was watching. Matt just wanted it all to be over.

"Show me what you got," he said just loud enough for the other man to hear. But Red just stood, savoring the moment. Matt knew he was still over confident. They always seemed to be. It hid the fear they were feeling inside. But none of this mattered. Matt was ready.

As time seemed to drag on, both men waited. But it had to end. Matt drew first, and then he hesitated and seemed to start twisting sideways in a defensive move. It happened so quickly that people watching questioned what they saw as Red quickly drew and fired. The bullet hit Matt in his left side. It spun him around so he landed face down. He lay in the middle of the street, not moving. Everyone watched as Red strutted off to the saloon with his buddy to crow about what he had done. There were plenty of witnesses to say it was self-defense, that Daly had drawn first. He was sure that if Matt weren't already dead, he soon would be. His practice had paid off..

# Book Two: Lavina

# Chapter 1

After Matt left the D Rocking D that ill-fated morning, Big John instructed the others to stay inside. The cowboys had all been sent out, scouting for grass on the parched range. They told to be careful, and none of them were to ride north. Matt was to hurry home were. It wasn't safe for him to be riding alone, but they were low on ammunition, and John wanted to know if there was any more information about Buehler's plans. He didn't think it would come down to a shootout, but there was no telling what Buehler would try. They all agreed it would happen soon though.

The hiring of the two killers had been done with complete secrecy. They arrived a couple days before, and slipped out to the Spade Ranch for instructions without being seen. It might have been considered overkill hiring two of them, but Buehler knew the men he was dealing with wouldn't go down easy. And he might need to do more thinning out if the neighbors disagreed when he took the Daly's range. Frequently one of the two men went outside and looked around. Lavina and Kirsten

167

went about their daily household chores silently. There was little talk and their faces were lined with worry. Jesse went down to the creek for water. The wood box was empty so John went out for an armload of wood.

Suddenly a shot rang out in the distance, followed closely by another from just outside the cabin. Then two more sounded only seconds apart from the ridge back behind the cabin.

"Jesse!" Kirsten grabbed the shotgun and stood waiting, waving Lavina away from the window. There was no other sound. She waited a long minute, then flung the door open and ran outside. Lavina glanced over at her two sleeping children, and followed.

A scream met her at the door. Kirsten had dropped to her knees next to the body of Big John. He was dead. A bullet had caught him in the middle of his forehead. He had gotten off one futile shot as the first gunshot rang out and Jesse went down.

Kirsten jumped up and ran towards the creek, screaming out Jesse's name. She found him lying in the creek, his blood staining the water red. "No, no, no." The word came out of her mouth over and over. Jesse was dead also, a slug had torn open his chest as he stood up after filling the water buckets. Kirsten pulled his body out of the water and collapsed next to it.

Lavina screamed also when she saw what had happened. Neither of their minds could begin to comprehend what their eyes were telling them. The two women looked at one another, almost pleading. They seemed to be asking one another to make the nightmare go away.

Finally they came to their senses. It was true. Big John and Jesse were dead. Lavina looked around. Where was Matt? She looked down the creek, wanting to see him come riding into the yard. Annie cried out, followed closely by Little John. She went inside and picked them both up. She held them both tightly, unable to release her grip as they cried louder.

The men watching from ridges, one to the back, and one to the side of the house, slid their rifles back into scabbards on their saddles. It had been easy so far. They had watched Matt ride off that morning, then waited until the other two men were both outside and picked them off. Now all that was left was to set a trap for the younger Daly.

They each mounted and headed down towards the creek from different directions. They rode cautiously, staying hidden in the trees as much as possible, but knowing where the other was at all times in case there was more shooting. A mile from the house they met at the road. Staying concealed, they waited.

It all went as planned, except Big Nose became impatient and fired before he had a sure shot, and Matt escaped. They knew it was useless to go after him, since he knew the country and they didn't. Buehler and a couple of his men were waiting up a draw to the west in case this happened. When they heard a single, faint gunshot from that direction they both swore, thinking their job was done, but that they had lost part of their fee since it had been finished by another.

They were to meet Buehler at a prearranged spot that evening. The two men had no desire to be seen by anyone. They wanted to get paid and be on their way. Arriving at the camping spot at dusk, they stopped just out of sight and waited. Horses were tied in the trees and men were moving around, but something didn't seem right. They had expected a fire and a hot meal. Cautiously they approached and let themselves be seen. Buehler wasn't there. Instead they found only his men waiting.

"Where's Buehler?"

"Daly killed him. What happened?" But the two weren't interested in swapping stories. Mean Monty Harris cursed. He was still angry at his partner's impatience. They both knew they wouldn't get paid at all if the man who hired them was dead.

"This isn't some kind of a setup, is it? Buehler going back on his word?" The man's eyes narrowed in his sinister looking face as he glared at the cowboy.

"Oh, he's dead. I've never seen anyone draw so fast. Bully had a rifle on him and Daly still shot first."

The two killers were unconvinced. They weren't impressed with the story either. It was probably an attempt to cover up bungling on the part of the cowboys. But Buehler's men told them where to find the body.

"You didn't even pack him out of there?" The question was to try and catch the man in a lie. He didn't care what happened to the ranch owner.

One of them shrugged. "We signed on as riders, not grave diggers. The only reason we showed up here was for fresh horses. We'll be riding out at first light."

"Well you never saw either of us. Say a word and you'll be lucky if anyone finds your rotting corpse."

One of the cowboys pulled out a bottle and took a swig. He passed the whiskey and said, "There's no moon, so we may as well get comfortable for the night."

***

Lavina and Kirsten spent a sleepless night, jumping at the slightest sound. They barricaded the door, and Kirsten sat with the shotgun across her lap. She wanted the killers to show their faces, and for her to be the last thing they saw before they died. They thought they heard Matt at least a dozen times, but when morning came, he still hadn't come home.

Finally a couple of cowboys returned home late that afternoon. When they saw what had happened, one of them caught a fresh horse and rode for town, while the other stayed at the ranch.

As word got around, neighbors began showing up at the D Rocking D. A couple of men went up on the hill to dig graves. Matt still didn't return and no one knew what had happened to him.

Curtis Hicks, the manager of the way station in Turkey Creek was also the town carpenter. He arrived a day later with coffins to put the dead men in for burial. Women sent food over with their husbands and the table and counter were soon crowded with covered dishes.

The end of the second day Kirsten finally thought about Eva, her milk cow. She realized the cow hadn't been up to be milked so she walked out to find her. Eva lay in the pasture. When Kirsten walked up she didn't move. The gentle cow was shot dead. Nobody knew if she had been caught in the crossfire or if it was intentional.

Lavina took care of her two small children as best she could, determined to stay strong in front of them. She held back tears as she thought of Jesse and Big John, and watched and waited for Matt to come home.

"Where is the sheriff?" The two dead men were buried and she wondered why the sheriff hadn't come out.

"Gone. The cur couldn't leave town fast enough when he heard what happened." Curtis spat on the ground after he answered her, unable to hide his contempt for the man.

"How will they catch the men who did this?"

Curtis looked down. "There's a good chance they won't."

"Well, we have to do something." Lavina felt desperate.

"We'll do all we can." He wanted to reassure the poor woman, but thought that, unless Matt returned to tell what happened, there was little chance the killers would pay for what they had done.

Theodore Lavold locked the door of his store, and he and Elizabeth caught the first train west when they got word of the shootings a couple days later. They left the two boys home, with Mrs. Larsen from next door to feed and keep an eye on them.

It was somewhat of a comfort to have her parents there for Lavina. They wanted her and the children to come back to Cedar Junction, but Lavina refused. She still had faith Matt was alive and would return home so she wasn't going anywhere. Plus, she had plenty of men around her since the hired hands weren't going anywhere either.

Joe, Samuel and the other cowboys still rode for the brand. They would be loyal to the end, even with the future of the ranch uncertain. The two women didn't seem capable of running the place. Lavina tried to make decisions, but was lost without Matt. But the men all stayed on, doing their jobs whether they got paid or not.

The following morning Joe and Samuel emerged from the bunkhouse. Both were feeling helpless and frustrated.

"What do we do?" Samuel asked Joe. When he came out west, he never imagined anything like this would happen.

"Whatever needs to be done," Joe answered. They decided to go out looking for sign, maybe tracks, something that would answer the question of what had happened to Matt, fearing the worst. The logical place to start was towards the east, where the trail wound through the rolling hills into a draw that was the easiest way through the rimrock.

From a distance, the two cowboys could see vultures circling overhead. They urged their horses into a lope, even though reluctant to see what was attracting the carrion eaters. What they found was the body of Bully Buehler.

Joe studied the tracks around the body. He could see that there had been horses tied to trees near the body. They had come down through the draw and left in the other direction. A single set of tracks went east. The horse had been going at a dead run.

"What do we do now? " Samuel asked again. He seemed to need Joe to give him some direction.

Joe shrugged, feeling relief not to have found Matt lying there, but a decision had to be made about what to do with the dead man. The body was already stinking in the summer heat, and animals had been chewing on it. There was no way to haul it out. Digging a hole in the rocky soil without tools was also out of the question. Even though neither of them had liked Bully Buehler, they didn't feel right about leaving him there. They finally covered the body with rocks before riding for home.

That evening, after discussing it with neighboring ranch owners, they decided it was time to call in a federal marshal to investigate the shootings. Frontier justice could only go so far, and no one wanted to risk an all out range war.

Since there was still no information about what had happened to Matt, Lavina remained hopeful that he was alive. Her parents left after a couple of weeks, failing to convince their daughter to come back to Cedar Junction with them. After a month went by despair began replacing hope.

The crew of a neighboring ranch headed out on their fall roundup. A D Rocking D cowboy volunteered to go repping and bring any wandering Daly cattle back home. The rest waited around to see what would happen. Lavina wondered the same thing. A single question circled in her mind, preventing her from thinking clearly. Where was Matt?

One day Kirsten said to her, "I can't stay here any longer. I want to go back home."

Lavina didn't blame her. Life on the D Rocking D had lost its appeal to her also. She woke each morning not wanting to face the day. The sadness would have overwhelmed her, except she had to carry on for her children. That night she made a decision.

The following morning at breakfast she spoke to Samuel. "Will you hitch the team to the wagon?"

While she waited, she walked across the foot bridge. Kirsten hadn't come over to eat. "You have to come over and watch the children." The words sounded harsh, but she needed to get Kirsten's attention. Once she returned to her home with her grieving friend, she took a matching skirt and jacket from her closet and changed into them. She secured her hair in a bun at the back of her head and used pins to fasten on a hat. She hadn't worn it since arriving at the D Rocking D four years before.

"I'll be back this evening," she told Kirsten as she hugged Little John and Annie goodbye. The other woman hadn't even asked where she was going. Samuel helped her up onto the wagon seat and they drove off towards a neighboring ranch.

Hubert Bailey lived about ten miles east of the D Rocking D. He was a wealthy Englishman who had crossed the Atlantic looking for adventure. The term remittance man was used for men like him who lived off allowances, as they frequently seemed to be waiting on money from relatives.

When he realized how much money could be made on the open range in America, Hubert convinced his father to invest in cattle. He then built a house on land that wasn't his and moved in. He bought a herd of twenty thousand head of cattle to stock the surrounding range and hired a manager so he could leave whenever he wanted.

It was pure chance he was home when Lavina and Samuel arrived. He had of course heard about what happened to Big John and Jesse. When rumors of hired gunmen circulated, he thought like most people, that Matt was dead also. And when his widow showed up at his house, he automatically assumed the poor woman was desperate to find another husband. In his opinion there was no better man than himself. He was rich, so what was not to like.

"Mrs. Daly! I'm so sorry to hear about your troubles." Bailey's dark hair was parted in the middle and slicked down. A full mustache and goatee hid a small mouth and weak chin. He pulled on a gold chain to reveal an expensive watch that he flashed in the sun for all to admire while he confirmed the time of day. Patent leather boots that had never seen mud covered his feet.

"Good afternoon, Mr. Bailey."

He helped her from the wagon and continued his condolences while admiring her figure. "Have you heard anything of your husband?" he asked, knowing she hadn't since he had heard the latest news in town the day before. Samuel drove the team underneath a large cottonwood to get out of the late summer sun.

"Won't you come in?"

"No thank you. We can talk out here."

"It's much more comfortable inside." Lavina glanced at the house. It was made of lumber that had been hauled seventy-five miles on wagons from the nearest mill. The two stories easily made it the most luxurious house around. She had been inside once, the Christmas before, when Bailey had thrown a party. It was filled with expensive furniture brought over from Europe. She hadn't been in that extravagant a home since coming out west. But she wasn't about to go inside with him. Once more she refused.

"Well, then what can I do for you?"

She got right to the point. Taking a deep breath, she said,

"I want to sell my cattle. Would you be interested in buying them?" She was determined to keep her composure.

"Wouldn't a partnership work out better for both of us?" Bailey was still scheming, and his smile had just the slightest leer to it.

Lavina understood the man's meaning. "I'm not interested in a partnership. I wish to get out of the cattle business." It was getting harder to go on with the conversation, knowing that she was giving up the life Matt and his father had worked so hard for.

"I'm uncertain of the laws in this country, but legally the cattle belong to your husband, I believe." Bailey wasn't done trying to persuade her. If she was trying to sell the cattle, she must think her husband dead. He made a mental note to check with his lawyer on the legalities of the situation.

Lavina was afraid that would be brought up. It was true Matt wasn't legally dead, but she was desperate.

"Please, I can't stay here." It was getting harder to hold back tears.

Bailey saw one opportunity slip by, but not another. After all, he was looking to expand. With both Bully Buehler and the Dalys gone, there was suddenly ample land to increase his holdings. If he couldn't have the dead man's wife, at least he could have his livelihood.

"Will you be selling the ranch headquarters as well?"

"No, not right now." The homesteaded acres were proved up, which meant the Dalys had lived there for at least five years and put a minimum of five hundred dollars into the piece of land. They owned the title free and clear.

But that insignificant acreage didn't matter to the Englishman. The thousands of acres of rangeland the Dalys ran their cattle on would be his to use. They agreed on prices for the six thousand or so head carrying the D Rocking D brand. Once the cattle were sorted and counted during the fall roundup, a final amount could be figured since cows, calves, steers and bulls all had different values. The brand would become his also, as well as the horses and the chuckwagon.

Lavina insisted on being paid in silver. There was too much worthless paper money floating around. Every new bank, and many of the larger ranches, used their own scrip. The temporary money was good only as long as the bank it was written against remained in business. Most of them didn't last.

She would be at her parent's in Cedar Junction. Bailey promised he would bring payment himself. They shook hands on the deal and Lavina walked over to where Samuel waited with the wagon, her face tense, as she fought back tears.

*** 

The fall roundup was the last one for the D Rocking D. Instead of the usual excitement, it was a somber event. Curly showed up to drive the chuckwagon and to cook one last time. Lavina appointed Joe as foreman. He had been with the Dalys the longest, and she trusted him to do a good job. He told her not to worry, that he and all the other cowboys still worked for her, and would as long as she needed them.

Kirsten agreed to stay until the roundup was over and Lavina had all the ranch affairs in order. Then they would leave together.

Once the cowboys had all returned in the late fall, Lavina reluctantly took the train to Miles City with Samuel. It meant burdening the grieving Kirsten with Little John and Annie once again, but receiving payment for the cattle would take some time.

Disembarking from the train, she and Samuel walked over to the Stockman's Bank. "Hello, I'm Mrs. Daly, and I wish to withdraw funds from my husband's account." Samuel sat on a bench and waited, at Lavina's request, while she conducted her business.

The teller had been hired only a few weeks before. Normally he would have still been working in the back, but the teller, who had been behind the counter when Matt came in two months before, was home with indigestion from eating a large pork supper the night before.

The young man facing Lavina wasn't sure how to handle her request. The names on the account were John and Matt Daly. Lavina explained that her husband and his father were both deceased, and that she needed to pay her help. He looked around. The manager was in a meeting and the senior teller was taking a late lunch. He was faced with what he considered a big decision. The large amount Mrs. Daly wanted would drain the account.

"How much do you need?" he asked again in a condescending tone. It was an obvious attempt to hide his inexperience. "Isn't there someone who could sign for you?" He glanced over at Samuel, believing women were incapable of handling financial matters.

Lavina looked him in the eye. "Are you questioning my intelligence or my honesty?"

Reluctantly he agreed to the withdrawal. He handed over the money after she signed the slip. That done, Lavina and Samuel took the train back to Compton. They had left the team and the wagon at the livery where a new proprietor had replaced Gust.

When they returned home late that night, the lantern was lit and hanging beside the door. Samuel jumped down to help Lavina climb down off the wagon. She went inside while Joe drove the team around to the barn.

Lavina carried the lantern inside. Kirsten was lying with the children on Big John's bunk. The three of them were asleep. Lavina envied the other woman. Kirsten had been able to curl up in a ball and shut out the world, while she had to carry on. Suddenly all she wanted was to go to the comfort of her parents.

The following morning the two women began packing. They could take only what would fit in the wagon. Furniture and other large items would have to stay behind to be dealt with later, if at all. The hired men were gone except for Samuel and Joe. Once they reached Compton the following day, Joe would drive the wagon to Cedar Junction, while Samuel rode the train with the two women and children.

There were only a few horses remaining, ones that had been their favorites. Among them was Lucky, Lavina's little black mare, and Jack, the gelding she had learned to ride on. She couldn't bear to sell them and there was only room behind her parent's store for the single team.

"What are you going to do with those horses?" Joe looked out at the few that remained as they grazed out in the pasture early the next morning. The wagon was loaded and it was time to leave. She had already given him his favorite mount from the remuda and had offered the same to Samuel, but the other man declined the offer.

"Wait here," she replied. They watched as Lavina walked across the pasture and opened the gate. The horses picked up their heads and trotted towards her. By the time they reached her, they were at a lope. As the horses ran by, their pounding hoof beats filled her ears. She watched the shiny coats and flowing manes and tails fly past. Cocked ears and flaring nostrils anticipated the meaning of the open gate. Soon they were at a gallop, racing across the prairie, at once wild and free.

Lavina watched them go, her heart feeling even heavier. Kirsten stood by the wagon beside Samuel, with tears in her eyes as she also watched the horses disappear in the distance. They climbed aboard the wagon with the children and Samuel took the lines, steering the wagon towards Compton. Joe rode ahead on horseback.

Samuel carried the two young children onto the train. He was continuing east with Kirsten after Lavina and her children reached Cedar junction. Being out of a job, he had decided to visit his family back in Boston.

"Won't you come and have something to eat? The train will be here for a couple of hours and my parents want to see you." Lavina pleaded with her friend. She could see her mother and father on the platform outside the train, waiting for her.

"No, you go on. I just want to wait here."

"I'll stay here too." Samuel didn't want to leave Kirsten's side.

As Annie began fussing, Lavina hugged her friend goodbye. She thanked Samuel for all his help and picked up her children. The tears finally rolled down her cheeks as she stepped off the train and into the arms of her family.

# Chapter 2

The Cedar Junction Mercantile had changed since Lavina had last been there. Theodore Lavold had added a second story to the building, and the upstairs was where he and his family now lived. There was an inner staircase at the back of the store, and outside stairs ran up one side. It was a fine looking building, Lavina decided as she saw the addition for the first time. The white paint looked fresh and the green trim contrasted nicely with the blue trim on Mother's Cafe next door. The sign had also been redone. Its gold lettering shone in the sunlight.

They didn't pause long outside, as the autumn air was chilly and the children were tired and hungry. Theodore carried both his grandchildren up the stairs and into the living quarters. It seemed spacious. There were two bedrooms, a larger kitchen, and a separate living area heated by the big stove downstairs. Business was good, and Elizabeth had added some of the finer things she had missed from their old home. There were colorful rugs on the floor, and more furniture. A bookcase lined one wall. Both boys were now going to school back east. They were staying with an aunt and uncle through the winter. Next summer they would return home.

Lavina settled in and tried to bring some kind of normalcy back to her life. Besides caring for her children, she once again worked in the store. With his sons gone, Theodore welcomed the extra help. She avoided people as much as possible, as she couldn't stand to see the pity in their eyes when they looked at her.

Cool fall weather arrived late and there was still no precipitation to speak of. But at last the haze in the air cleared off as fires finally burned out.

Theodore was concerned. Ranchers he talked to sounded worried. After the summer-long drought, little grass was left on the prairie. Even so, herds of cattle kept arriving from the south. The frenzy continued due to the amount of money being made and it seemed everyone wanted in on the opportunity. The herds just arriving were in poor condition from traveling all summer. There was little chance they would become acclimated to the northern range this late in the year, even if they had plenty to eat.

The tension was also building as established ranchers fought to keep newcomers off their range, so the cattle already there would have feed for the winter. Some cattlemen leased Indian land. Others found ungrazed land way up in Canada and were hurriedly pushing herds further north before winter.

In late November it began snowing. The moisture was welcome. But the snow kept piling up, and soon the prairie was covered with a thick layer. Then the wind began blowing. Cattle had begun to get hungry when their feed source became unattainable. It didn't take long before they began dying. First it was the newly arrived ones, longhorns from down south and bulls brought from warmer climates to improve existing stock.

In January, a Chinook wind blew from the southwest and the snow began melting. Ranchers breathed a sigh of relief. But it didn't last. When there was still a foot of slush on the ground, the wind turned again. As it howled out of the north, the temperature began dropping. There were reports of fifty to sixty below in places. The slush froze, becoming impenetrable. Behind it came more snow. The range from Canada, down through Montana and Wyoming, and all the way into northern Texas was covered by ice and snow the remainder of the winter. It was the same further east, through Dakota Territory, Nebraska and Kansas.

Cattle began dying by the thousands. The scene Matt witnessed in Texas was the same all over the western prairie. The northern-most range took the worst of it. Unprepared homesteader families froze to death in hastily built shacks. It was a faster way of dying than starving to death on the frozen land.

The frontier towns weren't immune to the effects of the blizzards. Hungry cattle wandered in, eating anything they could get their mouths around. Fences were pushed down and hay reserved for horses was devoured. Siding on houses, and even tarpaper was eaten. Bark was chewed off trees. It was a devastation no one could have imagined.

The Lavolds huddled around the wood stove and waited for warm weather. Lavina was in a fog as Matt had been, and not fully aware of what was going on around her until one day she saw cattle going after hay reserved for the team. She called her father and the two of them went out in the driving wind and snow to nail up more rails, reinforcing the fence before the cattle broke through. They fought the starving creatures until dark. Finally they retreated inside, freezing and exhausted. They could only wait until morning to see if they were successful.

They weren't. The next day the hay was gone, with the remnants of the fence trampled into the snow. The bewildered horses stayed, but there was nothing to feed them. The cattle were going at the sides of the store.

Theodore thought hard. There were sacks of flour and other grain inside, in the back of the store. He wondered if the cattle could smell it. Instead of selling the whole oats, they would have to feed it to the horses. But first they needed to save it, and the building. He thought of the strongest smelling liquid he had, coal oil. If they coated the building with it, maybe the desperate animals wouldn't smell the food.

He and Lavina bundled up and went back out into the cold. They dipped rags in the strong smelling fuel and rubbed it onto the building as high as they could reach. It worked. After tasting the foul-smelling wood, the cattle floundered off through the deep snow, to finally collapse and die.

Lavina climbed the stairs with her father that evening after running the cattle off, feeling emotionally as well as physically spent. She had tried not to look into their eyes, but she couldn't avoid seeing the scared, doomed looks. She hugged her children tight. At least she could protect them.

When the sun finally melted the snow and ice that spring, the water ran off in huge torrents. River banks and coulees overflowed, but not only because of all the water. They were choked with cattle that had starved and frozen to death during the winter.

Cowboys riding out in the spring found mainly rotting carcasses. Losses from various ranches went from sixty to over ninety percent. The cattle business in the west was devastated. Investors packed up and moved on to other, lucrative, business opportunities. At least the ones that weren't bankrupt. Many banks went under as well.

The smell of rotting meat permeated the air. The dead cattle were drug out onto the prairie, away from towns and homes, but the scent still came in on the wind, making even the strongest stomach feel nauseous.

***

Lavina woke up one morning feeling feverish and weak. She didn't know what was wrong with her. It must be from smelling the death all around her she decided. Annie and Little John seemed fine. They were now one and two years old, typical toddlers exploring and getting into everything they could reach.

When they went down for naps that afternoon, Lavina

told her mother she needed to lie down and rest a while also. It was four days before she woke again.

"Thank God!" Elizabeth started crying when her daughter opened her eyes, her fever finally broken.

Lavina felt weak and confused. "What happened?" were the only words she could manage.

Her father came into the bedroom, his face as sad as she had ever seen it. She tried to sit up, but was unable to until her father helped her. She looked around for the children. "Where are Annie and Little John?"

"They aren't here." Her father answered as her mother was too choked up to speak. They had no idea how to explain to their daughter that while she was sick, the fever had taken the lives of her two children. And that they thought they had lost her also. But she recovered, at least as much as she was able to.

Little John and Annie were buried in the cemetery amongst the dozen other people who had died in the epidemic, a fever that was blamed on all the rotting cattle. Lavina didn't think she would ever want to open her eyes to another morning. She could truly see nothing to live for.

The Lavold boys returned home for the summer. Lavina tried to make them take their bedroom back, but they refused. So she spent most of the day sitting in there alone, vaguely hearing the pleas of her mother begging her to eat.

One morning Theodore went into the bedroom where his daughter sat day after day. He believed that a good day's work was the solution to most of life's problems. "Would you like to help me in the store this morning?" He had enough help with his teenage sons home. Lavina looked at him as if not understanding. Then a little light came on in her eyes. The will to live struggled to the surface of her being. She couldn't understand why it was there, or even if she wanted it. But she nodded at her father, unable to deny it.

Theodore smiled. He had seen the spark and knew his daughter would live. She followed him out into the kitchen and poured herself a cup of coffee. Her mother still frowned on what she considered a nasty habit for women, but was relieved her daughter had actually gotten up and done something for herself.

Once again Lavina found herself following the same routine of helping her mother and father. But she never smiled or showed any enthusiasm. She began to believe that this was to be her life, and that there was nothing else to hope for.

Business had slowed in the store since the failure of so many of the ranches, but by now the town of Cedar Junction was big enough that the townspeople provided enough of the store's income to keep it going. The Lavold's were able to weather the economic decline in the area when neighboring businesses closed their doors.

## Chapter 3

A s the red-haired gunman and his partner retreated to the nearest saloon, two boys walked out into the street where Matt lay. They stared at the body with a morbid fascination. Coming closer, they jumped back when they heard a groan.

"He aint dead," one of them said. They continued staring. "Should we get help?" They looked around, but by now the street was deserted. No one wanted to be responsible for cleaning up after a gunfight.

The father of the boys saw them out in the street. "Get away from there!" He stood in a doorway and yelled.

"He's still alive."

The man walked over and rolled Matt over onto his back. There was a bloodstain where he had been lying and his face was deathly pale.

"I guess we better find the doctor." He walked over to the saloon and looked inside. The doctor was slouched in a chair, drunk as usual. The sheriff sat next to him in the same condition. Then more people had joined the two boys to gawk at the fallen man. "What do we do?" The father had come back over.

"There's the Indian."

"How do we get him out there?" Even though everyone thought Matt would be dead shortly, and most believed it was probably what he deserved, others didn't want the guilt of leaving him in the street to die.

The Indian lived ten or twelve miles from town. He had helped many people in the area heal from various injuries and illnesses. In fact he had a much better record than the doctor.

An eager young man spoke up. "I'll take him." He had a reason for wanting to travel in that direction. There was a girl he was sweet on who lived out that way. Here was an unexpected excuse to visit her.

He drove a wagon, borrowed from a store owner, into the street. Three men picked Matt up and heaved him into the back of it. He landed on the hard boards with a thud. There was another agonizing groan. No one could tell if he was aware of what was happening. Someone tossed his hat up next to him while another climbed into the back and stuck a folded feed sack under his head.

The young man drove off. He stopped at a homestead a few miles from town to invite his girl for a drive "Where are you going?" she asked.

"I have to deliver something," he replied. She looked in the back of the wagon.

"Who is he?"

"Some poor fella found himself on the wrong end of a gun."

Another groan was heard. The girl cringed. She was reluctant to ride with him, but the young man convinced her that the bloody stranger posed no threat.

They continued down the road. Near a stream, they turned into the yard of a small shack amongst the cottonwoods. "Hey, Injun Joe! I got somethin' for you."

An old Sioux came to the door. Two black braids hung down the front of his shirt. "Come here." The young suitor handed the lines to the girl before climbing down off the wagon. He looked at Matt, who had been quiet for a while, to see if he were still breathing. "Come help me," he demanded.

The Indian came over and peered into the back of the wagon. "No. I cannot take this man."

"Well that's too bad, because I aint hauling his carcass back to town. Get hold of his leg." They pulled Matt out of the wagon and carried him into the shack, laying him on a blanket on the dirt floor.

As the wagon rolled back down the road, the Indian examined Matt's wound. It had stopped bleeding, which was a good sign, but he had lost a lot of blood. The bullet had gone all the way through. The severity of the wound depended on the damage to his insides.

The Indian didn't know if Matt would live, but he had to try and save him. Although he despised what the white man had done to his people, he was a healer and considered all life sacred. He had to do his best to save the *wasicun* whether he liked him or not.

He went outside and collected two large fistfuls of the lush, new grass growing along the creek. Sitting down next to Matt, he put a small amount of the grass in his mouth, and began chewing. Once the juice was extracted from the coarse fiber, he spit the entire mouthful into the wound. He sat there for over an hour, repeating the process until both handfuls of grass were chewed. He packed the holes in Matt's side, knowing that the antiseptic quality of the chlorophyll-rich juice was the best way he had to prevent infection and encourage healing.

It was getting late. He covered the wound with his only other shirt. Then he ate a cold supper and went to bed, sleeping on the floor covered with his only other blanket.

The following day Matt opened his eyes. He tried to look around, but intense pain prevented him from moving. He was awake only long enough to drink some water while eyes that seemed both stern and gentle studied his face. The Indian repeated the process with the green grass.

After a couple of days Matt was awake for part of each day, and eating small amounts of soup his host made. The boiled bones were all that was left of a quarter of beef that had been hanging from a tree outside.

He still couldn't move, and he could barely open his mouth. There was no way he could chew. A large bruise covered one side of his jaw. The brightly-colored swelling distorted his face, pushing his right eye into a squint. The Indian couldn't tell if the jaw bone was broken or not. He made a poultice using crushed herbs and hot water. After applying the cooled mixture, he wrapped the side of Matt's cheek with a rag, tying it on the opposite side to hold it in place.

The pressure made his face throb with pain. But that wasn't all bad, Matt decided in his semi-conscious state. It took some of his attention away from the pain in his side.

What neither of them knew was that the force of the bullet had spun Matt all the way around and he landed on the right side of his face. When he fell, his face hit a rock. The slight sideways turn caused the bullet to glance off the outside of his lowest rib, taking a piece of the bone with it before it exited.

He barely remembered anything, except standing in the street wanting to die and then fierce pain as the bullet struck him. He felt ashamed.

After a few days of the Indian's care, he was finally able to look him in the eye and speak. "My name is Matt Daly. " It was the first time he had used his real name in almost two years.

"I am Gray Eagle." The Indian walked outside. He had no interest in getting to know the white man. His only concern was in how long before he would be well enough to leave.

Laying there with nothing to do, Matt watched as Gray Eagle went about his day. The Indian rose before the sun each morning to walk bare foot outside and pray aloud to his beloved earth. Since he spoke in his native language, all Matt heard were sounds. He didn't even know that Gray Eagle was praying, except he began recognizing the same phrases spoken each morning.

The Indian's possessions were few, and Matt realized that he was living in the worst poverty. Meals were simple and spare, prepared mainly from food passed out by the government. Cooking was done over a fire outside.

Some days Gray Eagle disappeared for long periods. When he returned, he carried bundles of herbs he had collected from the hillsides. He hung them from the ceiling to dry. His home had an aroma that reminded Matt of riding out on the prairie after a rain. Frequently Gray Eagle boiled one or another of the herbs and had Matt drink the tea when it cooled.

Matt felt a peace he hadn't known for a long time, living in silence with the old Indian. But as his side healed, he began feeling restless. He tried to get up off the blanket, and found himself too weak. Plus moving made him gasp in pain.

Gray Eagle watched his progress closely. He decided when it was time for Matt to get to his feet. It took some maneuvering, but finally he was successful in helping the injured cowboy stand up and walk outside.

Matt took as deep a breath of the fresh air as he could and looked around. The colors seemed brighter than he remembered. He had missed the sounds of birds and of water flowing over rocks. Suddenly he noticed his horse. Easy was picketed next to Gray Eagle's horse near the creek. He was happy to see the faithful animal.

"My horse." He looked at Gray Eagle. The Indian nodded.

The sheriff had brought Easy out to Gray Eagle's after he sobered up and was told that Matt was still alive. Matt remembered selling his saddle to pay for feed, thinking he would never need it again. The rest of his possessions were gone. His rifle, his coat and slicker, and his saddlebags had all disappeared. The thief wasn't so bold as to take a branded horse that he had no bill of sale for. Somehow his pistol had made it back into his holster, probably because, with the crowd out on the street, no one had been bold enough to swipe it either.

Easy lifted his head, still chewing a mouthful of grass,

and watched Matt walk over. He sniffed his owner as if reassuring himself. Matt looked the horse over. The gelding had started to flesh out on the green grass, but his feet were still chipped and worn from hard riding without shoes. Matt stroked his neck and then slowly walked back inside to lie down again.

***

After a month, Gray Eagle could stand it no longer. The white man seemed to have no desire to leave. He had become an even more unwanted house guest.

"You must go home," Gray Eagle finally told him one morning.

Home? Matt didn't even know what that meant any more. But he understood that the Indian could barely subsist on the meager rations he received, much less feed an invalid who contributed nothing. But where could he go? He had no idea if he were still being hunted, but there could still be wanted posters depicting his likeness scattered across the region. Matt no longer wanted to die, but he still had no plan for his life.

The next morning Gray Eagle was adamant. "You must go now. Go home."

Matt's gunshot wound was mostly healed, but the chipped rib was tender, and his strength hadn't fully returned. His jaw still had a slight discoloration and also remained tender. Nevertheless he put his wool vest on over his shirt. Both garments had been washed, but there was a brown stain on the shirt. There were also the holes through them. After he pulled on his boots, he painfully got to his feet and strapped on his gun belt. He looked around at the dismal shack that had been the closest thing to a home he'd had in a long time.

He wished there was something he could give Gray Eagle for saving his life, but he had no money. He still had his pistol, which felt uncomfortably heavy hanging from his side. If he could have, he would have given it to his destitute host, but leaving the shack nestled in the cottonwoods scared him. He might need the protection it provided.

Matt went out and bridled his horse, then slipped the rope off from around the gelding's neck. Gray Eagle watched from the door.

"Thank you for helping me. I live near the town of Turkey Creek, up north in Montana Territory. If you ever need anything, come find me."

Matt had made up his mind. He would take his chances and go back to the ranch to see if there was anything left for him there.

He led his horse over to a tree stump and from there eased onto his bare back as carefully as he could. The pain in his side tore into him, but he forced himself to sit up. He turned and lifted one hand in farewell. The Indian nodded, and then turned back inside. Matt rode off, once more feeling completely alone.

# Chapter 4

Elizabeth Lavold glanced over at her daughter. Lavina stood over a basin peeling potatoes for the mid-day meal. She watched as Lavina put the knife down and opened the firebox to the side of the oven to check the fire. An ember fell out and Lavina absently ground it into the floor. The aroma of roasting meat filled the kitchen.

"Why don't you help your father this afternoon? I noticed the windows could use a good scrub."

Lavina nodded and kept peeling. She was indifferent as to how she spent her days. As long as she kept busy she could minimize the amount of time she spent thinking about her children. It had only been three months since their deaths and she continued to grieve for them. Inside she felt ripped apart, demolished. She tried to suppress the feelings, but lived in dread that they would overwhelm her.

Once dinner was eaten and the dishes washed, Lavina took a bucket and poured water and vinegar into it. Picking up a handful of rags, she walked down the stairs to wash the windows at the front of the store. She started inside, smearing the glass with the liquid and then carefully rubbing each pane dry.

Outside she barely looked around. The fresh air used to invigorate her, but now she didn't even notice it. The people on the street were practically invisible to her as she worked. Once she was done, she emptied the bucket into the street and dropped the rags into it.

She was turning the door knob to go back inside when, out of the corner of her eye, something caught her attention. She turned to look. It was a man riding a dingy bay horse coming towards her. She watched, wondering why something about the pair looked familiar.

The man was slouched over. He looked liked a derelict, ragged and dirty. What was it about him? The man looked up, not seeming to see anything. He had a scraggly beard and as they came closer she could see for certain that his horse had no saddle.

Suddenly he saw her. The horse kept walking until he was in front of the store, and stopped at the hitch rail as if on cue. But his rider hadn't signaled him in any way. The man was still staring at Lavina.

She started down the steps. It couldn't be. Could it be Matt? She wasn't aware of her feet moving. Arriving at the side of the horse, she looked up into the man's eyes. He still hadn't looked away.

"Lavina?" His chest hit the horse's neck as he fell forward. Then he began sliding off.

Lavina realized he was unconscious and tried to grab him. With the help of the horse, who stood rock still, she was able to prevent Matt from falling, but she couldn't hold him for long.

"Help me!" She screamed out. Two men had been watching and were already grabbing Matt on either side. "Bring him in here." They carried the limp body up the steps and into the store.

Lavina burst into the store ahead of them. "It's Matt!"

Theodore was behind the counter. He hurried over for a closer look. The man didn't resemble the son-in-law he remembered, and he didn't believe it was him. But he said, "Bring him over here," and quickly cleared a table to lay the prostrate man on.

"I'll fetch the doctor," one of the men said after staring at the prone man for a moment. He hurried out the door. Lavina took Matt's hand. He didn't move. She stared at his face, even more sure that it was her husband.

The doctor had Lavina wait on the other side of the store with her parents while he examined his patient. Half an hour later he made his report. "The poor fellow seems to simply be exhausted and badly dehydrated. I doubt he's eaten in some time." He didn't mention the newly healed gunshot wound. Since there was no infection, he didn't consider it relevant. "Get some water in him when he wakes up, and some broth. I think he'll be fine."

Lavina went back to Matt's side, still not believing her eyes. She studied his face some more. It was so thin, and his complexion had the pallor of an invalid. The beard hid his mouth and chin. But she knew it was him. The brief look into her eyes as he said her name had confirmed it.

"Do you think we can get him upstairs?" She called out to her father as the doctor was leaving.

Theodore walked over to the table where Matt lay. Elizabeth stood next to him. She looked up at her husband. They still weren't sure it really was Matt. He looked so different. But wordlessly they decided to trust that Lavina would know her husband.

Glancing up the stairs, Theodore said, "I'll need help."

He went next door, where the word was already out. Matt Daly was back. Some wondered if he was wanted by the law. Most knew he wasn't.

"Hey, Earl, come help me, will you," Lavold called to a big, burly man sitting on a bench sipping coffee. Together the two of them grunted their way up the stairs to the living quarters with the now semi-conscious man between them. He wasn't nearly as heavy as a man of his height should be. They both had the same thought.

Once Matt was resting upstairs, Lavina told her parents she would be right back. She hurried down the stairs and outside. Matt's horse, Easy, stood patiently in front of the store where he had stopped. She walked up to him and petted him, noticing his thin sides and sunken eyes. But he seemed to have a satisfied look in his eye as he met her gaze. She led the footsore horse around to the back of the store. He drank deeply from the water tank, and then she led him inside the small barn. She fed him oats and hay, lots of hay.

He eagerly pushed his nose into the feed. Lavina stood watching him eat as tears slid down her cheeks. She couldn't imagine what Matt must have gone through for his horse to be in such poor condition.

*** 

Elizabeth Lavold was a caretaker. She never minded, and found satisfaction in helping others. After the doctor left, she immediately went next door with a jar, and asked Sophie Larsen if she had any broth ready. "Of course," the restaurant owner replied. She took the jar and started back to the kitchen, motioning Elizabeth to follow. Once out of sight of curious eyes, she asked about Matt. "Is it really him? How is he?"

"Apparently it is. The poor man is starved down to nothing, but Dr. Wilson thinks he'll be fine. I hardly recognize him." The two women shook their heads in sympathy.

"All I have is beef broth." She planned on using it to make soup the following day. "Chicken would be better."

Elizabeth nodded her head in agreement, but this was all that was immediately available. The two women talked for a few minutes, speculating on where Matt could have been. Then Elizabeth hurried back through the restaurant and outside. After dropping off the jar filled with beef broth, she went back out. Purposely, she walked down the street to the butcher shop and returned home with a freshly killed chicken. Back in her kitchen she began the process of making broth.

"Matt. Matt." Lavina began speaking to him as soon as his eyelids fluttered a couple hours later. He blinked and focused his eyes, still unconvinced he wasn't dreaming. His wife was sitting beside him, but he had no idea where he was.

"I, I thought you were dead." He reached out to touch her to be absolutely certain she was real. He was afraid to ask about his father.

Lavina was surprised, but she said, "Drink some of this broth." Matt sipped a few spoonfuls of the warm liquid and then he slept some more.

Elizabeth came into the bedroom to check on the two of them. Lavina looked at her mother. "He thought I was dead." They didn't know what to think, and would have to wait until he was stronger to hear his story.

Elizabeth couldn't help but look at his grimy clothes. He smelled like his horse and worse. Her nose wrinkled involuntarily. She couldn't imagine how he came to be in this condition. She only said, "I put some water on. Do you want me to find something for him to wear?"

The following morning Matt was awake and looking around when Lavina came into the room. "Where are we?" He had never seen the upstairs addition to the store. Lavina explained as he sipped the chicken broth. He vaguely remembered being carried up the stairs.

"Can't I have some food?" He had no idea when he had eaten last. It felt like there was a hole gnawed in his stomach.

What he remembered most about the trip home was that it seemed like endless wandering. He heard Gray Eagle saying, "Home, home," to him over and over as he rode. Once he fell off his horse and the pain he felt when he hit the ground took his breath away. He almost blacked out from lack of air. But the pain also shocked him awake. He got his bearings and continued north.

The only reason he ended up in Cedar Junction was because that was where the road he was traveling north on met the Yellowstone River. From there he intended to follow the river west, towards Compton. It never occurred to him, in his semi-delirious condition, that this was where his children would be. If he hadn't seen Lavina standing out in front of the store, he might have continued on by the Cedar Junction Mercantile without stopping.

Lavina smiled at him. She went out and brought back some soup with a few chunks of potatoes and chicken floating in it. He let her feed him. He was capable, but he wanted to focus on her face as she lifted spoonfuls of food to his mouth.

He didn't know what to say to her. He wanted to tell her he was sorry, but the words stuck. Maybe when he felt better.

"Where's Easy?"

"He's out back with Steel and Gray." She had turned the horse out into the corral, where he sniffed noses with his old friends.

The team. It was a reminder of before. Matt struggled to remember them. He wanted to ask her what else she had from their past. The children. He suddenly thought of them and looked around. "Where are Little John and Annie?"

It was the question Lavina had been dreading. She began crying. Elizabeth heard her and hurried in from the kitchen. "What happened to the children?" He began to feel anxious as he looked from one woman to the other.

"There was a fever last spring. Twelve people in town died." Elizabeth was also crying. "We almost lost Lavina."

Matt felt a wave of anger surge over him. He felt helplessness at not taking care of his family. There was one more question he needed to ask. "Big John?" He was afraid to hear the answer. Lavina told him the story about what had happened the day two years before when he shot Bully Buehler.

Once Matt was up and feeling stronger, Lavina and her parents could tell that things were not right with him. He sat and brooded, and acted sullen. Every noise startled him, and he seemed always on guard. They waited for him to tell them where he had been all this time. At least they could partly understand why he hadn't come back, but they didn't understand his silence.

He began helping in the store, ignoring people's questions and their curious looks. At night he again wasn't sleeping well.

"He's constantly waking up, and he thrashes around so I can't sleep," Lavina told her mother. They were alone in the kitchen, discussing how peculiarly Matt was behaving.

"Maybe he'll talk to your father."

The two men were in the store. Theodore told Matt about what had happened after the shootings at the D Rocking D. "You know they caught the imposter, that fool Booker who was pretending to be a sheriff." Theodore couldn't hold back the anger he felt over the situation his daughter had become involved in. If there had been a real lawman over in Turkey Creek the trouble might have been prevented. "He's in prison down in Wyoming. It's better than he deserves if you ask me."

Matt didn't respond. He walked over to a large crate that had been unloaded off the train the day before. He pried off the lid and began removing the shovels that were packed inside. He told his father-in-law nothing about the past two years.

One afternoon Lavina was in the bedroom she and Matt were sharing. She was filling a chest with clean clothes. Matt appeared in the doorway. "Make love to me." He used the same low voice that used to promise excitement. But today she heard desperation in his words.

"Not right now." She tried to smile. This was hardly the time. Plus, she was uncertain of her husband. He was acting so strangely since being back.

That night as she got in bed with him, Matt turned to her and she again felt his desperation when he touched her. She yielded to him, but there was no passion between them. She began to think she no longer knew the man she was sharing a bed with. He felt the craziness had returned.

There was also the scar. Lavina had seen it when she bathed him just after he returned. She had never seen a bullet wound before, but she knew what it was. Now she felt it with her fingers as he slept.

Almost two hours later Matt woke with a start, his heart pounding. "What's the matter?" she whispered.

"Nothing. Go back to sleep." His voice was soft, but she heard panic in it. He listened in the darkness.

They spent the winter living above the store with Lavina's parents. There was tension all around as no one understood Matt's behavior, and he wouldn't talk about it. Elizabeth and Theodore tried to be patient, as their daughter and son-in-law had endured so much sadness. But their nerves were also frayed. Lavina began sleeping in the other room. It angered Matt, although he understood. His depression deepened.

One morning at breakfast Matt looked at Lavina and said, "I want to go back to the ranch."

She looked at him, as did her parents, not knowing what to say. Part of her missed their old home, but part of her wanted the safety of her parents.

"I think it's a good idea." Normally Theodore wouldn't have offered his opinion, but he knew Matt was sinking lower. Something had to change. Maybe going back to the D Rocking D and doing what he enjoyed would lift his spirits.

Matt and Lavina made plans to leave the following week. It was now early June, and the weather was warm enough for them to make the journey comfortably. They packed the wagon full of supplies and started out before sunrise one morning. Easy followed behind, tied to the wagon. A saddle was cinched to his back. It and a new rifle were presents from Theodore.

The drive was somber. It seemed every coulee was still filled with the bones of cattle that had died the winter before last. They arrived at what had been their happy home late in the evening.

The ranch headquarters had an abandoned look and feel to it. The yard was overgrown with weeds and corral rails lay on the ground. Matt stopped the team, and they both just sat and looked. In front of them was the main cabin. Neither of them wanted to be the first one inside.

Finally Lavina climbed down, but she followed behind the wagon as Matt turned the team towards the barn. He stopped outside the leanto and jumped down. The horses remembered their old routine and tried to pull the wagon underneath the shelter, but Matt wanted to examine the structure first. It seemed sound.

He and Lavina peered through the doorway into the barn. The dirt roof had caved in, but it wasn't surprising. It had needed repairing before they left. The corral was in no shape to hold the horses, nor the pasture, so after unharnessing the team and unsaddling Easy, Matt picketed them in the grass near the creek.

Finally they walked up to the cabin. The door was ajar. Inside it had been stripped bare. Everything that could be removed was gone, including their beautiful cook stove and the wardrobe Jesse had made. Their bed was also gone. The bunk in the corner was full of mice droppings amongst the remains of the grass mattress.

They walked back outside and over to the bunkhouse to see what shape it was in. The small stove used to heat it had been taken as well. Matt looked at her and said, "I just don't know how we'll get going again." He felt defeated.

"We'll buy more cattle and start over."

"How? We have no money."

Lavina held her husband's gaze and took a breath. "Yes we do." She explained about selling the cattle and the horses. The money was still at her parents untouched. Actually she had added to it, since her father had insisted on paying her for working in the store.

She didn't know why she hadn't yet told Matt about the silver in her father's safe, except that for some reason she was afraid to. He seemed so unstable and the money represented the only certainty of their future. But now that they were back at the ranch, maybe they could begin rebuilding.

Matt actually smiled. It was just the hint of the way he used to grin, but it was the first happy expression she had seen on his face in a long time. Maybe everything would work out for them.

They camped outside that night and the next day began making the cabin liveable. Lavina pulled down cobwebs and swept the dirt floor. Matt mixed mud to chink the cracks between the logs of the cabin walls.

\*\*\*

A few days later they made a trip to Turkey Creek. It was practically a ghost town. The general store hung on, but The Palace Hotel had closed down. The streets were deserted as most the townspeople, and ranchers in the area, had left. It had become a one saloon town when Bobby closed the Blue Bear, pulled up stakes and moved on.

Silas Riggs tried to act cheerful about the situation, but knew he wouldn't be in business much longer. He knew he'd never find a buyer for the store. He had decided to hang on as long as possible, providing goods for the few remaining people.

He was happy to see Matt. "Where you been?" He greeted the couple as they entered the Turkey Creek Mercantile. Matt didn't even smile.

"I've been here and there." It was all anyone heard. Matt collected what he needed, placed the items on the counter and walked out, leaving Lavina standing alone with Silas.

"We can pay." She felt humiliation at having to explain their financial situation.

"Don't worry about it." Silas waved his hand in the air. He acted unconcerned, although lately he had heard all kinds of excuses concerning payment from financially unstable people. The Dalys were his friends though, and honest, and he would never cut off their credit.

Lavina was lonely and wanted someone to talk to. She told the storekeeper about fixing up the ranch headquarters, and that they intended to start ranching again. Silas hoped it would work out for them. He had heard about the young Daly children's deaths, and about how Matt had reappeared after everyone thought him dead.

"Where was Matt all this time?" He hesitated asking, but his old friend had told him nothing.

"I don't know. He won't tell anyone. I can't get him to talk at all." She was relieved to have someone to confide in.

"I suppose it will take some time," but Silas couldn't imagine that Matt had been through worse experiences than his wife.

"Our stove was stolen. We'll have to order another one." Silas told her there might be a wood cook stove in one of the abandoned homes at the edge of town, and assured her it would be all right to take it. He could order one for them, but it might take a couple months to receive it from back east. They needed one now.

Lavina said goodbye and walked outside to find Matt. He was coming out of the saloon carrying half a dozen bottles of whiskey, as many as he could carry. His breath smelled of alcohol.

They drove to the edge of town and began exploring the deserted buildings. The stove they found wasn't nearly as nice as the one they lost, but it worked, and Lavina no longer had to cook outside over an open fire.

Matt tried shoveling the dirt out of the barn from where the roof had caved in, but he could never seem to get any momentum going for the tedious and arduous task that needed to be done before he could replace the roof. He felt like a failure and was overwhelmed at the thought of rebuilding the D Rocking D. The main thing still on his mind was quenching the thirst that never left him.

Most mornings he saddled his horse and rode off, leaving his wife alone until evening. All the work that needed doing barely progressed. He never helped with household chores. After supper he sat on the porch brooding in silence while Lavina hauled water from the creek and scrounged for wood, since there was no longer a stack of logs cut and ready to split. This went on all summer. Lavina spent many days alone and frightened. She worried about her husband, but also about her own safety. Occasionally a rider or two showed up, strangers she was reluctant to let into her home. Matt never thought to leave the rifle and she had no way to protect herself if she needed to.

By the time the air had a hint of fall to it, things were even worse between them. Matt was drinking heavily. It was the only way he could sleep at all. But neither of them was getting much rest as his tossing and turning kept Lavina awake also. She felt she was near the breaking point.

The slightest nuisance caused him to become angry. One day Lavina asked him to help her. "Can't you do anything! When did you become so helpless?" He answered her back. She was shocked. He had never spoken to her like that. It frightened her and she began avoiding him as much as possible. Matt was shocked also. He had never acted like that with anyone, least of all his wife. It scared him, although he hid it behind a condescending tone. The silence between them grew.

"Talk to me! Why won't you talk to me?" Lavina's own anger and frustration finally burst out one evening. "Tell me what's the matter!" she demanded as he sat out on the porch.

"Nothing is the matter." His voice sounded indifferent, but inside he wanted to silence her any way he could. The feeling made his blood run cold.

"Yes it is! You don't sleep. You don't talk. Tell me what is going on!" Lavina screamed at her husband. He didn't even look at her.

Once she was silent, the only sound was of liquid swishing against glass as Matt took another drink. The darkness hid the white of his knuckles as he clenched the bottle. She turned and stomped back inside, fighting back tears. Matt's eyes followed the brief arc of orange light as he flicked the butt of his cigarette out into the yard.

A few days later Lavina awoke and looked around. It was still pitch dark out. Matt was up and dressed, and had a fire burning in the stove. The coffee water was on. Now, he was packing their belongings. He saw that she was awake.

"Come on. We have to get going."

"What?"

"Get up. Get dressed," Matt commanded as he stuffed belongings into gunnysacks.

Lavina stood up and began dressing. "Where are we

going?" Even though she felt apprehensive, she also felt relief that she hadn't woken having to face another day of her husband's surliness.

"I'm taking you back to your parents."

"Where are you going?"

"There's something I have to do." Matt would say no more. After coffee and cold biscuits, he went out and hitched the team to the wagon. They set out as the sun was rising on the hills, with Easy once again following along behind. It was a quiet ride as they took the back road to Cedar Junction.

The Lavolds were surprised when they showed up, but Lavina felt relief to see her parent's smiling faces. Matt unhitched the team, turned them loose in the corral, and pitched hay in for them. Meanwhile Easy was in the barn eating a quick meal of oats.

When the horse had licked up the last of the grain, Matt slipped the bit into his mouth. He didn't want to wait for morning before setting off on the journey he knew he had to make. He tied the horse to the hitch rail in front and climbed the stairs to the second story living quarters.

Inside Lavina waited with her parents. They all had questions on their faces. Before any of them could ask, Matt spoke. "There's something I need to do. I'll be back."

"When?" It was the only word Lavina could get out.

Matt walked over to her, and ignoring the question, said, "I need to talk to you." He led her into the bedroom. "I need a hundred dollars."

She blinked hard, but she didn't ask why. Technically it was his money, and she doubted he would tell her anyway. "It's in Papa's safe."

He followed her back down the stairs into the store where the safe stood hidden in a corner. Lavina opened it, took out a bag of coins and handed it to Matt. He counted out the amount he wanted and returned the bag.

"When will you be back?" she asked again.

"Just wait here." He gave her a quick hug, and then hesitated for just a moment. "Tell your parents thank you," he said and then he turned and walked out the door.

She watched him go, feeling confused and once again abandoned and scared. She couldn't tell him what she didn't yet know, that she was carrying another child.

# Chapter 5

M att rode south, down into Wyoming Territory. The mild weather continued, and showed no sign of turning, but still he pushed his horse, anxious to reach his destination. Both horse and rider were in much better physical condition than when they made the trip the year before. Easy also had a new set of shoes to protect his feet.

Close to a week later he reached the town of Kincaid. He vaguely remembered it, but hadn't been back since his meeting in the street with the red-haired outlaw. Bypassing the saloons, he went directly to the livery and had the attendant feed his horse. He didn't remember him as the man he had sold his saddle to, and he was relieved when the man didn't seem to recognize him. As the liveryman worked, Matt asked where he could purchase a pack horse. The man scratched his chin. "Well, I just got a horse in. How far you goin'?"

"Not far." The man led Matt out to the corral where a few horses stood. He pointed to a sorry looking sorrel. The horse's previous owner had worked him down to nothing, and then traded him in for a healthy horse.

"That's all I got right now." Matt felt disgust, looking at the pitiful animal. There was no excuse for letting that happen. He looked the horse over. There seemed to be nothing wrong with him that couldn't be fixed with adequate feed and rest. He put a halter on the gelding before prying his mouth open to look at his teeth. They were in decent shape, meaning the horse wasn't old, and that he would be able to chew his food.

"I'll give you ten dollars for him." The livery owner agreed. It would take a lot of feed and time to get the horse back in shape, so he doubted he was out anything, selling him so cheaply.

Matt led the horse over to the general store, tied the lead rope to the rail and went inside. He spent most of the remaining silver buying the food and supplies he needed. He asked for flour, beans, a side of bacon, coffee, a bag of sugar, and tobacco, mostly big bulky items he needed another horse to carry. Lastly he asked for blankets, a warm coat, and a soft rope.

Matt wrapped the supplies in the blankets and used the hemp rope to tie them on the horse, keeping everything as balanced as possible. It wasn't the best way to pack a horse, but it should work, he thought, since he hadn't far to go.

As he prepared to ride out of town he glanced over at a saloon across the street. He heard the sound of piano music coming from inside. It was enticing. He wanted a drink badly, but he resisted. Shortly after, leading the pack horse, he rode out. If anyone remembered him they stayed silent.

That evening he arrived at Gray Eagle's shack. The Indian came out when he heard the horses and frowned when he saw who it was. Why wouldn't the crazy white man leave him alone?

"Hello, Gray Eagle!" Matt called out to him. The Sioux just stood there. Matt felt nervous, but he was also desperate. "I thought you could use some food." He dismounted and began untying the rope holding the bundles in place. Silently Gray Eagle watched Matt carry everything inside.

"What do you want?" He finally asked.

"You saved my life." Matt didn't know how to explain what he was doing.

Gray Eagle looked at the food and blankets. "So this is what your life is worth to you?" He felt no compassion for the white man now that his bullet wound was healed. And he didn't want his charity.

Matt tried again. "Winter is almost here. I wanted to help you out."

"Well now you can go." Gray Eagle dismissed Matt and turned away.

"I had this dream." Matt blurted the words out. He knew the medicine man was the only one he could tell about it. "And at night you talk to me." Suddenly Gray Eagle was intrigued. In his experience, white people didn't dream. At least they never talked about it. But dreaming was a big part of his world. He turned back to Matt.

"What do I say to you?"

Matt felt silly. "You say, 'Home, home,' over and over in my ear."

"Tell me your dream."

"There... I, I was being chased by a demon or some sort of monster."

Gray Eagle thought. The demon wasn't chasing Matt. It was already inside of him. He had seen it when the tormented *wasicun* was here before. It wasn't unusual for white people. Most of them were carrying these spirits. It was much easier to heal the physical body. Healing the other, unseen parts of people was difficult. Most were unwilling, or unable, to observe these much deeper parts of themselves. Maybe this man was different.

"Come Matt Daly, Let's eat." Besides, Matt had brought gifts. He refused to acknowledge payment. He neither expected it, nor accepted it. It seemed a fine line, but it showed faith when people brought generous offerings when they needed help, instead of putting a price on his help afterwards.

Grateful as he was for the food, and the warm blankets

and clothing Matt had brought, he knew he hadn't yet seen what the white man's greatest gift to him would be. And he didn't know if he wanted it. "Thank you." He looked at Matt as he spoke. They ate and then they slept.

***

Lavina settled into her old routine once more. A life of drudgery and sadness seemed to be her destiny. Her parents wanted to help her change the situation, but were at a loss as to how.

The three of them discussed where Matt could have gone, but nothing made sense to them. Lavina remembered the prostitute in Miles City, and secretly worried that he had gone to be with another woman. He hadn't acted like he wanted to be with her. She tried not to think about it. He had told her he would be back. All she could do was wait.

When she realized she was pregnant, her fears became greater. She thought of Annie and Little John and wondered if she was capable of taking care of another child. It was still difficult thinking about her son and daughter, and yet she would have to go through their old clothing and dress the new baby in the same garments. At least she had some time to get used to the idea. When she told her mother about her pregnancy, Elizabeth didn't know whether to be happy or sad for her daughter.

Meanwhile, Matt was having doubts about why he had returned to Gray Eagle's home. As usual the old Indian didn't say much. Before the silence had been restful, now Matt fidgeted, wanting a drink as he waited desperately for some direction from his host. But Gray Eagle went about his days almost as if the white man wasn't there.

After a week, Matt could no longer keep quiet. "When I was here before it... the... I could sleep at night. Now I can't."

Gray Eagle knew. He had heard the *wasicun* moving around at night. He also knew why he had been able to sleep through the night when he was here before. "There is a plant I

210

know about. It helped with the pain also."

"Can you help me again?"

Gray Eagle was testing him. The silence was meant to see how serious he was about healing his mind. He also knew Matt needed to get the whiskey out of his body before doing anything else.

"If you were one of my people we would go to the hilltop for *Hanbleceya.*" He looked over at Matt to see if he was listening.

Matt had no idea what Gray Eagle was talking about. "What the hell does that mean?"

"Face the demon and see what it wants."

Matt turned and looked out. The late summer sun shone warmly through the open doorway. He was about an inch away from climbing on his horse and riding away. The old man wasn't making any sense.

Then he thought about how desperate he had become. His life had no direction. He remembered how he felt leaving Lavina again. "What do I need to do?"

Gray Eagle looked at him intently. "Go out on *Hanbleceya.*"

"On what?"

Gray Eagle didn't have the words in English to explain to Matt about vision quests. Instead he stood up and led Matt out the door. "First we gather wood."

There was a small mound back behind Gray Eagle's home, down closer to the creek. Matt had noticed it before, but had never really looked at it. The Indian walked over close to the small dome and said, "Pile wood here." He indicated a spot.

The woods nearby had already been picked clean of dead wood, so Matt foraged farther down the creek. He went and got Easy to help, and had the horse drag downed logs of decaying cottonwood back to the cabin. He still felt frustrated, but at least hauling the wood gave him something to do. While he worked, Gray Eagle crossed the creek and climbed to the top of a small hill to pray. He came back down after a couple of hours and indicated there was enough wood collected. He had Matt follow behind him as they approached the tiny hut. To Matt it looked like a large pile of blankets and hides. On one side of it was a fire pit.

"First we purify in the *inipi*." He looked at Matt sternly. "Do as I say." He was taking a risk, letting a *wasicun* come into his sweat lodge. It had to be treated with the utmost respect or the sacred energy would be lost. Most white people, he had found from experience, lost their connection with *Wakan Tanka,* the Great Spirit, without even realizing it.

After receiving Matt's assurance that he would do exactly as told, they began preparing. First Gray Eagle lit a sprig of dried sage and waved the smoking leaves over Matt. Then he walked over to the sweat lodge and pulled open a flap. He again motioned Matt to follow closely behind. They stooped to walk through the opening. Inside, Matt looked around. He saw a frame of bent willow branches holding up the blankets and hides. In the center was another pit full of rocks. One by one they brought the rocks out and placed them in the fire pit. The heavy rocks were already covered with soot. Then they piled the dry wood on top of them.

When all was arranged to Gray Eagle's satisfaction, he said, "Tomorrow we will begin."

The two of them lay on their bellies and drank from the creek, enjoying the cool water and the evening air. They ate from the pot of beans and salt pork simmering on the coals outside Gray Eagle's shack. By the time it was completely dark, they were wrapped in blankets and asleep.

A couple hours later Matt woke with a start. What was that noise? He lay there listening in the darkness, his heart pounding. The rest of the night he tossed and turned, occasionally dozing off, only to wake a few minutes later.

Gray Eagle was purposefully not explaining to Matt what was intended. He would go in steps. If Matt made it through the inipi, they would go on.

In the morning he allowed Matt only water. They went outside to say morning prayers. While the Sioux medicine man was thanking the earth for providing him a place to live, and the rising sun for giving life, Matt was wondering what he had gotten himself into. He could leave anytime, he thought. But leave and do what? He pulled his attention back to Gray Eagle. He saw the humility on the man's face, and there was knowingness in his eyes.

Once he was done, Gray Eagle instructed Matt to take a bucket to the creek and fill it with water. When he came back, they drank again. "No more talking," he told Matt just before he lit the pile of wood.

Gray Eagle's movements had become slower and more purposeful. Matt wondered if he was in a trance. But the Indian was perfectly lucid. He was also having doubts. It didn't seem right to lead a white man through his sacred ceremonies. He had prayed for the troubled young man before deciding to help him.

Once the fire burned down, Gray Eagle began undressing, motioning for Matt to do the same. Then he had the *wasicun* enter the *inipi* and sit on the side opposite the opening. Silently Matt sat on the fragrant sage scattered on the dirt floor.

Gray Eagle used a rusted pitchfork with no handle to bring the hot rocks into the sweat lodge. It took a while as he handled them one at a time. When he finished, he closed the opening behind him and sat down, facing Matt across the large mass of heat. The small enclosure heated up quickly.

Gray Eagle prayed out loud again, in his own language. He put sprigs of sage and small bunches of sweet grass on the fire, adding other aromatic herbs one at a time.

The heat continued to intensify and Matt began to sweat. The lodge was tight, so little of the hot air escaped. The two men sat silent and still for a while, and then Gray Eagle reached into the bucket of water, scooped out a small amount and carefully poured it onto the rocks.

Breathing in the hot steam, Matt's nostrils burned. As he sat there, with sweat beading on his skin, he felt an energy he had never noticed before circling around outside the small enclosure. He felt safe, as if in a womb. Gray Eagle listened for any reaction from Matt at the surge of heat. He wanted to go easy on him. At the first sign of distress he would open the flap and allow cool air inside.

"What are you grateful for, Matt Daly?" Gray Eagle's voice broke the silence.

Matt didn't know what to say. He hadn't thought about being grateful before. "My wife," he finally said. He thought some more. "I'm grateful you saved my life." But he didn't think he had much to be grateful for lately. And there was little feeling behind the words.

The silence began to feel oppressive and the perspiration trickling down his sides and back tickled. He felt uncomfortable in the heat. Gray Eagle sat silent in the darkness.

Finally the medicine man pushed back the flap. As the cool air flowed in, the two men exited. Matt followed Gray Eagle down to the creek. They waded in, and when at the deepest part, sat down to let the water flow over them. Matt's skin tingled and he felt invigorated. They retrieved their clothing and dressed.

"Now, are you ready to face your demon, Matt Daly?" Gray Eagle's tone grabbed Matt's attention. He looked up into Matt's eyes, demanding an honest answer. The younger man hesitated. He still didn't know what the Indian was talking about. But the thoughts that seemed to be making his decisions lately once again took over. What was his option? Go back, to what? Keep running, where?

"Yes, I'm ready." He tried to make his voice sound confident, but the words came out sounding hoarse. There must be a little rust in his throat from all the silence, he decided. But he looked Gray Eagle in the eye. Satisfied, Gray Eagle told Matt to catch the horses. Fifteen minutes later they crossed the stream as their riders guided them up into the hills.

Three hours later, when the sun was low in the sky, they came to a lone butte pointing skyward. The bottom of it was covered with ponderosa Pine. Above, sheer cliffs made the flattened top inaccessible.

They followed a game trail through the trees and up into a canyon at the base. Reaching the head of it, Gray Eagle stopped his horse and looked around. Once again he was concerned about taking a white man into the sacred canyon. Could Matt Daly feel the closeness of the spirits?

They dismounted and Gray Eagle instructed Matt on *Hanbleceya,* the Vision Quest. He would stay here for four days, alone and with no food, praying to his tormentor, asking why it stayed with him. Then he would wait for an answer.

"I'm not sure how to do that."

"Be silent and listen."

"Okay, I'm ready." He had already become good at the silence part, and he spent most nights lying awake listening. He gave a sigh of resignation.

Gray Eagle left him under a giant, grandfather ponderosa with a canteen of water and his clothing. When his people went on a vision quest they had neither, but this was a white man. He rode for home, leading the extra horse.

Matt sat under the tree. The cushion of needles was soft and he lay down.

A sudden gust of wind woke him as it roared through the trees. He sat up startled. He felt no air moving on his face, and realized there was no wind. Fully awake he listened in the darkness. He lay down again, but the pointed ends of the needles poked him and he could no longer get comfortable.

In the morning he felt irritated and hungry. What was he doing out here? He looked around. Nothing moved in the absolute quiet. Where were the birds? He could start walking or he could tough it out for four days. He stood there and considered his choices. A typical cowboy, he hated walking, and he'd been without food for long periods time of before. He decided to sit and wait.

\*\*\*

Lavina had mixed feelings about her pregnancy. The thought of bringing a new life into the world began growing on her. She decided that mostly she was happy about it. She still grieved for her other children, but that would never end. Although she worried about Matt, she felt less stressed than when they had recently been together.

What bothered her most was the way people looked at her. Her husband had come home after disappearing for two years, gotten her pregnant and left again. The judgment in their eyes angered her. Therefore she rarely left the store. She got little fresh air and her face was pale. Both her mother and the doctor were concerned because she was so thin. She just had no appetite. She told them that except for being tired, she felt fine.

Teddy and James were back in school, so there was a bedroom for her to sleep in. The Lavold's living space was much larger than Lavina had out on the D Rocking D, but it felt more confining.

*** 

Matt lay under the huge pine tree and looked up into the swirling pattern the branches made against the blue sky. His hunger had gone, and the warm air felt pleasant. He was trying to remember what Gray Eagle had told him, but his mind kept going blank. He stood up and walked around, sat back down, and had a sip of water. What was he doing here? He questioned himself one more time. He looked up into the sky. Was he supposed to be asking or listening? The day kept getting longer and longer.

Gray Eagle couldn't help but chuckle to himself as he went about his day. The *wasicun* was probably thoroughly confused by now. Even though he was helping Matt in all seriousness, he still saw humor in the predicament he had put the white man in. He knew the cowboy was in no danger.

He had no expectations one way or another about what Matt would experience. Not everyone who went on a vision quest was successful. Some went on many and never received a message. It wasn't necessary to be on a quest to have to have a vision either. In fact Matt's dream was a vision, but he didn't understand it. Gray Eagle was simply helping Matt to understand what he already knew, but wasn't yet able to acknowledge.

Suddenly Matt woke up. It was dark, and once again he had heard the wind whistling through the trees. He sat up. There was no wind. He jumped to his feet and yelled, "What do you want!?" Immediately he felt foolish. He stood in the darkness, wondering for the hundredth time what kind of a ridiculous situation he had gotten himself into.

The next morning was cloudy and cool. A breeze came up at dawn and Matt sat against the tree on the downwind side. He hadn't slept again after waking hours before. He was tired and his hunger had returned.

He tried to remember how long he had been there, but his mind couldn't seem to be able to think back that far. He thought about Lavina, about how beautiful she was. Suddenly he was with her. They were making love. He wanted to stay in that moment forever, but knew something would disturb him before it happened. He snapped awake, listening. What had he heard? Again there was no sound, and he became angry.

He jumped up and began yelling down the canyon. He cussed at the circumstances that had ruined his life. He cussed at Bully Buehler for what had happened to his father, and at God for taking the life of his children, feeling the emptiness the deaths of his family brought to his life. He shouted down the canyon at the unfairness of his life. He let loose with a couple of blood curdling screams for good measure. Tears ran down his cheeks as he sobbed. Once more feeling humiliated at his outburst, he sat back down, wishing the ground would suck him up and end his torment.

"Listen. Listen." Gray Eagle's voice continued pestering him. He fell asleep and woke at dawn when birds began twittering in the trees above him.

He was in a daze. It was the confusion of waking from a deep sleep. The only time he'd experienced that recently was after drinking heavily. Soon boredom set in again. He stood up and looked at the top of the butte and wondered if there was a way to reach the top. He sat back down. The day droned on.

Matt was being chased by evil looking men carrying

rifles. He ran through a narrow canyon. It forked and he paused, wondering which way to go. There was a sharp crack as one of his pursuers took a shot at him. He turned and continued his mad dash down the dark, twisting canyon. There was another shot. He turned to look and saw the angry figures coming towards him. "Go away! Leave me alone." Fear almost overtook him, but he held his ground. The shadowy shapes were large and menacing, coming closer. Still, he stood. As one, they pointed their guns and fired.

A flash of light and the sound of the shots woke Matt. Another flash of light allowed him to see the cliff in back of him for just an instant. The immediate crash of thunder sounded as he jumped to his feet. Rain assaulted him as he ran for cover underneath the cliff. It took a few more moments to remember where he was. He watched the sheets of rain soak the ground until the lightening passed and the bright flashes no longer illuminated the ground.

Finally he fell asleep again, curled up in a tight ball to hold in body heat. There was a faint light in the east when he opened his eyes. He had slept through the remainder of the night. Feeling stiff and cold, Matt stood up and peered out. The rain had stopped and he could see the last stars. The air smelled fresh.

Matt remembered his dream. He still felt the terror of being hunted by the dark figures. He had no idea what it meant. What did any of it mean? How long had he been up here? The hours ran together, turning day into night into day again.

Gray Eagle appeared the afternoon of the fourth day, riding his bald-faced sorrel and leading the bay. He found the cowboy fast asleep near where he had been left. The white man didn't wake until he dismounted, walked over and touched him on the shoulder. Matt sat up, looking relieved. Never had he been so happy to see another person. Seeing his dry lips, Gray Eagle handed him a canteen of fresh water.

They found a bare spot on the ground for a fire. Gray Eagle pulled a small pot from the gunny sack he carried on his horse. He poured water into it and put it on the coals. They drank hot coffee and ate the cold pancakes Gray Eagle had fried before coming for Matt. They said little. Gray Eagle seemed to have no interest in hearing about Matt's experience. Watching the white man he saw all he needed to. After rolling and smoking cigarettes, they mounted their horses and headed back down the trail to Gray Eagle's. He had collected more wood and prepared for another purifying inipi. The same procedure was strictly followed. Matt still felt frustrated. It seemed he had accomplished nothing during his four day ordeal.

Late that night, after completing the sweat lodge by bathing in the creek, they ate again. Afterwards Gray Eagle finally asked Matt what he had experienced. Matt looked at him, reluctant to tell him about the fears, both in and out of his dreams, but mostly he was ashamed about the outburst that had led to his crying like a child. It just wasn't something grown men admitted to.

He took a deep breath and began. Much of his time in the canyon was hazy, but he told of his dream where the men turned monsters chased him. Gray Eagle nodded as he talked. Finally he finished by telling about the tears he had shed. Gray Eagle nodded one last time and looked into the fire, deep in thought, wondering what the white man would understand.

"Well," Matt waited.

People always needed words to explain their experiences. Indian people were no different than the *wasicun*. Their minds wanted to be kept busy figuring it all out. He had never asked Matt about who had shot him or why. The circumstances around the cowboy's craziness didn't concern him.

"The monsters chasing you in your dream are the fears inside of you. You can let them go now. It has already happened because you faced them. The rain came to help you."

Matt still didn't understand, although he remembered feeling relieved breathing in the air the rain had cleansed. Gray Eagle walked inside his house to sleep. Matt sat looking into the dying fire for a while longer, appreciating its warmth and companionship after his four days alone. Finally he emptied the coffee pot on the coals before going in to sleep.

## Chapter 6

Matt made preparations to leave. He felt more at peace when he was with Gray Eagle, and was uncertain what would happen after he left. "Tell me something," Matt said. "Why are you living here? Where is your family?"

The Indian's face darkened. It was none of Matt's business, but he replied. "I have no family. They are all dead."

Matt asked no more about it. But he felt sad for the old Indian, living here all alone. At least he had food for a while. After mounting Easy, he looked over, and said once again, "If you ever need anything, come find me." After repeating where he lived, the cowboy turned and rode off.

Matt headed north. He had loaded the pack horse with more food then he would need for just the trip home. It was late summer, and the weather continued warm, so Matt was in no hurry. He enjoyed the trip. It felt good to be riding cross country with provisions and a purpose. As much as he missed Lavina, he couldn't see her yet. Instead he bypassed the town of Cedar Junction and continued on to the D Rocking D. He intended to stay there alone until he was sure he would never mistreat her again. He felt something had changed in him, but had to be sure the past couple years were behind him. He also wanted to stay away from the temptation of alcohol. Could it really be as easy as sitting hungry under a tree, and then having a dream?

His main concern with staying at the ranch for the winter was that he didn't know if there was enough grass left in the fenced pasture to feed the two horses. Instead of putting up hay to feed over the winter, he had kept busy trying to stay drunk all summer.

The cabin was as they had left it. Matt lit a fire in the wood stove after turning the horses out onto the meadow. Thankfully, he had repaired the fence around it so no cattle had strayed in to graze it down.

He spent another lonely winter. At least he was home, even if his family wasn't here. He felt the presence of Big John and Jesse, and went up the hill to visit their graves. For the first time he mourned their deaths. He thought about his small children and tried to imagine what they would look like now if they had lived.

A lot of the time he slept. The long nights made it easy. It helped restore his confidence in himself that he could lay down at night wrapped snugly in his blankets and not wake until morning.

Daily chores were simple. Stepping out the door each morning with the water buckets, he would first check the direction of the wind and scan the sky. Then he'd walk down to the stream to break the ice and fill the buckets, leaving a hole where the horses could drink. After breakfast he replenished the wood box inside and put the beans he'd left soaking overnight on the stove to simmer.

After that there was a lot of idle time. He reread the few books that had been left behind and thought about Lavina. He sat and waited to see if the craziness returned. Instead he felt the peace he had first felt at Gray Eagle's home slowly beginning to grow inside of him. It was a huge relief, and Matt began planning for the future for the first time since his father had died.

Spring came and the sun melted the snow, from a late storm, one last time. Matt had a strong urge to ride for Cedar Junction. He really missed Lavina, plus he wanted to be out and moving around. Early one morning he saddled Easy, and leading the pack horse, set out. He would be reunited with her by nightfall.

*\*\*\**

The afternoon before Lavina had come into the kitchen to make tea. She felt so tired, and hoped the tea would revive her. A lot of her days were spent lying down as she endured the end of her pregnancy. Both her mother and the doctor forbid her to climb the stairs and she felt imprisoned and bored.

She put tea leaves in the pot and poured in hot water, waiting for her mother to come join her. Finally she went to the top of the stairs and called down. "Mother, tea's ready."

"You go ahead. I'll be up in a minute," her mother called back. Elizabeth was looking through bolts of fabric that had just arrived.

Lavina poured tea for herself in the dim, late afternoon light and stirred in sugar. As she reached for the cup, a sharp pain caused her to catch her breath. She knew immediately the baby was coming, and it was early.

Ten hours later she was still lying in bed, with her mother helping the doctor deliver the baby. She didn't remember feeling this much pain, or seeing this much blood before.

Dr. Wilson didn't say much, but Elizabeth could tell he was as worried as she was. Lavina was bleeding way too much for a normal delivery. She no longer had the energy to push. At times she seemed semi-delirious. The baby should be out by now. In fact it was becoming critical. Elizabeth removed one more blood soaked rag, and then looked at the doctor.

"Go make some tea and put in plenty of sugar." He was

hoping that, with the extra energy, Lavina would have the strength to finally push the baby out.

Elizabeth went out into the kitchen where Theodore waited. "Not yet," was all she said at his questioning look. But it was hard not to notice the bright, red-stained towels and linens that were being removed from the bedroom.

She brought the cup of tea back in and approached her exhausted daughter. "Drink this." She held the cup to Lavina's mouth and practically forced her to take a few sips. Lavina just wanted it all to be over. The pain was overpowering her, and she was so tired.

"Push," the doctor encouraged one more time at the next contraction. The sweetened tea did its job and she pushed with all her might. The baby came, and with it another surge of blood. Elizabeth took the baby as the doctor frantically tried to stop the bleeding. But there was nothing he could do. Lavina lay there white as a ghost, not moving as the blood drained from her body. The baby began crying and Elizabeth brought it over for her daughter to see and hear.

"Here's your daughter." She tried to keep her voice calm as she looked at Lavina. She had to come close to see if her own daughter was still breathing. Hopefully hearing her crying baby would encourage Lavina to fight for her life. The bleeding slowed and finally stopped, but she didn't move.

There was also another problem. Elizabeth had recognized early on that, thin as her daughter was, she doubted there would be milk for the infant. She was correct, but she was also prepared. There was a family of Russian immigrants living on the edge of town. She had seen their herd of goats, and had gone out to visit them. The wife and her eldest son communicated to Elizabeth, using signs and the few words of English they knew, that there would be fresh milk soon. When she realized it was for an infant, the smiling woman promised to save some of the crucial first milk for the baby.

Elizabeth breathed a huge sigh of relief as she started back home. Her grandchild wouldn't starve to death. She thought about the next dilemma as she walked along the dusty street, how to get the milk into the infant. It had taken some experimentation, but she figured out a way.

Now the baby was here and she was hungry. She sent Theodore to the Russian family's home to buy milk and began preparing. Without hesitation she pulled out one of her best napkins. After cutting the finely woven fabric into smaller pieces, she stuffed enough of the material in a narrow necked bottle until the milk slowly seeped out. Now all she had to do was teach the tiny infant how to suck the crude breast replacement.

The doctor prepared to leave. "It's in the hands of God now." It was his pessimistic way of saying he didn't believe she would survive. All they could do was wait and see if Lavina recovered.

\*\*\*

Matt reached town as dusk was falling. He rode straight to the store, anxious to see Lavina, and uncertain how she and her parents would react to his showing up after the long absence. The door to the store was locked. He knocked on it when he saw Theodore moving around inside.

The store owner looked surprised as he came over and opened the door. His tone was somber when Matt greeted him. "You better go upstairs."

Matt hurried up and met a surprised Elizabeth in the kitchen. "Matt, hello." Her tone was also serious, way too serious.

"Where's Lavina?" He thought everyone was acting strangely because they were upset with him. Elizabeth didn't say another word as she led Matt into the bedroom. He was shocked when he saw his wife. She lay in the bed pale and not moving. He didn't remember her being so thin. He thought about the fever that had made her sick before and was suddenly scared.

"What's the matter with her?" His voice was a whisper. Elizabeth went out and picked the newborn up from where she lay in a basket near the stove. She was content and sleeping, with a full belly of nutritious goat's milk. Matt saw her and became confused.

"Here's your daughter. She was just born today." Her voice was also low.

Matt looked from the baby back to Lavina. "Is she all right?" He bent over and picked up her limp hand. It was so cold.

"We'll have to see. She lost a lot of blood." Tears came to Elizabeth's eyes as she remembered carrying out the blood soaked sheets and clothing. "Just let her rest."

Matt took the tiny infant and sat in a chair holding her, hoping for his wife to wake up and look at him. The baby seemed so small. Frowning, he counted back the months and also realized she was born too soon.

He sat there all night long, relinquishing his daughter to her grandmother only once, when she fussed. She was the only one who slept. Matt, Elizabeth and Theodore kept watch, checking frequently to see if Lavina was still breathing.

Dawn came. Matt stood up from the chair and blew out the lamp, still holding the baby. He looked down at the miracle of his tiny daughter, then over at Lavina. Her eyes were open and she was looking at him. He hurried to the side of the bed and knelt down.

What could he say to her? Once again it seemed he had failed his family. Lavina lifted her hand and touched his face. It was icy cold. He laid the baby next to her and took her hand, wanting to put the warmth back into it.

Lavina seemed confused. "Where, what?"

"Shhh. Look." Matt showed her the baby girl and she remembered. "See how beautiful she is." Matt felt relieved at Lavina's weak smile. She couldn't comprehend why Matt and her parents kept staring at her with such worried expressions.

After a while the doctor came and had Matt wait outside while he examined the mother and daughter. "She'll live as long as no infection sets in," he said as he entered the kitchen. It was as optimistic as he could be about Lavina. "The baby seems healthy for being premature." He gave Elizabeth a bottle of blood building tonic for Lavina. That, along with his parting words of, "Keep her fed," was all he had to offer.

That evening Lavina was awake, but so weak that she spoke only a few words. As Elizabeth spread another blanket over her daughter, she told Matt, "You can sleep on that corner bed," indicating the extra bed over by the kitchen.

"No, I'm not going anywhere," Matt told her.

"You'll be a lot more comfortable." Elizabeth tried to persuade Matt, believing that an invalid needed privacy. But Matt didn't budge. After she left the bedroom he undressed and slid in bed next to his wife. He snuggled up close, carefully wrapping himself around her to share his warmth. He never intended to leave her again.

The third day Matt rode to the edge of town to buy goat milk, he decided he may as well buy the doe. He paid a whole five dollars for her. After he went and got the wagon and brought her home, he still had to figure out how to milk her. The poor thing was terrified by the time he got her back to the barn behind the Lavold's store. He'd had to tie her in the wagon and hoped she wasn't too traumatized. Taking a pail from Elizabeth, he cornered the doe in a corner, wishing he'd paid more attention when Kirsten milked her cow. He knew the general concept of milking, but it was hard with the squirming animal doing her best to escape. Finally, with Theodore holding her squeezed against a barn wall, he was able to keep her hind legs still enough to squeeze the teats and get some milk into the pail.

"She'll settle down once she gets used to being here," Matt optimistically told Theodore. It had been a procedure they both hoped wouldn't have to be repeated every day in order to have milk for the baby.

During the next few days Lavina began to grow stronger, but her mother insisted she remain in bed. She was taking no chances after nearly losing her daughter for a second time.

Elizabeth was still irritated at Matt. She felt he was responsible for what Lavina had been through. But both she and Theodore had noticed a change in him. He seemed like his old self. He smiled as he sat and talked to his wife.

Finally Lavina could stand it no longer. Her mother was treating her like an invalid, but she had to get out of bed. Theodore and Elizabeth heard laughter early one morning as they came out into the kitchen. Lavina sat in a chair near the stove holding the baby. A blanket was draped over her shoulders. After moving the pot of boiling water to the far edge of the stove, away from the fire, Matt added coffee.

"Good morning." Matt straightened up. Elizabeth wanted to be upset. She was still feeling protective of her daughter and wanted her to stay in bed longer. But she relented when she looked at Lavina's smiling face. The baby had been fed and was sleeping.

Theodore walked over and looked down at the infant. "What are you going to name her?"

"We've decided to call her Kirsten."

"That's a good name." Theodore took the baby and held her as she slept.

That afternoon Matt and Lavina were alone in the kitchen. Theodore was down in the store and Elizabeth had gone out.

"Kiss me." Lavina sat near the stove. Matt leaned over and kissed her on the forehead.

"No, kiss me." Lavina emphasized the word. He didn't have to be told again. Taking her hands, Matt pulled her out of the chair. He wrapped his arms around her and kissed her on the mouth, long and passionately.

Lavina felt a surge of joy run through her body. The man she had fallen in love with was back. She was fairly certain when she looked into his eyes after he returned, but she wanted to make sure. She hugged him and never wanted to let go.

Matt sat her back down. Pulling another chair close to her, he sat also. "I have to tell you something." The serious look on his face made her suddenly nervous.

For the first time he talked about what happened the day Big John and Jesse were killed. Lavina looked horrified as he told her about killing Bully Buehler. He told her how lost he became when he heard she was dead. Admitting he was a hunted man, and that he killed twice more and ran away more times than he could remember, was hard to talk about.

Thinking about the two lonely years away from her brought back difficult memories. The endless wandering and his attempts to obliterate the pain made him feel shameful, but the hardest part was telling her about wanting to die, about how he had let the red-haired outlaw shoot him. Lavina's face showed absolute shock when she realized how close he had come to dying in the street.

He forced himself to tell the entire story, with one exception. He never mentioned the girl who had died while he cowered behind her bed. He intended going to his grave without ever speaking about that. When he finished, they were both silent for a minute.

"Thank you," Lavina whispered. As horrifying as the truth was, it was easier to hear it than to endure stony silences each time she asked about it. "Where were you this time?"

Matt hesitated. "I'll tell you when the time is right." "All right," she agreed.

They began making plans for moving back to the ranch. Matt became excited when he talked about restocking the D Rocking D with cattle.

Lavina remembered the carcasses and the stench of the thousands of cattle that had starved and frozen to death during the winter two years ago. "How will we take care of them?" She asked apprehensively.

"We'll only have as many as we can feed. We'll put up enough hay for when the snow gets deep." He saw that the ranches that suffered the least losses during the blizzards were the ones who put up hay to feed their livestock when the grass was unattainable. The days of a quick buck were over in the cattle industry. Sustainability was the way of the future.

The fencing of the west had also begun. Mile after mile of barb wire was being strung as ranchers began claiming public land as their own. Almost all of it was illegal, but everyone hoped that eventually, by using the land, they could acquire it.

\*\*\*

As Lavina recovered from the birth of little Kirsten, Matt became restless. One morning at breakfast he announced that he wanted to ride out to the D Rocking D to check on it.

"No!" The word shot out of Lavina's mouth. They all stared at her. "You can't leave me." Her look was one of desperation.

"All right. I'm not going anywhere," Matt reassured his wife. He was surprised at how she clung to him, and wanted to be annoyed. But it made him realize how hard the past few years had been on her. He had been so wrapped up in his own misery that he hadn't seen it. Suddenly he felt guilty about all she'd been through.

A month later Matt, drove the wagon towards the D Rocking D. Lavina sat beside him holding little Kirsten. The nanny goat was tied in the back, which didn't leave much room for their belongings. They bypassed the town of Turkey Creek and headed for the ranch. It was a beautiful midsummer evening. Rain the day before had cooled and cleared the air. Both Matt and Lavina were happy to be going home again. It was a noisy trip as the doe bleated her dislike of her predicament the entire way. At first it was amusing, but the noise became annoying as the miles started dragging by.

A couple miles from the ranch headquarters, something caught Matt's eye. Lavina saw it too. "Is that...?"

"It sure looks like Lucky." Matt finished the thought. There was a black mare standing on the ridge above them looking down, watching, a foal at her side. After a couple of minutes the pair disappeared. "Do you think she knew it was us?" Lavina asked.

"It's hard to tell." Suddenly they were both excited about getting back to the D Rocking D, knowing that the mare was still on their range. If she had been unbranded it would be different. There were never enough horses around and any that showed no proof of ownership were captured and put to use.

"Do you think she'll come home?"

"Not without help, but we'll get her." Matt promised.

They reached the ranch headquarters and once more pulled up into the yard and stopped. Matt looked over at his wife and sleeping daughter and smiled. Unlike the last time they had returned home together, he was full of optimism. "Well let's see how it looks." He jumped down and went around to the other side to take the baby while Lavina got down.

They walked over to the cabin. Inside it looked the same as Matt had left it. "Somebody must have stayed here," Lavina remarked after she looked around.

Matt only nodded. He wasn't sure why, but he was hesitant to tell her that he had been here all winter while she was in Cedar Junction. "It looks like the first thing I'll be doing is cutting wood." Together they looked around to assess what other work was a priority.

Lavina stood frozen in the middle of the cabin holding baby Kirsten while Matt took care of the horses. She felt scared whenever he was out of her sight. She knew he would be up when he finished, but her throat felt tight and she was unable to function. Finally he came through the door and she could again breathe.

*** 

The first thing Matt wanted to do was to see how many cattle were using the range near the D Rocking D. The grass nearby hadn't been eaten down, so that was a good sign. The large ranches in the area were gone. Hubert Bailey had quit the country after losing a large sum of money when most of his cattle died in the blizzards during the winter of 1886-87, as had another outfit to the east. The Spade Ranch broke apart the day Matt shot Bully Buehler. According to the men he talked to, big ranching was over. With the wealthy investors gone, the little guy now had a shot. Small ranches were cropping up all over, claiming the range once again, only in smaller pieces.

In some areas homesteaders had begun moving in, farmers who plowed up the sod to plant crops. It was leading to more dissension, as everyone had their own ideas about what was the best use of the land.

Word had gotten around that the D Rocking D was restocking and there were a few cattle around for sale. But Matt wasn't interested in the rangy longhorn cattle. He believed the future of ranching lay in producing a better quality of beef. The longhorns were hardy. They calved easily on their own and could get by on less feed than the stockier breeds. But Matt had eaten enough of their tough stringy beef to realize that in order to sell it to markets back east, the meat had to have a consistently good taste and texture. He began looking into bringing English breeds out to Montana from back east.

*** 

One morning, shortly after they returned, Lavina woke with a start. Matt wasn't in bed next to her. She reached out and touched Kirsten, who lay sleeping next to her. Panic rose in her. Just then the door opened and Matt entered with an armload of wood. She felt foolish as she rose and began dressing.

That summer was the first time Matt and Lavina spent any time alone. The solitude was hard for her sometimes. Plus she still worried that Matt would leave again. He wanted to be out riding more, but instead, stayed with his wife most of the time. Gradually the fear left her, and the couple began enjoying their time together.

Although the money from selling the cattle was mainly intact, they agreed it was to be used for restocking. And with no income, they were reluctant to hire any help. The barn roof still needed rebuilding and Matt was resigned to doing the work alone. So he toiled by himself, shoveling dirt out of the barn from the collapsed roof. He spent long, tedious hours removing it one wheelbarrow full at a time.

One hot day they carried their dinner down to the

cottonwoods by the creek to eat. It was pleasant sitting in the shade on the cool grass. They lingered after they finished their meal. Lavina dozed lying alongside Matt, her head resting on his arm. She woke when he shifted. Sitting up, she sighed. The baby would need to be fed soon, and there was laundry on the line that needed to be taken inside and put away. Then it would be time to start the evening meal. Matt would want to get back to work on the barn.

She looked down at him. He looked back at her. "Come here." The intense desire in his eyes gave her goose bumps as he reached for her. She leaned down and kissed him. He was so grateful that the passion he had felt for her when they first met had returned.

It was an hour before they returned to their work, and that was only because little Kirsten woke up hungry from her nap. Matt and Lavina retrieved their clothing and dressed, feeling reluctant to leave their spot near the creek.

On hot afternoons they stripped down and splashed in the creek to cool off. No one was around to see them, or to hear their laughter as they played in the water. At night they made love out under the stars.

Matt was still sorry he had hurt the beautiful woman he was fortunate to have as his wife. He wished he could build her a real house. For now all he could do was improve what they already had.

He was nowhere near the carpenter Jesse had been, but he banged together a crude table and two benches so they no longer had to eat sitting on the bunk in the corner. Eventually they wanted to buy another, bigger stove so Lavina wouldn't have to bend over the small one they had salvaged from town.

# Chapter 7

Lavina worked in the kitchen. She had a dutch oven on the stove. In it simmered the bones from a deer Matt had shot a few days before. The fresh venison had been welcome. Matt had hauled half of it to town and given it to Silas Riggs, as the store owner could sell what he didn't eat before it spoiled. It was a way the Dalys traded off some of the balance they owed the store.

In the summer heat it didn't take long to spoil, and Lavina had served the meat at every meal in order to use it up. Now, the bones were becoming soup.

She peeled an onion, then chopped it up and added it to the pot. Next she added potatoes and a couple cans of tomatoes. She was making a large pot, and although not the most filling, with biscuits, it would make a meal. She was happy to be preparing enough food for the next day also. She still hadn't recovered fully from the birth of her daughter. The tiredness never seemed to completely leave her body, nor had her strength fully returned. Sleep didn't refresh her, and it was easy to become overwhelmed by the unending chores of running her household.

She lifted the heavy iron lid off the pot to see that the soup still simmered. It smelled delicious and she hoped Matt wouldn't be long. She opened the firebox next to the oven and added another piece of wood before closing the vent to keep the heat in the oven. After checking the temperature by sticking her hand in the oven for an instant, she slid in a tray of sourdough biscuits. She wiped the remaining flour off the counter and scrubbed the spot where she had rolled the biscuits out. Finally she poured herself a cup of coffee from the fresh pot sitting on top of the stove.

Lavina sat down, relieved that her infant daughter still slept. The hot coffee tasted good despite the heat in the cabin. She felt energy returning as she sat there. Hoof beats sounded out in the yard. Before she could get to the door a voice called out.

"Hello! Anybody home?"

There were four riders, men she didn't recognize. They sat their horses until asked to get down. She invited them to come in. Introductions were made as she poured coffee. They had ridden over from a neighboring ranch to welcome the Dalys back.

Lavina enjoyed having the company, even when their loud voices woke Kirsten. She went and picked her daughter up.

"Is your husband needin' any help riding?" One of the men asked as he stirred sugar into his coffee. The D Rocking D still had a good reputation.

"You'll have to talk to Mr. Daly." Lavina walked to the door with the coffee pot and threw the grounds out onto the dirt, looking around for Matt. She poured water from the bucket into the pot and put it on the stove to begin heating.

The four men were a happy bunch. They entertained Lavina with stories that needed to be told and retold to perfect them with the right amount of embellishment. They took turns holding the little girl, entertaining her also as she stared, fascinated at the strange faces and at the brightly colored scarves around their necks. She grabbed hold of whatever she could reach, including mustaches.

Matt had ridden out that morning feeling happy, like in the old days. He thought about his father for a moment, as he did every day. Then he shifted his attention back to the grass swaying in the breeze. He decided to go north, all the way to the ridge that used to separate the D Rocking D from the Spade range.

He was riding a new horse, one he had picked up from Curtis Hicks, the manager of the way station in Turkey Creek. With Easy, and Jerry the pack horse, Matt had the beginnings of a new string of horses. He loped the horse across a meadow towards a tree line of ponderosa on the far side, forgetting about anything except the job at hand.

The sun was low in the sky when he finally returned home. He was concerned when he saw horses in the yard, but after seeing a familiar brand on all four geldings, he realized it was a social call. Everyone streamed out of the cabin. Matt scanned the cowboy's faces and recognized one of them.

"Howdy, there Matt!" The man called out. "You think it's safe leaving your wife alone where the likes of us no-goods can have a chance of stealing her away?"

Matt smiled. "Hey there, George! I'm surprised she didn't smell you from a mile away, and isn't out of the country by now." He wasn't concerned that any of these men posed a threat. In fact he was glad they came by while he was gone. But he hated leaving Lavina alone. He had meant to be home sooner, but had ridden further than he realized.

He dismounted and walked up onto the porch. "Do we have anything to feed these bums?" He asked his wife good-naturedly.

"Of course." Lavina was happy to feed the hungry men, even though her plan for the soup lasting longer than one meal was shot.

The four cowboys went down to the barn with Matt when he took his horse down. Then they all came up to have supper.

Lavina served the soup in whatever they had, a small pot, two bowls, and deep tin plates.

"Be careful," she warned one cowboy as he took a plate. It wasn't meant to hold soup, and the hot liquid sloshed over the edge onto the table as the man set it down in front of him. He soaked it up with a biscuit.

The six of them ate, crammed together on the two benches. Lavina brought an apple pie over to the table and divided it into six slices. She wished there was another one.

As the men rolled cigarettes after the meal, one of them again asked, "You needin' any help?"

Matt looked at him. There was nothing he wanted more than to hire a couple of cowboys to ride for the D Rocking D, but there was no need. He had bought a couple hundred head of Herefords, heifers and some young bulls, to try the breed out. "Maybe next spring. All I can use now is a carpenter, and maybe a nurse maid." He grinned as he teased them, knowing he'd have no takers. The only job these men wanted was to ride, just like Matt wanted to do. "Isn't ol' Lantern treating you right?"

"He's a tight-fisted old coot," George replied. The other three nodded their heads in agreement. Of course being frugal with his money was the reason their neighbor had survived the hard winter. Unfortunately it also meant his hired hands were less than content. Besides, they would lose their jobs once fall roundup was over.

"There is one thing you can help me with. There's a mare I need to catch."

"The black one with the colt?" They had all seen her roaming the prairie. She had been trapped once, but when her brand was identified she was set free. This wasn't her only foal. The first one had been claimed with a hot iron and now belonged to another outfit.

The four said goodbye as the sun set and rode off towards their home ranch after making plans for the following week to help hunt Lucky and her colt. Matt shut the door and looked at his wife. "Are you all right?"

She nodded and said, "I'm just tired." The water buckets were empty and the wood box needed filling. She had washed the dishes as the men talked. Kirsten began crying. She picked her up and began heating milk to feed her.

\*\*\*

Catching Lucky turned out to be easy. She was found only a few miles from the ranch headquarters. The riders hazed her towards the fenced pasture, pressuring her only enough to keep her and the colt traveling in the intended direction. As they approached the gate, one rider rode around in front of the pair while the others formed a half circle so the mare's only option was to turn and go through the opening into the pasture. The colt followed close behind. Having been born a domestic horse, Lucky wasn't overly concerned with being surrounded by a fence once again. Her main concern was for her foal's safety.

Matt left her out in the pasture to start her becoming accustomed to people again. One day he lured her into the corral with grain, and then went to get Lavina. They couldn't see much of the colt as he hid behind his mama and peered out from underneath her neck at the humans staring at him. Both horses stayed at the far side of the corral.

"Will she ever be tame again?" Lavina asked about the mare.

Matt assured her it wouldn't take long. "I may have to drop a loop on her to help her remember, but she'll come around."

In fact he intended to start working with her immediately. A cowboy could never have enough horses, and the mare was another addition to his string. He wasn't concerned that she was still nursing the foal. She was in good condition and the foal could come along on short rides.

A couple weeks later, as fall began to take hold, Lavina paused for a moment in the open door. She started as she realized there was a rider waiting outside. It was an old Indian. He was astride a bald-faced sorrel horse. She hadn't heard him ride up, so had no idea how long he sat there waiting.

Lavina looked at the man. She had seen few Indians during her time in Montana. While on the train she had looked out at sad faces on thin, hungry bodies. Matt told her they mainly stayed on the reservations, starving on government rations. But here was one in her yard.

"Is Matt Daly home?" She was even more surprised when he asked for her husband by name.

"He's not here right now. I'm Mrs. Daly. Won't you get down?"

Once the Indian was off his horse, Lavina continued. "He'll be back soon." The horse looked as hungry as the man so she had him lead the animal into the barn where she fed him some of their precious hay.

"Come up to the house and have a cup of coffee." She didn't know if he understood, but he followed her to the cabin. She wasn't sure how to treat him. She had heard stories about Indians becoming pests when you fed them, but she couldn't turn away anyone who was hungry.

"I am Gray Eagle," the man told her. Just then Kirsten made a sound. The old Indian saw her and smiled. He walked over and began talking to her in his native language. Lavina watched, and then turned to pour a cup of coffee and put a plate of leftover biscuits down on the table.

She invited him to sit, and then watched him eat, at a loss for words. He only nodded as he finished off the food. She poured him another cup of coffee, plus one for herself, wishing Matt would hurry up and get home.

Finally she heard hoof beats outside. She hurried out the door and reached the horse before he stopped.

"What's the matter?" Matt was alarmed.

"There's someone here to see you." Matt didn't see the horse in the barn, so had no idea who it could be. He dismounted and went inside. When he saw his friend, the concern on his face vanished.

"Gray Eagle!" He smiled as he greeted the man who had twice saved his life. "Have you met my wife?" Gray Eagle nodded. His face remained solemn. He didn't know if coming here was a good idea, but for some reason he was still connected to Matt Daly.

"Why are you here?" Matt got right to the point. He knew the old Indian wouldn't have traveled this far for a social call, especially to visit a *wasicun*.

"My house is gone. Men came from town and burned it." The sadness in his voice told the story. He shook his head, not comprehending how white men had so little compassion and could so easily force him out of his home. Matt had thought it was only a matter of time. It was much too desirable a spot near the stream to let the old Indian live there undisturbed. He had only been left alone this long because of his reputation for healing people in the area.

A bunch of men had ridden up to run him off. They allowed him to collect a few belongings, and once he was on his horse they torched the shack. They did the same to the medicine man's sacred sweat lodge.

As sad as it made him, Gray Eagle recognized that it was time for a change in his life. He wanted charity from no white man, but Matt had invited him. And he was different than most white people. He seemed to feel somewhat of a connection to the earth. It was something his people had, but seemed to be lacking in the white man.

An Indian off the reservation was suspicious, but his medicine had remained strong on his journey. It had kept him hidden during the four day trip, and he hadn't been harassed on the road.

"You can stay here as long as you like." Matt saw Lavina's eyes widen at his words. He hoped she would understand that he could never turn Gray Eagle away.

She kept silent; but she remembered all the stories she had heard about Indians. She looked at him. He was no dirtier than any man who had been riding for days. And he had treated her with respect when she invited him into her home. Once more she'd have to trust Matt to know what he was doing. But he had more explaining to do. She went inside to prepare supper as Matt showed Gray Eagle around. No one was using the bunk house, so he could stay in there. She wondered if he needed blankets.

Gray Eagle had no problem fitting in at the D Rocking D. He was left alone to do as he pleased and his hosts expected nothing in return. He thoroughly enjoyed the baby, and held her and sang to her while Lavina worked.

One morning shortly after he arrived, he came to her with a bundle of dried herbs. His eyes missed nothing and he had seen how tired and run down she was. He instructed her to put some of the plant, root and all, in water and boil it, then strain it and drink the tea once it had cooled. She was told to do this every day until it was gone. Lavina thanked him and put the bundle down on the counter.

When Matt came in later she showed it to him. The plant was familiar to him, as he had seen it growing on the hillsides. "If Gray Eagle says it will help you, then do it," he said to his skeptical wife.

"Who is he?" She asked. Matt had only told her that he was a friend.

He paused before he answered. "That's the man who saved my life." He hadn't told Lavina much about what happened after he was shot, about waking up in Gray Eagle's shack and being nursed back to health by the old Indian. The time spent there had seemed almost dreamlike, and he didn't know how to talk about it. He merely told her that once he recovered he had decided it was time to come back home.

Now he told her about both his experiences with Gray Eagle. He gave her no details of his time alone in the canyon at the base of the butte, as Gray Eagle had told him not to. But he assured her that the medicine man had helped him find his way back to her.

Lavina drank the tea every day for a week and began feeling stronger. She awoke feeling refreshed and ready to start her day for the first time since she could remember. Shortly after, she became pregnant again.

Once again, she worried about carrying a child and then

bringing it into the world. She remembered her last pregnancy and was scared. She tried to talk to Matt about it, but he didn't know what to tell her. Finally she got up the courage to talk to Gray Eagle.

"I'm going to have another baby." She explained what had happened before, feeling embarrassed to be discussing anything so intimate with a man, and one she barely knew.

Gray Eagle looked into her eyes and told her, "You will be all right, and the baby also. I will help," he promised.

Lavina thanked him, feeling better. She realized that she could trust him.

## Chapter 8

One afternoon Matt drove the team home from town. The wagon was loaded down with lumber for the new barn roof. A keg of nails sat at his feet. It was a beautiful fall day. The sun warmed him. He noticed the reds and oranges on the hillsides that were becoming more vibrant with the frosts they'd been having at night. Curing grass waved in the breeze. He couldn't imagine a more perfect day.

The horses moved at a slow pace because of the load they pulled. Stopping on the crest of a hill to let them catch their breath, Matt looked around. There was a horse and rider approaching at a trot from behind. Immediately he felt apprehension, remembering his days of being hunted. Watching to see who followed him, Matt recognized the horse first. It was a solid bay he knew belonged to the way station in Compton. Someone had rented the gelding. Curious, he squint his eyes, trying to identify the rider. The man had a big grin on his face. "Sam Yule! Where in the devil have you been hiding?" He smiled as he recognized the man who had once worked for him and his father.

Mathew Daly! It sure is good to see you!" The other man yelled back as he came close. Leaning over off the horse, he held out his hand for Matt to shake. His exuberance at seeing his old boss alive and well caused the normally reserved Samuel to show unusual emotion.

An hour later they arrived back at the D Rocking D. Lavina heard Matt call out, "Come see who's here!" By the time she had rubbed the dough from her hands, Matt was in the doorway. With him was Samuel.

"Sam Yule!" She automatically pronounced his name as Matt had. "It's so nice to see you. Come in."

The quiet young man had matured since they had seen him last. He was no longer frail looking, but carried himself with the confidence that comes with experience and hard physical labor. Both Lavina and Matt wanted to hear what he had been doing the past four years. He told them he had been traveling around, getting work where he could, and seeing the western part of the country.

He could have stayed in Boston and worked in his father's accounting office. Living out west had spoiled him for that kind of life however. He preferred freedom, even if it meant financial insecurity, over the safety of a steady job. He hadn't made much money, but he had seen and experienced quite a lot.

The three of them spent the evening catching up. Gray Eagle came in the house to eat, and then left again. Matt and Lavina both insisted Samuel stay with them, as long as he didn't mind bunking with an Indian.

Samuel laughed at their concern. "It will give me something to write home about, although my family will probably worry I'll get scalped in my sleep." They laughed at the thought of the gentle old medicine man harming anyone.

Samuel had never heard the whole story about Matt's disappearance, since the other hadn't felt the need to explain himself to anyone but his wife. But one day Samuel brought up that he had run into Curly out in Portland a few years back. "He owns a bakery out there. He told me he's been working there off and on for quite a few years. After..." Samuel wasn't sure how to phrase it without bringing up painful memories. "After that last roundup, he bought the business."

"So that's where that old bugger hid out when he wasn't cooking for us. How's he doing?"

"He found himself a wife."

"Good for him." Matt was happy for the cook, but dreaded the subject that was coming up next.

"He says he ran into you down in Texas, at least he thought it was you."

Matt remembered. He had spied Curly while walking down a busy street in a town whose name he didn't remember. It was when he was on the run. An instant after their eyes met, Matt disappeared, running for cover behind a building. He was afraid of being recognized, and also ashamed. So he hid from his friend. The memory brought up uncomfortable feelings. And now he didn't know what to tell Samuel.

"Yeah, it was me," he finally said, but his tone told Samuel he didn't want to talk about it. Samuel let the subject drop.

He ended up staying for a month and got along just fine with his bunk mate. He helped Matt put the new roof on the barn. Once it was finished, it was the best looking building on the place.

Another day he asked about Kirsten. Lavina had never stopped thinking about her, and also wondered where she was. She and Samuel crossed the bridge to look at the cabin that still belonged to her friend. It was in good condition and could be livable with a few repairs.

They all knew Samuel had been attracted to Kirsten. He could only watch her from a distance however, as she had been married to Jesse. "Do you know where she is?" Lavina asked him. She remembered the somber train ride he had taken with them when they left the D Rocking D, the day she had said goodbye to them both. Lavina pictured Kirsten, her smiling face and the blond braid that hung down her back.

"You might be able to find her," Samuel replied. "Her

family lives in eastern Nebraska, Lancaster County is where she got off the train. I'm not sure where she went after that." He remembered a young man she said was her brother meeting her at the train station. She didn't really talk about it. "Jesse's family lives there too."

Lavina remembered Kirsten telling her that. It seemed so far away. "I wonder if I could get a letter to her. Of course she could be anywhere after all this time." She didn't know what would happen to her friend's homesteaded land and cabin.

***

Late fall arrived. The distant mountains already had a covering of snow. Final preparations were being made for winter. Matt looked off into the hills. In past years he and Big John would have been finishing up the fall roundup. He sighed and swung the axe again. Samuel stacked the split wood against the side of the cabin one arm load at a time. Periodically they switched jobs.

After supper Samuel announced he was leaving in a couple of days. All he said was that he had something to do. Matt and Lavina figured it was time for him to move on. They'd enjoyed having him at the ranch and told him he was welcome anytime. Matt tried to pay him for his help, but Samuel refused to take money. He was happy to help out his friends.

The Dalys, along with Gray Eagle, settled into their winter routine. Matt checked the small cattle herd frequently. It was easy for him to do alone. A few years ago a couple hundred head would have barely been worth his while. Now he was happy just to be ranching again, even on a small scale.

After mulling it over in his mind for a couple of months, Matt made a decision. Samuel had told him the name of Curly's bakery, and the street it was on, so one night he sat down and wrote a letter By mid winter he received a reply. Curly was happy to hear from the Daly Ranch and wrote all about his life as a married businessman. The two of them began a correspondence, writing one another a couple times a year. Each urged the other to come for a visit.

Baby Kirsten was now crawling and Gray Eagle seemed pleased to have the job of babysitter. She loved the patient elder. He played with her and sang to her as she fell asleep. Lavina worried about whether he was spoiling the little girl. Matt looked at it as giving their daughter another grandfather.

As Lavina felt the new baby grow inside of her, she gradually lost her fear of having another child. She had never felt healthier, but still wondered if it wouldn't be wise to go to her parents when the baby's birth got closer.

Matt had continued milking the nanny goat into fall, but she gave less and less milk. They fed her hay and oats, but it wasn't the optimal feed for her. She would have preferred to browse the shrubs and forbs on the hillsides.

One morning Matt went out to milk her. Shortly after, he came back in with an empty bucket. "Well, that's it. There's no more fresh milk."

"We'll get by on canned milk." Lavina tried to sound optimistic, but she was concerned how her little girl could thrive on the monotonous food choices that were their winter fare.

*** 

The winter snow had melted except where it drifted deep into the coulees, and on the north facing hillsides where there was still little sunshine. The air felt warm as Lavina stepped outside to empty a tub of dirty dish water. She could see Gray Eagle up on the hillside with little Kirsten waddling alongside of him. The little girl was falling down more than she was walking, but she kept getting up and trying again.

Matt had gone to town for the day. The ground had dried up enough for the wagon to make it over the rutted tracks to town. They were running low on flour and other staples.

The baby wasn't due for another month, but they wanted to be ready when the time came. Lavina was too far along to safely travel, so the baby would be born at home. It concerned them both, but heavy snow all winter had prevented travel except by horseback. The nearest doctor was in Compton, and he refused to travel that far to deliver a baby.

Lavina looked around one more time before going back inside. She wondered if she would ever get to ride a horse in the hills or across the prairie again. She lowered herself onto one of the benches to rest a minute before preparing supper.

Gray Eagle came in carrying the sleeping child. He smiled at Lavina. "She is strong, this one." He sat on the bunk still holding her, singing softly.

Suddenly the door was flung open from the outside. Standing in the doorway was a grinning Kirsten. Lavina shrieked with delight and hurried to her feet to hug her friend as the baby woke and began crying.

Kirsten patted her swollen stomach. "I heard you had another one on the way," she said after greeting her friend. Suddenly she noticed the Indian sitting in the corner. "You must be Gray Eagle." He sat and stared at the boisterous white woman as Lavina picked her daughter up off the bunk.

Lavina was puzzled how she knew so much about happenings at the D Rocking D. Then she saw a shadow on the porch. Samuel appeared in the doorway. She was even more delighted.

"Come in," she told him. She remembered him telling her and Matt that he had something to do. Laughing she said, "You little sneak."

Samuel came inside, tickled that his plan had succeeded so well. He and Kirsten stood side by side. Taking his hand, and still beaming from ear to ear, she said, "We were married last month." Lavina hugged her friend once more, feeling overjoyed for the two of them.

After Kirsten held the child named for her, she and Samuel went back outside. They walked across the foot bridge to investigate the cabin on the other side. Lavina watched them go, still smiling. They had asked her to come along, but she thought it best they go alone. She used the excuse of her pregnancy and not wanting to cross the narrow bridge.

When Matt arrived home, he heard the laughter of a noisy celebration coming from inside his home. He opened the door and saw Kirsten sitting next to Samuel holding the baby. He smiled and greeted them, the surprise at seeing the two of them showing on his face.

"We were trying to decide whose name to change so there won't be two Kirstens to confuse us." Lavina attempted to explain the laughter.

"So, you're staying?" Matt asked.

"We both are." Kirsten once more told of her and Samuel's marriage. She seemed like the old Kirsten, exuberant and unrestrained. Matt also expressed his happiness for the couple.

"Well, what have you come up with?" Matt returned to the subject of name changing.

"Kirsten the Big is out. So is Kirsten the Little." The laughter resumed as they continued their silly conversation.

"Am I going to get any supper tonight?" Matt finally asked. It was getting late and he still had work to do.

Lavina got to her feet. "No, let me," Kirsten insisted as Matt and Samuel went out to unload the wagon and tend to the horses.

Gray Eagle had disappeared. Matt found him in the bunkhouse. "Supper is ready." The old Indian nodded and stood up.

"You have good friends Matt Daly," he said as they walked over to the main house, appreciating the warm spring air. He sounded satisfied. Matt wondered what he was thinking.

With Kirsten there, Lavina and Matt both breathed easier about the baby that would soon be coming. They couldn't believe the timing of the other couple's arrival.

Samuel and Kirsten cleaned up the unlived-in cabin and moved in, making plans to begin ranching on the small spread. Samuel made the same arrangement with Matt that Jesse had with Big John. They worked the two places as a partnership, exchanging labor, and helping one another out.

Once more Lavina had a best friend. With Kirsten's strength and energy, the daily chores seemed like nothing. In fact Kirsten wouldn't let Lavina do much at all.

The baby finally arrived with no complications, a boy. They named him after his father. Matt and Lavina couldn't imagine how they could be any happier, as he held his son, and she, tired yet exhilarated after giving birth, looked around at the smiling faces of their friends.

# Epilogue

The old man pushed aside the screen door as he stepped out of the kitchen, and looked up. He scanned the sky. It was still cool out, but one of the first mornings of spring when there was no frost on the ground. The early morning sun already felt warm. He took a deep breath of the fresh air and looked up at the blue sky once more.

Pausing at the bottom of the steps, he had to think a minute to remember where he was going. Oh yeah, he was off to saddle his horse. He walked slowly over to the barn, admiring it as he approached. The big, red building was still his favorite structure on the ranch. It had replaced the original barn years ago. There were eight tie stalls for horses, plus it housed wagons and other wheeled equipment. Up above in the loft many tons of hay had been stored through the years.

Once inside he paused again, allowing his eyes to adjust to the dim light. In front of him two cars were parked. He wrinkled hi nose at the smell of oil and gasoline. There were no horses waiting to be saddled or harnessed. He walked between the cars, feeling confused, and wondering where his saddle had been put. At last he went back out to find his son. The younger man was over at the machine shop repairing a tractor. He didn't ask why as he led his father to the door of the tack room. Inside, one end of it was filled with racks holding saddles. Harness and bridles lined the walls. Rows of collars hung above. Matt breathed in the familiar scents. This was more like it, leather and horse sweat. He spotted his old, worn saddle immediately. It sat cleaned and oiled, waiting to be used. Every year someone performed the maintenance on it out of respect for him. They knew it would never be used again.

He walked over and grabbed the horn, the feel of leather bringing back memories of horses he had ridden. He looked up, again having to pause and think about what he had been doing. Suddenly he felt tired. He walked back out into the sunshine and crossed the yard over to the cabin.

The small, two-room cabin looked the same as when it was built almost seventy years ago, except for the roof. A few years before Matt had tried to open the door, but it was jammed by dirt from the caved-in roof. Rose, his daughter-in-law, had seen him pushing on it and hurried over. "That's not safe anymore. Come away from there." But Matt hadn't left it at that.

That evening he told his son he wanted a new roof put on the cabin. He had seemed his younger self, taking charge and giving orders. They hired the job done. Laborers came and cleaned the dirt out of the cabin and tore out the rotting timbers. The ends were built up, with new logs forming a triangle shape to attach a real roof to. They decided to add a wood floor, finally covering up the packed dirt that all of Matt and Lavina's children had crawled, and then learned to walk on. The porch was repaired and the cracks between the logs re-chinked, making the structure as good as new.

Matt moved back into the cabin during the summer, sleeping once again in the room he had brought his bride home to sixty-six years before. The iron bed still stood in the bedroom, with a new mattress to replace the one mice had destroyed. Out in the main room, the worn-out cook stove had been replaced with a wood heating stove. Near it the box still held wood, split for his use. It was hard to manage an axe since injuring his shoulder.

He started a fire before flinging the used coffee grounds out the open door. He poured water from a pitcher into the old enamel pot. The water wasn't hauled from the creek in buckets any longer. Rose brought it over from the kitchen for his use. He rolled and smoked a cigarette while patiently waiting for the fire to heat first the thick, cast iron stove and then the water. The can of coffee sat on the shelf where it had been kept when the cabin was lived in. Of course now it came already ground. But he didn't mind since it would have been hard for his arthritic hands to manage the grinder.

The water boiled so he got to his feet. He poured the coffee into the palm of one cupped hand to measure it before carefully dumping it into the pot. He still made it the way he had first tasted it, like it had been prepared on cattle drives, adding cold water to settle the grounds after it had brewed.

Matt studied his hands as he again waited. They were gnarled and misshapen from hard work. He could no longer completely straighten his fingers because of damage to the tendons caused by many hours spent clutching a rope during brandings. The skin was mottled with scars and there were lumps and gouges causing further deformity. He no longer remembered how he received most of the injuries. He poured himself a cup of coffee and sat down.

His family had put a bed in one corner of the living room for him after the last fall from a horse when he broke his hip, since he had trouble with steps. But he didn't like it. Only during the colder months did he consent to sleeping there. He had slept upstairs with Lavina since they had built the house over fifty years before.

The cabin suited him just fine. There were no steps to negotiate and it still felt like home. He hobbled over to the big house for meals, but there was always a pot of coffee on the stove in the cabin for visitors. He sat at the head of the well-used table in the straight back chair that had replaced his father's.

Recently his son bought him an easy chair. At first he resisted when the red, upholstered chair was carried into the cabin. But his daughter-in-law convinced him to try it. He had to admit it was comfortable, especially when he put his feet up on the matching footstool. He sat in it more and more, watching the activity out in the yard through the open door, or dozing with his chin resting on his chest.

Besides family he didn't get much company the last few years. It seemed everyone was gone. Kirsten and Samuel were dead, buried across the creek. Their children still ran their ranch, but the partnership between the two places had evaporated a while back.

Ever since that last horse had planted him in the ground he didn't get around real well. He also banged his head pretty hard that fall and had never ridden after that. He thought back, but he couldn't be sure. Ten or twelve years ago he figured. Lavina had died a few years before.

Matt wished he would have a visitor. He enjoyed sitting back and talking about the days of the open range. For the most part it had been a good life. He and Lavina had raised six children, three boys and an equal number of girls. His oldest son Mathew ran ranch the now and he did a good job. Of course he'd be sixty soon. One day he'd turn the ranch over to his oldest son, Garrett. Matt worried about that some. His grandson was in his late twenties, and didn't seem to have the same passion for ranching as the three generations of Daly men before him. But he would inherit the D Rocking D and be expected to run it until he turned it over to his oldest son, never the less.

Matt thought about his two younger sons. One married into a ranching family and the other bought his own place forty miles east of Turkey Creek. Two of his daughters had left, but one of them, the youngest, Millie, lived with her family on a homestead house that was now part of the D Rocking D spread. Her husband worked for the Dalys.

It still amazed Matt that he could hop in an automobile and be at his son's ranch in an hour. Forty miles used to be a good day's ride. The cars were convenient and made life easier, maybe too easy. But thinking back on when he was courting Lavina, it would have been nice to have had a warm car to zip back and forth between the ranch and her father's store. It would have meant more time visiting her.

He never told anyone how close he had come to freezing to death that night when he got caught in the storm returning home. He had shrugged it off as if spending the night out in the snow was no big deal, but secretly he believed the image of Lavina's face in his mind, and wanting to see her again, had kept him alive.

Mathew opened the door and stuck his head in. "Hey Dad, want to go to town with us?" Matt nodded and rose to his feet. Why not, he had nothing better to do.

With his son driving, and a grandson in the back, the three of them sped down the road. The car stopped at the highway, just over the bridge that now spanned Turkey Creek. They accelerated past the town because, except for ruins, it no longer existed.

The roof of the old store had fallen in years ago. But Matt still looked over at the disintegrating building as they drove by, remembering when it was filled with the necessities of frontier life. It had been the settler's main link to civilization. He could almost see the buckboard sitting out front, the team tied to the hitch rail. The automobile had finally put Silas Riggs out of business since it made traveling to bigger towns so much easier. The store owner had shut the door for good and ridden the train east, never to be heard from again.

There were fences strung all along the highway. They seemed to go on for an eternity. It seemed to Matt that every time he drove to town there was another cross fence. Fencing and driving their cars, it seemed it was all ranchers did anymore.

Compton was now the nearest town. It had grown to a few thousand people and the ferry had been replaced by a bridge across the Yellowstone River. The old livery barn still stood, but it was also abandoned. Matt ignored it as they drove by. He didn't want to remember the emptiness he felt when he had been inside it and heard his family was dead.

The three men drove to the tractor dealership for the part they needed, and ran a few other errands before stopping at the coffee shop for some socializing. Matt walked in the door and looked around. He knew everyone who sat scattered around the restaurant.

"Mornin' there Matt, Mathew, Jimmy," a gray haired old man greeted the Daly men.

"Mornin' Charlie." They slid into the booth with the man, one of their neighbors.

A waitress walked up with a coffee pot and poured each man a cup without asking, while greeting them. "Can I get anyone anything else?" They all shook their heads. This was the mid morning coffee hour, too late for breakfast and too early for lunch.

"How's it going out at your place?" Matt asked once the waitress left.

"Well I tell you, Matt, I can't complain. That rain last week sure helped." The four men talked and sipped coffee, greeting others as they walked past.

"Well we best be getting along. That tractor won't repair itself." Mathew stood up after leaving change on the table.

The car ride home was way too fast for Matt. He couldn't take in all the detail. His eyesight was still fair, but at the speed they traveled everything was a blur.

Once they returned home, the two younger men went over to the shop where the tractor sat. Matt had never had much to do with anything that wasn't horse powered, and not having anything else to do, he decided to go up to the house and see what was for dinner.

Whenever he opened the kitchen door he still expected to see Lavina. Instead he saw Millie and Mathew's wife Rose. Pork chops sizzled on the stove as they prepared the noon meal. Rose smiled when she saw Matt.

"Back from town? Come sit down. Dinner won't be for a while yet." She poured him a cup of coffee as he hung his hat on a peg near the door before sitting at one end of the long table. His son had done well when he married. Both he and Lavina loved Rose as if she were their own daughter. The two women had run the household together, cooking for the expanding family and the hired cowboys as well. That had all changed though. Now the hired hands were mostly married men who lived with their own families in houses on the ranch.

The old bunkhouse was used only when they took on extra help during haying season, and in the spring when they branded. A bathroom with plumbing had been added not long after the same had been done to the main house. It had a new roof also, but anyone staying there still ate over at the big house.

Through the years the house had filled with growing children, and then emptied as they left home, only to fill again with grandchildren. Now a new generation was starting. Garrett was recently married and his wife, Ursula was expecting their first child. Matt was going to be a great- grandfather soon.

The young couple lived in a house just down the road, another one a nester family had built. Matt bought the homestead when the family went broke back in 1918 after a year of drought. The house was amazingly well built, given the distance from town and the difficulty of obtaining lumber. It had been used by the Daly family ever since.

"Where's that wife of Garrett's?"

"She stayed at home." The baby was due any time.

"Oh." The girl was only nineteen and didn't seem to care much for the life of a ranch wife, even though she had been raised on a ranch south of Compton. Matt remembered Lavina pitching in on her first day as his wife, and never stopping.

When the other men came in to eat, Matt asked his grandson, "How's your wife feeling?"

Garrett shrugged his shoulders and replied, "Okay, I guess." He sounded like he didn't really care. Matt wondered about the unconcerned reply.

There were nine of them at the table. Millie and her family ate the noon meal with the rest of the family. Her husband, Walter, had started working for the D Rocking D right out of high school, and the two of them had married soon after.

"Why aren't you kids in school?" Matt frowned as he looked down the table at his three grandchildren.

"It's Saturday," Millie reminded him. The days of the week no longer had much meaning.

That afternoon Matt walked back outside and looked around again. He spied the root cellar door sticking out of the side of the hill. It had been dug out over sixty years earlier, and the walls were lined with rock quarried from a sandstone outcrop back in the hills. It was still used for storing potatoes and carrots, plus home canned vegetables. He smiled when he remembered the first garden Lavina and Kirsten had put in. Being a die-hard rancher, he hadn't wanted anything to do with farming, but the women had persisted. The garden helped feed them through two wars and a depression, plus other hard times. Rose still planted vegetables every year.

Lavina and Kirsten had also planted apple orchards on either side of the creek so they didn't have to rely only on dried apples for pies any longer. Some of the fruit was put up as apple sauce, and added to their winter stores. Matt remembered the fragrance of apple blossoms on the air in the springtime.

He looked up the hill, above the root cellar. The tops of the trees that grew near the graveyard could just be seen. He walked up there from time to time to have a talk with Big John and Lavina. There were stones to mark their graves, as well as Jesse Branson's.

Matt remembered the day Lavina died. He had risen early as usual. When his wife hadn't come down within an hour, he knew. There was only one thing that would keep her in bed that late. Lying beside him, she had died peacefully in her sleep. He felt like part of him had gone with her.

That was the first time he had felt the finality of his life. The second was when he could no longer sit a horse. He hadn't thought he could go on living this long without the two things he loved most, but he had. He sighed, making a promise to Lavina that he would come visit her soon.

Matt looked across the creek. He could just make out the ruins of the cabin Kirsten had lived in, first with Jesse, and then with Samuel. The foot bridge had washed away years ago. Now there was a regular bridge half a mile downstream where the two driveways divided. The left fork led across Turkey Creek to the K Hanging S, as Kirsten and Samuel had named their ranch after the brand they designed. The ranch headquarters had been built just over the bridge where it was more accessible.

The right fork led to the D Rocking D. Between the two ranches they now owned both sides of the creek, almost all the way to where the town ruins were. They also controlled all the water in Turkey Creek. Together the two ranches put in a reservoir up above so they could save water for irrigating their hay meadows throughout the summer.

Kirsten had milked a cow almost to the end. Finally her hands had become too arthritic to squeeze the teats and she had to quit. By then she had spent years walking with a bow in her back from bending over. Part of her had given up when she could no longer milk her last, beloved cow.

Matt had felt domesticated when he started putting up hay to feed cattle over the winter. It felt stifling, going from being able to ride out in any direction as far as he wanted, to stringing his own fences, plus respecting his neighbors' fence lines. But he began breeding Percherons, big draft horses, for pulling the haying equipment. Now the horse drawn mowers and rakes sat out back along with other discarded equipment, rusting as weeds grew up around them.

When Matt turned the place over to his son, the younger man had begun buying tractors and other newer equipment. Both Mathew and Walter considered themselves modern ranchers and wanted to keep up with the times. Recently the ranch had purchased balers that bound the hay into neat, manageable bales.

Instead of handmade stacks that resembled huge loaves

of bread, dotting the fields, the bales sat in big rectangular stacks. The huge loft on top of the barn was no longer filled with sweet smelling loose hay to be pitched down into the mangers in front of hungry horses.

But the family members had worked well together for years, with Matt and Mathew doing the riding, while Walter managed the irrigating and haying operation. Matt had recognized it was time to let his son have full control while he was recuperating from his last accident. Still, he shook his head thinking about the changes. It seemed to him things had been working just fine the way they were. And he wondered if it was a good idea to be putting men out of work with all the machines.

Now Matt felt useless and helpless a lot of the time. He still remembered where all the springs were and where there would be grass any given time of the year, but if he ever went out on the prairie, he had to drive. It just wasn't the same. Riding in an automobile was a poor way to travel cross country. The tracks turned into roads that washed out when it rained. Plus there were so many fences dividing the range that he could no longer travel in a straight line, but had to go from gate to gate.

They had all learned to drive automobiles though, even Lavina. Kirsten had been as wild behind the wheel as when she rode. Matt smiled again, remembering her flying down the road with a cloud of dust following her.

The prairie was different from when he and his father arrived. First it had been overgrazed by cattle and sheep. Then the homesteaders had moved in, plowing up the sod to plant wheat and other crops. Many of the newcomers were immigrants from foreign countries who had been lied to about the climate. They were told that there was an abundance of rainfall to grow grain. After the first drought year, with no crop, most had gone broke. As fast as they moved in, they left again, selling what they considered worthless land for practically nothing. Matt bought up all he could, sometimes an entire section was had for the price of a train ticket east.

Of course it had been marginal land by then. The bare top soil had blown and washed away until there was nothing left in places. Much of the prairie had been replanted with imported species that stood up better under heavy grazing pressure than the native grasses, but the soil still had nowhere near the fertility and productivity of before. Matt had babied thousands of acres, but the rugged country supported a fraction of the number of animals it had before the white man came. A lot of it was taken over by sagebrush, cactus, and introduced weeds, plants considered worthless because livestock refused to eat them.

He remembered the first years he and his father lived in Montana. The prairie had been so much more alive. It had been full of wildflowers, a wide assortment of bright colors, pinks, yellows, purples, oranges and blues swayed in the breeze amid the tall thick bunchgrass. There had been a lot more wildlife also, not just game, but smaller animals. Even the butterflies had all but disappeared.

The land that used to be part of the Spade Ranch was now D Rocking D land. A nester family claimed it and had lived there for a couple of years before selling out. Matt had burned the remnants of the buildings. They were already in ruins, but he wanted to erase the bad memory more fully.

The drought years of 1917-23 had ruined a lot of people's dreams. Of course the dirty thirties were worse. The Dalys always had enough to eat, but sometimes not much else. They hung on, and even expanded through others' misfortune, but Matt owned nowhere near the amount of land he and his father controlled in the days when it was open range.

He credited Lavina for much of their success. If she hadn't sold their cattle when he left after shooting Bully Buehler, things might not have turned out so well. Otherwise they would have lost everything as had so many others. She had "liquidated their assets at an opportune time" a banker once told him. He still chuckled at the fancy words for pure luck.

Matt's urge to visit Lavina became stronger. The pain in his hip was worse today or he might have attempted the walk up to the graveyard. Instead he went looking for the photo album.

Settling into a comfortable chair in the living room, he opened the worn book. The first picture was the one he and Lavina had sat for in Miles City so many years ago. Lavina had taken it off the wall of the cabin when she saw it beginning to fade. Matt smiled looking at it. They were so young. He thought about running into Lily and started chuckling. He still squirmed a bit when he thought of the day he'd had to introduce the two women.

He had run into Lily when he was in Billings. It was after Lavina died. Rose had insisted he go to the doctor because his hip was bothering him. It turned out that Lily was seeing the same doctor that day.

She had moved from Miles City and bought a house with her savings when she retired. Now she was living out her last years comfortably. It was so good seeing her that Matt told his son that he would meet him later. The two old friends went to a corner cafe to eat and reminisce.

"I hope you don't expect me to make an honest woman out of you," Matt said after he told Lily of Lavina's death.

She laughed. "Hell no. It's much too late for that." They spent a couple hours talking about wild times in the cow towns, and about people they had known, while dining on roast beef with mashed potatoes and gravy.

"Well my kid will be out looking for me soon." Matt finished his coffee.

"You don't have time to go back to my place for a drink?" They both laughed. What had been a pick up line was now a joke. Matt said goodbye and went to find Mathew.

Sitting on the couch, Matt continued turning the pages of the photo album. There was a picture of him sitting on a horse, the bay, Easy, who was still his favorite after all these years.

Just then one of his grandchildren walked by. "Hey, do you know what this is?" He asked, pointing to the horse.

"It's a horse, Grandpa," the little girl said as she climbed up on his lap to look at the picture. Her name was Dorothy and she was Matt's youngest grandchild. Millie became pregnant with her when in her late forties.

"It's not just any horse. That was my courting horse. I was riding him when I met your grandma. The two of us looked so good together that she couldn't resist me."

"Is that you?" Dorothy was too small to remember her grandpa other than as an old man.

"It sure is." The two of them sat together looking at the old photographs together.

There were scenes of life on the ranch through the years. Every so often a photographer had come through, traveling around to take pictures of life in the west. The family usually obliged and posed in front of the camera. If they had any cash to pay for prints, they received the photographs through the mail.

It was one way ranch life on the frontier was preserved. The photographers probably didn't look into the future and realize that this way of life wouldn't last long. It was just an interesting way make a living while seeing the country.

The little girl got bored and squirmed to get down. Matt put the album away and walked outside again. There was action down at the corrals. He hobbled across the yard and leaned on the fence to peer through the rails.

The corral that had been behind the barn was now the center of the cattle operation. It had been expanded into an extensive set of pens for holding and sorting cattle. They branded in chutes instead of on the open ground, using fewer men and horses. The roundups were also a thing of the past. Now it was a matter of circling a herd in a fenced pasture and pushing them towards the corrals. The uniformly brown and white Herefords were a lot tamer than the longhorns, which also made working them easier.

Two hired men on horseback were attempting to sort cattle. Matt couldn't figure out exactly what they were trying to accomplish, there was so much hollering. Dust filled the air. He stood there for a while watching and thinking.

Cowboys today were much better riders. Hell most of

them grew up riding, not like when he was a kid. He remembered his first cattle drive. There weren't horses around for him to ride as a youngster living in town, so he had been on a horse only a few times before spending his first summer horseback. It had been a matter of having to quickly figure out how to get the horse going in the direction he wanted while staying in the saddle.

Yeah, they were better riders, but sometimes he thought they knew nothing about working cattle. They got the animals agitated and running. It took four of them to trail as many as he could alone on a good horse. And this exhibition in the corral was pitiful. Feeling a little disgusted, and also sad, he turned away.

Back at the house, Matt decided he wanted to see his and Lavina's old bedroom. He made his way up the stairs slowly and painfully. Rose met him at the top.

"I was wondering what all that noise was. Where are you going?"

"To my bedroom." He hadn't been up the stairs since he broke his hip, and doubted it would look the same.

Rose started down the stairs while Matt continued on to his old bedroom. To his surprise, nothing in it had been changed. He wandered around, looking at Lavina's brush on the dresser, and at the curtains she had made to match the quilt that covered the bed.

He opened the closet door and looked at Lavina's clothes. They hung as they had when she died. He thought it strange, but apparently the extra bedroom hadn't been needed. He sat down on the bed, then lay back to rest for a moment.

He woke with a start. He had dreamed of Gray Eagle. "Home, home," the Indian whispered in Matt's ear as he slept

Matt lay on the bed thinking about his old friend. Gray Eagle had lived with the Dalys as one of the family until he died a very old and peaceful man. He had helped raise all the Daly and Sheldon children, and was a patient teacher. A small herd of children seemed to always follow him, and they hung around with him down at the barn. He was Grandpa to all of them.

Lavina and Matt had tried to get him to move into the house, but he refused. Instead he slept in the barn during the summer and moved into the bunkhouse when it got cold. Matt smiled remembering a cowboy he hired who had quit when he found out he had to eat at the same table as an Indian.

Gray Eagle was buried next to Big John. Matt had cried when they put his body in the ground, something he had done only one time since. That of course was when Lavina passed away.

He thought about his children's other grandparents. The Lavolds had finally moved out of the store in Cedar Junction after building a house on the edge of town. Their two sons had taken over the store, and had done well enough that they bought a store in Compton as well. Elizabeth and Theodore were buried next to his own children who had died from the fever so many years ago. The stores had eventually been sold. Matt wasn't sure what had happened to Teddy and James, but he knew some of their descendants, his relatives also, who still lived in the area.

Finally he thought about his children's other grandparent, his mother Libby. He had seen her one last time when the children were small. She had come to Montana to visit her son and to meet his family. She acted old and crotchety. Sitting all that way on the train made her bones ache and she complained the entire visit. Still, he was glad to see her, and happy his wife and children got to meet her. But after two weeks it was a relief when she left. She acted no differently than when he lived with her as a child.

He looked around the bedroom one last time, wondering if Lavina had been happy being married to him. He realized that she had felt trapped a lot of the time, running the household while he rode horseback every day. She seemed content though, and he knew she loved him and their children.

The two of them had done a little traveling after the children were grown. They rode the train west to Portland once when Curly finally talked them into coming for a visit. They had stood on the coast of the Pacific Ocean, looking out over the vast, expanse of water in silent amazement. It was the only time either one of them ever saw an ocean. He remembered the salty air and the excitement on Lavina's face.

Matt sighed, then stood up, not looking forward to negotiating the stairs one more time. But he managed, slowly and painfully taking one step at a time. At the bottom, after a deep breath of relief, he wondered where everyone had gone. The coffee pot sat on the electric stove, but it was cold. He went out the back door and headed down to his cabin once again. He faced the breeze, wishing he was on the back of an eager horse, riding out to check his cattle. He thought he smelled the sweet aroma of chokecherry blossoms on the air.

Instead he went inside the cabin and spotted the whiskey bottle. It also sat where it always had, above the counter to the left of the door. He considered pouring a glass, but disliked drinking alone. Just the thought of it turned his mind back to the dark times of his life.

He had spoken of his days as an outlaw only one other time after he told Lavina the story. Back in the twenties a journalist had come around interviewing old cowboys living in the area about their experiences trailing cattle into Montana. Matt decided it was a good time to set his family straight about what had happened since there were stories floating around about him, mainly untrue gossip, about all the men he had killed.

He gathered all six children in the living room. Lavina was there also, along with Kirsten, Samuel, and their children. Sitting in front of them, with the reporter writing everything down, he started with the shooting of Bully Buehler and ended when he was shot down in Wyoming. He left out a lot of detail, especially about how he came to end up lying in the street, but he admitted to killing three men in self-defense.

They all sat and listened wide-eyed, the reporter most of all. Matt didn't know what he was planning on doing with the story; he didn't really care. But a week later the man was killed in an auto accident. Matt never heard another word about it. He didn't know that Lavina and Kirsten had pulled the other family members aside and told them that his story wasn't to be repeated, as it could only hurt the Daly family.

Since that time Matt only drank socially and little at that. He put the bottle back on the shelf, frowning and rubbing his jaw, which still ached in cold weather. He had never fired a pistol since then either. His had been put away some place, along with the holster and he didn't know if it was still around or not. He had packed a rifle when he rode, for hunting, but that was the only use he had for firearms. He had seen their dark side and was lucky to be alive. Even though he could no longer recall the faces of the men he had faced with a gun, he still felt the guilt of not protecting his family.

Loneliness overtook him. Outside once more, he walked down to the horse corral. There were a few saddle horses standing idle. They were all nice looking animals. They still bred a few mares every spring, but horses were no longer in short supply.

When the homesteaders left, most of their horses were abandoned. Within a few years the range was full of the now feral animals. Ranchers had no tolerance for them as they gobbled up grass that was meant for cattle. Thousands were rounded up and shipped to butchering facilities. It was an ugly sight, the once proud horses, bruised and bleeding, loaded onto trucks, terrified. Matt hated it, and had never participated in the roundups. He had "Winchestered" a few of them though, to cut down their numbers.

Matt remembered the black mare, Lucky. He thought there were still descendants of hers on the place, but he wasn't sure.

His son had gotten into breeding the registered Steel Dust horses. They were pretty to look at, and good at their jobs, but they weren't as tough as the cow ponies he had ridden.

So much had changed. The big, black Percherons were gone. Once there had been a pasture full of the heavy workhorses. Gradually their numbers dwindled as their jobs became mechanized. Matt had refused to get rid of the last pair.

They lived out their retirement in the pasture and died with dignity after giving so much of their lives to mankind.

A gelding wandered over to where Matt was standing and sniffed his arm where it rested on the fence. Matt stroked the blazed face, still feeling lonely. Finally he made up his mind.

He looked up the hill towards the graveyard, full of resolve. He started walking, slowly and steadily, determined to ease his loneliness by having a talk with his wife and father. It seemed to take forever, but he made it to the graves. He bent over to pull out the grass that was growing over the carved headstones.

He told his beloved Lavina all that was happening with their family, and about the great grandchild that was soon to be born. Then he told Big John all that was happening on the ranch. In turn Jesse heard news from across the creek.

He didn't know what to say to Gray Eagle, so he just stood silent with his hand resting on the headstone that marked his friend's final resting place. The Indian had taught him gratitude, and in later years he realized that he had a lot to be grateful for. What more could a man ask for than to look out over the land he loved, knowing his family would continue caring for it. Deep down he knew that he had looked out for it the best he could, just as he had his family. He felt satisfied.

Matt eased to the ground, resting against an ancient juniper. The gnarled trunk felt hard against his spine and he shifted around until he found a place where the contours fit his back comfortably. He pulled his tobacco pouch from a vest pocket and slowly rolled a smoke. His stiff fingers were steady as he held the paper and filled it with tobacco. After licking the edge of the paper, he pressed it into place. He looked around and smelled the air before he struck a match and lit the end of the cigarette. The cooler air felt refreshing in the lengthening shadows.

As he smoked, the loneliness left him, riding off on the breeze. He carefully crushed the end of the cigarette out on the sole of his boot, making sure the fire was completely out. For the first time that day he felt peaceful.

He turned his head and smiled as Lavina walked over to him. She was wearing the dark, blue traveling suit she had worn the first day he had seen her stepping off the train in Miles City. She greeted him and put her hand out to take his. He rose and went with her.

That evening he didn't push his hat down onto his head as the wind gusted. When the hat blew off and rolled across the hillside, he didn't move.

At dusk, his son found him sitting there, propped up against the tree with a smile still on his face. Afterwards they joked that he didn't cause them the work of hauling his body up the hillside to be buried when he died. He was already there.